INTERSECTING PATHS

CHARM CITY CONNECTIONS BOOK 2

ROXANNE BLACKHALL

BLACK LABEL PRESS

To those who encouraged me to be free with this book (& everyone like them!)
Keep living outside the box.
Keep pushing against expectations.
Keep being your glorious selves.

CONTENT NOTES

This book is intended for adults and contains content that may be upsetting for some readers. Detailed information can be found on the author's website.

www.RoxanneBlackhall.com/content

INTERSECTING PATHS

New Year's Eve in New Orleans is the perfect getaway for Charlie Jones after a disastrous relationship with a coworker who turned out to be married derailed her career plans. Proof she should keep things casual—like she always had before.

A one night stand might be just the ticket to jumpstart a better year. And she's got her eye on the ideal candidate.

Deke Wallace has every intention of enjoying what he sees as his last year of freedom before he has to settle down and think about marriage and satisfying his parents' nagging for a grandchild.

He'd be more than happy to ring in the new year with the sexy redhead in a sparkly dress.

No last names. No phone numbers. Just adult fun. Except things don't go as planned.

♥

CHAPTER 1

The soft breeze was a welcome relief after the crowd on the main-level dance floor. Charlie Jones propped her elbows on the balcony railing and stared down Frenchman Street. She hadn't had a New Year's Eve off in years and she intended to enjoy it. What better place than New Orleans.

A woman's throaty laugh floated through the air and Charlie glanced over to see a model-perfect platinum blonde draping herself around a smiling man leaning against the rail at the other end of the balcony.

Him again.

She'd spotted him early on. Even in the crowded bar, he was hard to miss. He looked like a Greek god decided to come to earth and walk among the mortals. Dark hair and smoldering brown eyes sat in a ridiculously handsome face, and his shoulders strained the seams of a button-up shirt that looked custom tailored for his body.

It didn't hurt that he'd left more than the top two buttons

open. Or that he'd rolled the sleeves up, showing off forearms that were the stuff of legends. The blonde was the third woman Charlie had seen him with—not that she was counting. Besides, she'd danced or hung out with an equal number of men, plus a couple of women. This was the last stop on a New Orleans bar crawl. Getting a little wild was expected.

Still, she had no desire to sit here and play voyeur if those two started making out. She made her way back to the bar, found an open spot, and caught the bartender's eye.

"Boulevardier, right?" He tossed a paper coaster in front of her as Charlie nodded.

"Good memory."

He took another order, then made her drink and placed it on the coaster. "Like I'd forget that. You know how many sazeracs I've made tonight?"

"I can imagine. Never been my drink of choice." Charlie dropped cash in the tip jar and surveyed the room, letting the vibrant energy wash over her as she sipped her drink. This was why she liked running events—she loved helping people create happy memories.

She needed some happy memories of her own to wipe away the last few weeks. Hell, the last twelve months. Years of being staff had trained her to be an observer—and that meant spotting potential problems before they blossomed. She was halfway through identifying who might cause a stir later when she stopped herself. Fuck it, she was here to be social, not sit on the sidelines watching everyone else have fun. This wasn't work. She finished her drink and stood.

She stepped away from the bar and dodged a laughing woman who wasn't looking where she was going. Charlie backed into what felt like a wall that she was very sure had not been there before.

She turned and looked into the deep brown eyes of the Greek god. At five foot ten, she wasn't a small woman. Her heels put her over six feet, and she was eye to eye with him. His mouth curled into a lopsided smile.

"I wondered when I'd bump into you again."

The warm, rich baritone of his voice sent pleasant shivers down Charlie's spine. *Down girl.* He was trouble she did not need. In her experience, if a man was as sinfully handsome as this guy, they were either toxic, terrible in bed, or both.

Or he could be just the right kind of trouble for tonight.

"Can I get you a drink?" He had leaned close to speak and the view only got better.

If she was being sensible, she'd switch to soda, or water. Nothing about the impromptu trip to New Orleans was sensible. Instead, she nodded and the Greek god turned toward the bar and asked for a second of whatever she'd had and another for himself.

"You don't know what I'm drinking."

"Nope." He followed that up with a chuckle and a widening of his grin.

"What if it's something awful?"

He shrugged as he pulled out his wallet to pay for the drinks. "Then it's an adventure. It's New Year's Eve. Gotta live a little dangerously, right?"

A week ago, she would have disagreed with that sentiment. Tonight, she wasn't living by rules. He scooped up both glasses and gave her a 'c'mon' gesture with his head, and damned if she didn't follow. She was a sucker for a little swagger and confidence. This guy had them to spare.

He skirted the crowd and headed for the small patio in the back. Miraculously, they found two chairs and he waited for her to sit, then joined her, handed her a glass and raised his own.

"To new friends," he said as he clinked his glass against hers, then took a sip. "Oh, whiskey girl. Nice. Good choice. I'm Deke. Pleased to meet you."

Not for the first time, she wondered if name tags might have been a good idea.

"Pleasure. I'm Charlie."

Deke sat back and eyed her over the rim of his glass. She couldn't help feeling like he was appraising something.

"You're a bit of a social butterfly. I've seen you all over tonight." His eyes traveled from her face, down her body, and back up.

"I could say the same of you," she countered.

"Touché." He stretched long legs out and crossed them at the ankles. "Isn't that the point of this kind of event? Meet people. Make friends. Have fun."

If he could check her out, she figured turnabout was fair play. She let her gaze roam down his body. She suspected that was why he'd positioned himself the way he had—it gave her an unfettered view of broad shoulders and chest, flat abs, and narrow hips. The slim-fitting pants he wore did nothing to conceal a very prominent bulge. Plus those long legs.

She got back to his face and he winked. Yeah. He knew damn good and well she was looking and knew she'd liked what she saw. *Definitely trouble.*

"So, we're in a tourist town and everyone here is from somewhere else, but I can't place your accent. Where are you from?" He leaned forward, his drink cupped in one big hand and an expression of rapt attention on his face.

Charlie shifted in her seat, a move that put her legs in contact with his. Not that she was complaining.

"Blame college in Massachusetts and working literally all over Europe for the lack of accent. I'm another tourist—just in town for the holiday."

His eyebrows arched up. "Yeah, me too. Flying back home tomorrow."

The last thing she wanted to think about was the world outside of this bar tonight. He was hot as fuck and just as charming, and that was all that mattered right now.

She nudged his knee with hers and braced an elbow on the table. "Quid pro quo. I don't hear an accent from you."

He threw his head back and laughed, then leaned in until he was very close. "Catholic school—the nuns were sticklers for diction and proper pronunciation." He tipped his head and smiled. "I always give at least as good as I get. Often better. Your turn. What do you do?"

The smirk he gave her as he sat back needed no translation. He'd meant every bit of that as an innuendo. Too bad he had to go and ask that question. Reality rearing its ugly head was not on her agenda.

"I make people's dreams come true." That was how she viewed planning a wedding—she helped each couple bring their romantic ideas into reality. Deke gave her a quizzical look and Charlie flashed a smile. "I'm a wedding and events coordinator. You?"

"Cool. I'm a teacher."

He reached forward and snagged her empty glass. She hadn't even realized she'd finished her drink. Deke set them on the table and offered his hand.

"Dance?"

Why the hell not.

She slid her hand into his and he pulled her to stand. The song ended as they came back inside and the band slowed things down when they stepped onto the dance floor. Charlie didn't hesitate when he opened his arms. She laid one hand on his shoulder and Deke leaned close to her.

"You okay if I touch your waist?"

"As opposed to...?" She trailed off and batted her eyelashes at him and got a hearty laugh in return. He stepped closer and laid his hand high on her waist. After the cool of the outside air on the patio, the dance floor felt hot and stuffy.

"So tell me more about you." His breath ruffled her hair as he spoke.

Another couple bumped into Charlie and Deke turned so they'd hit him if they did it again.

"Who says chivalry is dead? I think I'm gonna need more detail first. What do you teach? What's your subject? And what grade?"

"High school students, and I teach advanced math."

Should not have asked that question. Get back to flirting. Maybe another drink.

"Huh, I'd have guessed coach. I pegged you more as an athlete."

She trailed her hand down the bulge of his biceps.

"I did play sports—pretty much all of them—but was never anything special as an athlete. I like being active, but it's not my life."

The firm muscles under her fingers said he was being modest. She gave his arm a squeeze. "Uh huh. You wanna try that again? This says otherwise."

That pulled another laugh out of him. "I work out to maintain a body I feel good in and that I know women find attractive—fit, but not too fit. Well muscled, but not gym-bro bod."

"I mean, you're not wrong." She gave another squeeze to his biceps and slid her hand back up to rest on his shoulder. "I do yoga and swim. I'll never look thin, no matter what weight I'm at. Some people don't like that, and that's okay. There are plenty who do."

He stepped back a little and his eyes roamed her body top

to toe. When he got back to her eyes, he gave a slow smile and pulled her close again.

"Count me among those who like that."

The rough rumble of his voice sent another cascade of shivers through her and conjured up images of getting him out of his clothes. A subtle shift in the music said the band was about to change things up again. Deke tipped his head and his lips brushed her ear.

"Think we can find a quiet spot?"

She stepped closer, bringing her body into full contact with his and it was electric. The beat dropped and the crowd around them cheered. Charlie made a face and Deke laughed again.

He pulled her away from the dance floor and they climbed the stairs, bypassing the crowd on the second floor before turning up narrow steps to the roof deck. The universe must have been smiling on them because it wasn't as packed as the rooms below.

"You wanna grab a table back there and I'll get drinks?" She pointed at the far end of the deck where a few tables sat in a dimly lit corner. More importantly, most of the people on the roof were clustered around the bar. Deke gave her a thumbs up and she turned to get drinks. Miracle of miracles, the wait wasn't too bad and she quickly joined Deke with fresh drinks in hand and two bottles of water tucked under her arm.

He stood by a tiny table tucked away from the others but only one chair. When she approached, he took the drinks from her and sat them on the table, then circled his hands around her waist and dropped into the chair. Gentle pressure from his hands encouraged her to sit.

She wasn't about to complain about getting closer to him,

but she'd never just sat on a man's lap. She did what she'd always done—half sat and half perched on his knee.

"Really? You're going to prop yourself up like that?" Deke tipped his head toward the foot she had braced for balance. "When a man invites you to sit, he doesn't mean hover. May I?"

He held his hands out and she nodded, trying not to think about all the possible meanings of what he'd just said. Deke leaned forward, scooped one hand under her knees and the other around her waist and lifted. Charlie let out a little yelp of surprise, then sighed as he settled her onto his lap.

"Better? There are reasons I work out that have nothing to do with looks."

Oh, it was better. And worse. Or at least more distracting. That little shift meant she was close enough to catch an intoxicating combination of sandalwood and spice and to feel that his legs were as well muscled as his arms. Not to mention that the bulge she'd noticed earlier was now pressed against her hip.

He reached around her and retrieved the bottles of water, handing one to her before he settled back in the chair.

"So why here for New Year's?" Deke uncapped his water and took a long swig. The muscles in his throat flexed as he swallowed. "And why a bar crawl instead of a big party?"

"Can't beat the weather." Charlie cast her eyes up to the clear sky overhead. It was unseasonably warm, even for New Orleans. There were patio heaters circling the roof, but most of them weren't even on. Deke gave her a look that said she could do better than that. She imagined he had some students, and likely parents, swooning.

"Would you believe me if I said it was cheap? It was spur of the moment. I knew I wanted to get away and just... be.

Have fun. Not have to think. If any of that makes sense. I got a good deal. What's your excuse?"

He tapped the unopened bottle in her hand and watched until she twisted the lid off and drank a quarter of it.

"Like you, last-minute thing. I had other plans but if I'm being honest, my friend with benefits got pissed that I didn't propose at Christmas. Not gonna lie, I came to party."

At least he's honest. Not like I wasn't thinking the same.

He swapped his water for the cocktail and took a long sip. His eyebrows went up and he took another taste. "What the hell are we drinking? It's good, but I'm not sure what it is."

Charlie sipped more water, hoping staying hydrated would minimize the inevitable hangover she was going to have at this rate.

"Basically, Scotch and soda meets whiskey highball, with a kick. The rest is honey and fresh ginger. And it's Glenmorangie. Which is probably why you couldn't figure it out."

She turned her head and found him closer than she thought. Another hint of spicy wood filled her senses. She switched her water for her cocktail and took a deep drink. It was that or wrap her arms around Deke and kiss him. Tempting as that was, she wanted to catch the fireworks at midnight. This trip was all about self-indulgence, though kissing Deke might be better than fireworks.

The crowd on the roof grew and the music pumping through the speakers changed, making conversation difficult. Not that Charlie wanted to talk, anyway. Judging from the way Deke's eyes kept traveling to the vee of her dress, then down her legs and his hand, warm on her knee and the other curled around her hip, he didn't care either.

She wasn't sure at what point he'd put his drink down, but she sure as hell didn't mind his hands on her. Her own glass was half empty already. She was going to pay for this in the morning, but she did not care.

A handful of staff members spilled onto the roof, handing out shiny bags of NYE accessories and plastic flutes of champagne. They deposited two on the table in front of Deke and Charlie.

Someone blew a paper horn and Charlie laughed and snagged the bags. She pulled out beads, a glittery headband adorned with feathers, and an equally sparkly top hat. Without a word, she stuck the top hat on her head, then leaned in and secured the headband on Deke's. She tossed the beads and glow stick bracelets back in the bags and did the same with the paper horns.

An employee pointed a camera at them and they both broke into broad smiles as the flash went off.

"It's getting close to midnight," Deke said into her ear. "Do you want to get closer to the front for a better view? Will we be able to see the fireworks from here?"

Charlie scanned the crowd now pressing at the railing overlooking the street and had no desire to move. She tipped her head back and tried to recall the last time she'd been in New Orleans for New Year's Eve. She'd still been in college.

"I think we'll catch a bit of them from here. Do you want to..."

She didn't finish. The countdown started and the crowd was yelling along. Deke shifted her on his lap and wrapped his arms around her waist.

The first firework went off at the end of the countdown and Charlie half turned toward Deke. Her lips were a breath away from his. She whispered, "Happy New Year" and closed the tiny distance.

She had thought to give him a quick kiss, nothing wild. The kind of thing people exchanged at times like this. But if his voice had sent shivers through her, his kiss was like an electric current. Charlie wasn't sure if the fireworks she felt were coming from inside her or the ones booming over their heads.

Deke's hands clenched on her waist. His tongue traced her lips until she opened her mouth to him. The sounds of the crowd and the thumping music faded as he filled all her senses. He tasted like honey and whiskey and he smelled like all things masculine and sexy. She was certain she could hear their heartbeats, or maybe it was just her own.

He pulled away, just a fraction of an inch, but Charlie wanted to reach up and grab him back. Deke pressed his forehead against hers and she knew what was coming. He'd said he'd come here to party, and she wanted to have fun and forget herself for a night. Deke seemed like the perfect way to do just that.

The last fireworks went off and some announcement came over the speakers about the band continuing for another hour. The crowd on the roof started to thin out.

"I think this is where I ask your place or mine." Deke cupped her head in his hands and Charlie was ready to agree to anything he suggested. "The street is gonna be a madhouse for a bit. Why don't we give it a few, then get out of here?"

The upside of technically still being an employee, she got room discounts at the Four Seasons and she'd somehow lucked into a river view room with a giant bed and a deep tub. That seemed like a better idea than going to wherever he was staying.

Honking horns and cheering echoed from the street below. Getting a car now would be a nightmare.

"Mine," she replied. "We'll have to call a car."

DEKE

The look on her face had his cock throbbing in anticipation. *Fuck.* He'd had his eye on Charlie all night—her lush curves and the sparkly outfit had caught his attention, sure. The cascade of dark red curls and gorgeous smile didn't hurt, but it was the way she carried herself that had him entranced.

Her dress hugged her body like a glove and showed off impressive cleavage and even more impressive legs that he was looking forward to wearing as earmuffs.

"Sounds like a plan," he replied.

Charlie shifted off his lap and stood. Her gaze traveled his body and the slow smile that curled her lips left no doubt that she'd noticed the effect she had on him. Deke didn't bother trying to hide anything. He was pretty sure they thinking the same things and he'd make damn sure before things went too much further.

She strolled to the front and leaned over, looking at the street below. Her skirt rode up, exposing creamy skin that he wanted to touch. Deke didn't need to look to know the streets were crowded with people, most of them very drunk and shouting "Happy New Year" at anyone and everyone, but he joined her at the rail.

He'd come down here with every intent of kicking off the last year of his twenties with a hell of a good time. He got the impression Charlie had a similar idea. It wouldn't be the first one-night stand of his life. After the debacle of trying a long-term friends-with-benefits thing, a one nighter had its appeal.

Not things he cared to think about when he was standing next to a goddess in human form. In her heels, she matched his height. He knew from holding her in his lap that she was soft in all the right places.

Charlie shivered and Deke wrapped his arms around her.

The night was mild, but there was a cool breeze up here that hadn't reached them when they were at the back of the rooftop. It was the most natural thing in the world to turn his head a tiny bit and kiss her. She ran her hands up his sides then around his back and pressed her body against his.

Fuck she feels good.

Back in college, he'd have been suggesting they find a bathroom and seeing how freaky they could get before people started pounding on the door. Those days were behind him, but damn she was tempting. He lifted his head and she bit her lip then rose on her tiptoes and leaned over the rail and his view got even better.

"It's a busy night, we'll have a long wait for a car. We could walk it, but..." She held up a foot encased in a silver sandal with sky-high heel.

"No need." He caught her hand and turned her to face him, hooking his thumb at the now almost empty rooftop. "Another minute and we'll have this space to ourselves. Looks like everyone's going back in for the band."

Every time the door opened, the music got louder. Charlie peeked around him then chuckled and pointed at the bar. The bartender was shutting down and telling folks the roof would remain open but they'd have to go downstairs for drinks.

"That's your reason."

"C'mon." He took her hand and moved away from the brightly lit front. Instead of returning to the table they'd occupied, he pulled Charlie to a dark corner created by the stairwell and the adjacent building. Out of easy sight and away from the cooling breeze.

As soon as he stopped, Charlie brought her hands up, curled them behind his neck and pulled him to her for a kiss.

All thought left his brain as his blood headed for points south. In seconds, he had her backed against the brick wall, his leg pressed between her thighs and his mouth on her neck. He reached down and cupped her ass, shifting her tighter against him.

Charlie clung to his shoulders and let out a tiny gasp as his teeth skimmed her skin. She lifted one leg and wrapped it around his waist. He slid a hand under her dress, up smooth skin and the curve of her hip until his fingers grazed a barely there thong.

It would take seconds to get that off of her. He could be inside her warmth with a few tugs of clothing and the condom in his pocket. In years past, he'd have been doing just that.

She arched against him, her fingers coiled in his hair and pushed down. He took the hint and trailed kisses along the swell of her breasts, nudging the fabric aside until he could pull a nipple into his mouth.

"Oh fuck, yes."

Her breathy voice and the rocking of her hips against him were all the encouragement Deke needed. He cupped her ass and lifted her higher, pressing her harder against the wall. Her dress slid down, exposing more of her magnificent breasts, and Deke wasted no time lavishing them with attention. He shifted his grip to slide his arm under her leg.

Charlie trembled at the first touch of his fingers over the silken fabric of her thong. He hooked a finger under the edge of the material and found wetness. She rolled her hips as if trying to get closer to his hand and Deke chuckled.

"Don't stop. I like that."

Nothing in the world could make him stop right now. He sucked her other nipple between his lips, eliciting another soft cry of pleasure. What he wouldn't give to be somewhere more private. Deke slid his finger along her silken folds—warm and slippery wet with want.

The thought of sinking to his knees and burying his face

between her thighs was tempting, but this was not the place. He wanted to feast on her until she begged him to stop. Instead, he stroked his fingers over her, coaxing her open while he treated her nipples the way he wanted to treat her clit.

She rolled her hips again and his finger slipped between her pussy lips. Her hands clenched in his hair, holding him tight against her breasts. He teased his finger along her entrance and she moaned softly. He didn't care that they were a few feet from a handful of stragglers still on the roof or that anyone who came around the corner would see them in the shadows.

Deke pressed a finger into her and was rewarded with a clench of her muscles around him. At this rate, he'd be having to count backwards from a hundred to keep from coming about two seconds after he entered her.

"Oh yes. Fuck yes."

Charlie ground down onto his hand until Deke slid a second, then a third finger into her. Her moans got a little louder and she clamped one hand over her mouth. She was so fucking hot that Deke was about ready to come in his pants.

He shifted his hand until he could press his thumb over her clit while his fingers still pumped into her. The swollen bud was hard under his touch and he pushed the hood back a bit more.

"Harder! Oh my god. Harder please."

Deke wasn't sure if she meant sucking on her nipples, finger-fucking her tight pussy, or the thumb on her clit, so he opted for all three. He let his teeth graze her skin and flicked his tongue over her nipple and rubbed her clit in time. Not one to do things halfway, Deke curled his fingers forward until he found her g-spot and stroked smooth and hard.

Charlie's entire body arched. Her head tipped back and she let out a cry before stifling it with both hands over her mouth. Her pussy walls clenched around his fingers. He was pretty sure he had her on the verge of orgasm. Hopefully, the first of many tonight. He just needed to keep it up and push her over that edge.

Someone set off firecrackers in the street and Charlie stiffened at the popping sounds. Her hands came out of his hair. Deke lifted his head and eased his fingers from her, using his body to shield her from view, even though the roof was deserted.

She straightened her dress and grabbed her phone.

"Lemme check on a car." She tapped the screen then scowled. "Um... shit. It's gonna be a while." She held the screen for him to see the estimated forty-minute wait.

The look she gave him had him wanting to say screw the car, I want you right here, right now. Her eyelids were heavy and her lips swollen and red as if she'd been biting them. He could imagine those lips wrapped around his cock, and he wasn't even all that enamored of getting head.

He should ask if she was okay. He was usually all about clear consent and always asked. Tonight, he had assumed. *Not drunk enough to blame the alcohol.*

Her body language made her desire clear, but that didn't make it right. Still, something told him if he straight up asked, she'd take it the wrong way.

"Show me what you want."

Deke let go of her, took half a step back and spread his arms wide. The pout she gave him was almost his undoing, then she tilted her head to the side and smiled. She trailed one hand up his leg before leaning in and pressing her lips to his throat. Her fingers teased over the buttons of his jeans then along the length of his cock—hard and throbbing and aching to be let out.

She nipped his ear with her teeth as she worked her hand

into his waistband and down. Slim fingers slid around his shaft. Charlie sucked in a sharp breath then let out a whispered "fuck." Her grip tightened and she groaned a little.

"You're... that's umm... a lot."

It wasn't the first time he'd heard that. He'd had a handful of women change their minds after seeing him—he had no problem with it and was always happy to make sure they still had fun. Charlie didn't look worried. In fact, she looked like she was ready to get naked right where they stood.

Her fingers tightened on him again, then loosened and slid until she circled the head of his cock. She teased along the ridge until he was gritting his teeth to keep from pinning her against the wall and fucking her senseless.

Instead, he braced himself in the corner and pulled her closer.

"Let's play a game. Put your back against me."

He opened his arms and she nestled her deliciously round ass against his crotch. *Fuck me*.

"Spread your legs."

Charlie's legs parted and Deke draped one arm over her shoulder, letting his fingers trail down inside her dress. He pushed a leg between hers, nudging until she spread even wider, then brought his hand up Charlie's leg and brushed his finger over the soaking wet fabric of her thong.

"Don't come. No matter what. We're going to play until the crowd thins out before going back to your room, where I plan to lay you back on the bed and make you come with my mouth."

Charlie shivered and let out a soft gasp.

"Tell me if you want that."

"Yes." There was no hesitation and she shifted against him, bringing her breasts higher and spreading her legs even more.

"Good girl." Deke teased her nipples with one hand as he

17

slipped his fingers into her thong. She was still slippery wet and arching against him. He pinched her nipple and thrust fingers into her in one stroke. Charlie covered her mouth with her hand and her whole body tensed.

Fuck, she likes it rough. This was going to be an amazing night.

He backed off to feather light touches before building up to almost punishing pinches and strokes as more firecrackers and small fireworks went off and the noises from the street got louder. Deke nipped her ear lobe and she whimpered.

From what he could tell, Charlie's brain had switched off. She was lost in sensation. As much as he loved and craved that, he wasn't sure how much was conscious choice and how much was alcohol. Tempting as it was to fuck her on the rooftop, that wasn't going to happen.

He brought her hand around and pressed her palm over his hard on. Charlie squeezed and wriggled her ass against him.

"To be clear," Deke whispered in her ear. "Once we get to your hotel, I want to make you come, repeatedly. Then I want to fuck you. Are you okay with that?"

She turned in his arms, pressed her lips against his. Her fingers tightened on his cock.

"I am very okay with that," she replied. "I want you, and I don't care how long the wait for a car is."

In seconds, she had her phone in her hand and the ride app open. Deke wasn't the type to look for signs, but when the expected wait was less than ten minutes, he'd count that as a win. Charlie wiggled the phone and gave him a grin that confirmed again—they wanted the same thing.

"Take off your thong." He held his hand out and waited.

Charlie tucked her phone into a tiny purse and took half a step back. Her eyes never left his as she reached under her skirt and slid the barely there thing down her legs, then put the scrap of fabric in his hand.

Deke pocketed the thong and pulled her closer, then spun so she was pressed into the corner. He slid his hand between her legs and cupped his fingers over her mound, squeezing gently, relishing the feel of skin on skin. Charlie moaned and lifted a leg to curl around his waist.

"You've got five minutes before we need to get downstairs. What do you want?" Deke knew what he wanted. More than anything in the world, he wanted to feel her wrapped around him with no clothing in the way.

Charlie lifted her other leg and locked her ankles behind his back, trapping his hand against her. *Fuck me.* His pants were the only thing between his cock and the delicious softness of her pussy. He slid his fingers into her, eliciting a moan of pure pleasure. Charlie curled her hips up and Deke settled into a slow rhythm with his palm flat against her and his fingers pressing deep inside.

She arched and ground against his hand, her head thrown back against the bricks and her lips parted as little gasps escaped her. The frantic energy of earlier had mellowed into something richer, deeper, and Deke was all for it.

"Oh, that's so good."

He didn't care how long it took, he wanted more of that. Hell, he wanted more of her. She was lost to the world as she rode his hand. If he shifted and paid more attention to her clit, she'd probably come in seconds.

Not yet.

He'd promised to make her come with his mouth, and he had every intention of keeping that promise.

Her phone pinged and Charlie's eyes opened. She blinked, smiled at him, and slowly lowered first one leg, then the other.

"Guess we should get downstairs."

Her grip on his hand was tight as they navigated the steps. She paused on the second floor and pointed at the bathroom.

"No line. It's a miracle. Be right back." She disappeared through the black lacquer door and Deke turned for the other bathroom.

Their ride pulled up just as they stepped into the street. Charlie stumbled getting into the big SUV, but Deke managed to steady her before she went down. He wasn't sure whether it was the state he had her in, her shoes on the uneven pavement, or the drinking.

He'd damn sure find out before getting naked. She settled against his side in the backseat, then angled her face up to kiss him and all thought left Deke's head. They bumped and jostled at a snail's pace along the crowded street. Tempting as it was to continue what they'd started, the driver had the interior lights on—probably to discourage that behavior—and Deke wasn't into putting on that kind of show.

Charlie shifted in the seat and her head rested on his shoulder.

Sleepiness has hit.

He chuckled and curled his arm around her, pulling her closer. He had sisters, and had dated enough women in college to know the pattern of tipsy to sleepy.

By the time they pulled up at the hotel, Charlie was half asleep. Deke helped her out of the SUV, into the lobby and to the elevators. All thoughts of sexy times got shoved to the back of his mind. Sure, he loved the idea of making her lose herself, but he wanted her awake and fully aware to start.

"What floor?" Deke pushed the button and waited for an elevator to open.

"Sixth," Charlie replied. Inside the elevator, she pulled out a keycard and handed it to him. She was steady on her feet as they walked down the hall but stumbled again as he unlocked her door and ushered her inside.

"I may have had too much to drink." Charlie sank to the bed. She reached up and pulled something out of her hair, sending the rest of her curls tumbling around her face.

Deke knelt and took off her shoes. By the time he rose with the sparkly sandals in hand, she was asleep, or passed out.

Well, shit.

He had a morning flight, so the idea of staying until she woke up and picking up where they left off wasn't on the table. Plus he didn't imagine she'd wake up in the sexiest of moods.

Instead, he placed the shoes in the closet and pulled her up so she was in the bed before tucking a blanket over her. She didn't move during any of it. He found a notepad and pen and tried to decide what to say.

She'd never told him where she was from. Or where she lived. He'd taken his cue from her and been equally evasive. Maybe she wanted strictly anonymous sex. He glanced at the bed—her curls spilled over the pillow. Her lips were puffy from kisses and he'd left a few red bite marks on her neck.

Shit. Didn't mean to do that.

On closer look, they were minor and would likely fade by morning. He turned back to the empty notepad.

> *Charlie,*
> *Thank you for making my night. Meeting you was an amazing end to one year and an even better start to the next. If you're ever in Baltimore, give me a call.*
> *Deke*

He added his cell number, folded the note in half and stuck it under a bottle of water on the nightstand. He found her phone and plugged it in, stuck her panties and the hotel keycard next to it and the water bottle, then turned off the lights and let himself out of the room.

The door snicked shut behind him and Deke made his way down the hall as if in a dream. She had to be some figment of his imagination. He should have gotten her number earlier. He should have made her come. That was his only real regret of the night—that he hadn't gotten to experience her orgasming from his touch.

The elevator opened and Deke checked the time. It wasn't too late. He could probably go out and find some willing woman. He wound up going back to the same bar. The music was coming from a DJ instead of a band and the crowd had thinned but the dance floor was still crowded. Except Deke wasn't feeling it. He turned to leave, dodging a drunk couple weaving their way to the door, and came face to face with a picture of Charlie sitting on his lap.

Oh yeah. The photographer earlier.

The picture was stuck to a board with others from the night—each featuring smiling people. He flagged down a staff member, bought the picture, and left. As he walked back to his Airbnb, every woman he passed paled compared to Charlie. He climbed the steps to his room and sat looking at the photo.

It was the kind of thing you'd get at an amusement park— a little grainy, not the greatest quality print, but a fun memory. He had one hand on her hip and the other on her bare thigh and her legs looked about a mile long. They were both smiling and leaning into each other. They looked like a happy couple.

He dropped the image and ran a hand through his hair— he could still smell her. Her scent was in his clothes. Some floral perfume that had an edge to it and the intoxicating scent that was her. If there was a heaven, this is what it would smell like.

Deke stripped for bed. His cock still throbbed and he'd have to do something about that before he could sleep. He knew what he'd be imagining as he came—Charlie with her head thrown back, tits in his face, and his cock buried in her wet pussy.

Fuck.

He closed his hand around his cock and stroked.

CHAPTER 2

Her cell rang and Charlie fumbled to silence it, knocking over a bottle of water she didn't remember putting next to the bed. Come to think of it, she didn't remember getting into bed.

"Shit." She crossed her fingers the bottle had been capped, then realized she'd hit the answer button by accident. Her head throbbed, making the screen hard to read. The professional sounding voice on the other end asking for Charlotte Jones snapped her to attention despite the entirely deserved hang over.

"I apologize for calling so early on a holiday, but our events manager had to take early leave and you're listed as available for short-term placement. Is now a good time to talk?"

Charlie rubbed her eyes and forced her brain to engage.

"Yeah. Ah, sorry. Yes. You said your events manager?"

Half an hour later, Charlie had agreed to come to Baltimore for an in-person interview the next day. She hung up the phone and looked at the time.

Shit.

Almost noon. She had to check out in twenty minutes and somehow get her head together enough to schedule a flight back to her hometown.

And why the fuck was her thong sitting on the nightstand?

Deke.

The thought of him brought a flood of memories from the night before. Or early this morning. Whatever. The man had been hot, and she had to go and pass out on him. At least, that's what she assumed happened.

She remembered the ride to the hotel, and that was it.

Her stomach twisted into a knot as she tried to recall anything after that. She remembered everything leading up to that moment—she definitely recalled wanting him. The making out on the rooftop. Kissing him during the car ride.

But what happened after that?

She was still wearing her dress, but where were her shoes? She found them placed neatly in the closet next to her suitcase. Fuck, she didn't have time for this. She hauled her bag out and threw it on the bed.

There was no time to shower, but she'd at least wash her face and change clothes. A quick self-assessment in the bathroom and she was reassured they had not had sex. Not that Deke seemed the type to do that, but what guy did?

From what she recalled about what he was packing, she'd be feeling it today if they had.

The knot in her stomach uncoiled a little and she focused on getting out of the hotel room. She'd revisit whatever the fuck happened last night after she'd secured a flight. Which, come to think of it, was something the hotel concierge could help with.

Miracle of miracles, the concierge got her a non-stop flight leaving in a couple of hours. The only downside was she have time to eat before heading to the airport. She could deal with where to stay once she landed. The hotel would honor her employee rate if there were rooms available.

Or I could just call Ryan.

Urgent matters dealt with, she climbed into the hotel's airport shuttle then texted her childhood best friend to let him know she was making a whirlwind trip back home.

> Holy shit! I'll pick you up. And hell no you're not staying at the hotel. You're staying in the guest room. No arguing.

She hadn't seen Ryan Grant in over a year. Not since she'd taken the job in Geneva. Not since she'd started seeing Noah. He only knew some of what had happened and why she'd left the day after Christmas. It was Ryan who had encouraged her to do something for herself. Go somewhere she loved and spend a week just enjoying life. She could figure out how to pick up the broken pieces and move forward after some much needed down time.

Fine job I'm doing of that.

Memories of being pressed against a brick wall and finger fucked on a New Orleans rooftop by some man she had just met her brought a mix of shame and arousal that heated her cheeks and had her squirming in her seat.

And she still had a pounding headache.

Once through security, she found a place serving all-day breakfast and ordered eggs, hashbrowns, and bacon. She needed hearty food. Screw the calories and fat. She planned to sleep on the plane. If she was lucky, by the time they landed in Baltimore, she'd feel human again. Meanwhile, she had to deal with the nagging questions in her head.

Like, why did he just disappear? And why didn't he leave his number?

She knew the likely answers.

What else was he supposed to do? Who leaves a number when it's a one-night stand?

They'd both avoided too much personal information. He'd said he was leaving the next day. Today. Everything about their interaction screamed hookup.

She was fine with that. Hell, it's what she had preferred ever since college. Until Noah. Which was the very reason she'd been looking to forget herself for a while and enjoy a New Year's Eve where no one knew her and there were guaranteed to be lots of people drinking and having a good time.

The flight was uneventful and Charlie slept the whole way. She deplaned feeling a little more like herself. Ryan was waiting for her outside of baggage claim and his rib-crushing bear hug was a balm to her soul. The cute, slightly awkward boy had grown into a truly gorgeous man with a smile that could light up the heavens.

"Hey, when did you get buff?"

It was a running joke between them. In college, Ryan had been lean and fit. After graduation and moving for jobs, she'd watched him transform via his regular updates on social media and pictures he texted. Still, when he'd come to visit, she'd been shocked when she hugged him, and those were the first words out of her mouth.

He stepped back and held her at arm's length as he looked her up and down.

"Are you okay? Let's get out of here."

Leave it to Ryan to spot something wrong. The years melted away and they were besties, back in college, rushing to grab a bite between their packed class schedules. Except

Baltimore wasn't Amherst, and they weren't starry-eyed undergrads anymore.

Once settled in his car, Ryan filled her in.

"Practical things first," he said. "You'll stay in our guest room for a few days. The unit above ours is a short-term rental. The owner usually leaves it vacant in January so they can do maintenance and stuff. They agreed to hold it until you get confirmation on the job."

Charlie shook her head and let his enthusiasm wash over her. Ryan had always been the more outgoing one. Not that she was a wallflower, but compared to him, everyone else was quiet and mellow.

"I can't wait for you to meet Bradly. You are going to love him. He's dealing with some family stuff but he'll be back Saturday."

Once in the city, he found parking and led her down a pretty block facing a park with a fountain, then up the stairs of a big brownstone.

"Walkup, I'm afraid. Third floor."

Charlie had no problem with stairs. When she'd worked in Europe, her apartments were almost always tiny and up at least three flights of stairs. They stopped on a landing and Ryan opened the door marked 3A.

"This is us."

He opened the unit and Charlie gasped. Tall ceilings and huge windows set off a smallish living room. She stepped in and looked around. A short hall led to two bedrooms and a bathroom.

"We got lucky when we found this place. It's a terrific building and the owner is very chill. So, here we are. The hall bath is all yours—there's another bathroom in the main bedroom. The place upstairs is smaller, just a one bedroom. It'll be perfect for you."

He dropped her bags onto the guest bed then led the way back to a small kitchen with a cozy table at one end where he encouraged her to sit while he bustled around making tea.

"You look hungover," Ryan observed as he put a steaming mug in front of her. "So which first? The whole story about what the fuck happened in Geneva? Or whatever has you looking like this?"

She wasn't sure she was ready to talk about Geneva and the fact that she'd walked away from the job she'd had for nearly ten years.

"New Orleans was... well... it was New Orleans. I met a guy." Everything spilled out over tea. At some point, Ryan retrieved cookies Bradly had made. When she'd finished, Ryan had a big, goofy grin on his face.

"I swear straight people do not understand hookup culture." He braced his elbows on the table and rested his chin in his hands. "You said it yourself—what else was the guy supposed to do? You'd given him minimal personal details and not pushed for more from him. It sounds like a classic hookup. Honestly, I'd be more worried if he'd kept your underwear—hot when it's a partner. Kinda creepy when it's some stranger."

He straightened up and snagged a cookie. "And I'll give him points for having the decency to take your shoes off. In all seriousness, I'm glad you're okay. That could have gone all sorts of wrong."

Charlie didn't want to think about that side of things. She'd done enough of that when she'd woken up and realized what had happened. She reached across the table and squeezed Ryan's hand. They'd been inseparable since childhood and everyone figured they were destined to marry each other.

Ryan came out to her at the end of middle school and swore her to secrecy. Throughout high school, they acted like they were dating. He didn't come out to their families until their freshman year of college. Neither set of parents took it well. To her knowledge, Ryan barely spoke to his family and hadn't seen hers since. A fact she considered a blessing. Hell, she avoided her family at all costs.

"I'm not going to tell you shit about Geneva until you spill what's up in your life. You've told me about Bradly—but something's changed. I can tell. So let's have it."

She knew she'd hit on something when Ryan blushed and a little boy grin crossed his face.

"We're getting married."

Charlie jumped up and hugged her best friend. "I'm so happy for you! When did that happen? Have you set a date yet? Picked a spot?"

Ryan rolled his eyes then kissed her forehead. Charlie grabbed another cookie and settled back in her chair, eager to hear all the details.

"He proposed the day after Christmas. That's why I didn't tell you. And it's kinda whirlwind," he replied. "With schedules and the busy summer season, we didn't want to wait till next year. So, it's March 15—we got lucky with calendars. We can do the rehearsal dinner at the hotel and the ceremony and reception at the Baltimore Museum of Art, because that's where Bradly works. And that's all the news. That's it. Life is pretty routine otherwise. And now it's your turn."

She'd avoided it as long as she could and she knew it. Charlie hauled in a slow breath and braced herself for the ugly.

"So, you know I was dating Noah. First time since college I decide to fall for a guy. Turns out he was engaged. Got married in early December, but I didn't find out any of that until Christmas."

Ryan's mouth fell open, then he closed it with a snap. His

eyes went round and sad. The man could never play poker—his emotions were all over his face.

"Long story short. We were coworkers and it started out like my usual—strictly casual. Things kinda grew from there. I should've known something was up. We only met at my place; he never answered his phone at night. He told me he was doing a two-week vacation with his family just before the holidays. In hindsight, it was obvious."

She took a deep breath and looked down at the last bite of her cookie. "I got called in on Christmas to cover for someone who was sick, and Noah and his new wife were there with their families. He saw me and cornered me in a supply closet. He figured we'd still see each other. When I said no, he got pushy. Nothing happened, but it was gross."

The sad puppy eyes morphed to righteous anger and Ryan leaned forward as if ready to defend her right here and now. How she wished she'd had friends like that in the moment. Charlie steeled herself to tell Ryan everything.

"He uh... he reminded me I couldn't report it because no one would believe me. They'd see it as a woman trying to get revenge. Icing on the cake, his new wife shows up as we're exiting the supply closet and goes ballistic. In front of guests."

"Please tell me you reported him." Ryan clapped a hand over his mouth and waved with the other, telling her to go on.

"Yes and no. I wasn't as loud as I should have been and it turned into a human relations nightmare. They refused to fire him and I was threatened with disciplinary action, so I threatened to get a lawyer. The regional manager got called in and he put me on un-paid administrative leave pending review."

"What an asshole!" Ryan's indignation on her behalf soothed her nerves and Charlie took a deep breath before continuing.

"I did fight that. I compromised more than I should have, but I didn't have it in me to do more. Which is why I'm here. I'm still an employee, active on the on-call list, and I can go for any jobs as an internal applicant. Luckily, I have a solid relationship with my previous manager, so I still have glowing letters of reference."

"I am so sorry. I can't believe they didn't fire his ass."

Charlie had thought the same thing. It boiled down to a lot of politics, misogyny, and family connections. Faced with limited options, Charlie had chosen the quickest way to get herself out of the situation with her dignity at least semi-intact. *Acquiescence.*

"You know the drill," Charlie said. Ryan was an out gay man. He'd faced plenty of discrimination in his life. He knew things weren't always fair or right. "I could argue it, but getting him fired wouldn't make me feel any better about it all. So, here I am. Assuming I land the position tomorrow, I'll be here until the end of March. Hope you don't get sick of me."

Ryan squeezed her hands.

"Never. I'm glad you're here. And all of that sucks. Any time you need to vent, I'm all ears."

Charlie swallowed hard, willing herself not to cry. Just being able to talk about it without judgment was a relief. She sniffed and squeezed his hands back.

"On a more pleasant topic. Tell me more about your wedding. You've got a lot to do in very little time."

His face lit up and he reached for his tablet and laid it on the table.

"Inspiration images." He thumbed open a photo album and turned it to Charlie.

She swiped through the pictures. No surprise, the vibe she got was elegant with a side of extravagant. She loved when couples brought in lots of pictures. It helped her see things through their eyes and gave her a place to start asking questions.

"What's the story with the event manager leaving suddenly?"

The last thing Charlie wanted to do was step into more drama, and since Ryan worked in human resources at the hotel, he might know the details.

"It's nothing salacious, don't worry. I can't believe they didn't tell you. Okay, backstory."

He wiggled his fingers at the iPad. "So, you know when you schedule an event at any of the major hotels, you get a coordinator. Well, short notice, the holidays, blah blah blah. The first one was horrible. I was trying to be flexible and understanding and all, because hey, I work there, too, but..."

He waved his hands like he was erasing a chalkboard, as if that could dispel the negative thoughts so clearly painted on his face. "We clashed. Without warning, she hands me off to her manager, and DeeDee is an angel. Unfortunately, she was in a horrible skiing accident on New Year's Eve. Broke a leg, an arm, and dislocated her other shoulder. She'll be fine, but she's taking a few months off for recovery. So, here you are."

He tapped the screen and opened another folder. Charlie flipped through images of the Four Seasons and another space that had to be the museum, but she hadn't been there in years.

"What do you still have to lock down?"

"We have everyone set for dates, except for the cake."

Okay. Not bad.

"But, we have a short list of places and need to do some tastings. We've both just been..."

Charlie nodded. When busy professional couples decided to get married, it was easy to get lost in the details, or let things slip through the cracks. There were a lot of moving parts.

"I can help with that," she said. "Assuming I get the job,

sounds like I'll be taking over the rehearsal dinner anyway, but aside from that I can be your social secretary. If you'll both share your calendars with me. What about flowers? Got those done?"

"We have the florist, but haven't decided on what yet. Ditto the DJ. And the food. And pretty much everything."

The conversation bounced between personal, professional, and wedding planning. When they finished, Ryan leaned across the table and caught both her hands in his.

"I have two things to ask."

"Anything for you," Charlie said. She meant it, but she still braced herself.

"Come out to dinner with us this Saturday. I want you to get to know the man I'm going to marry."

She'd wondered when he'd get around to that. "Come on. You know I'd love to. Of course I will."

Ryan bit his lip and looked across the table at her with wide, puppy dog eyes. A sure sign he was about to ask something outrageous.

"I want you to be my best person. And I know that's a big ask, so I just want to be sure you're okay doing that. With everything you just volunteered to do and working... I know it's a lot, but..."

Charlie glared at him until he stopped talking.

"I would be honored. And I can't believe you thought you had to double check that one."

Her best friend let out a squeal, jumped out of his chair, came around the table and wrapped her in another bone-crunching hug.

He had other friends he could ask. She knew that much for sure. Ryan was friendly and outgoing and made connections easily, but she understood why he asked her. Hell, if she ever walked down the aisle herself, she'd want Ryan to be there for her.

Not that it's ever gonna happen.

Once she was settled in the guest room, she dug through her bags to find a t-shirt and shorts to sleep in.

The mixed blessing of spending so many years moving around.

Charlie's entire life could be crammed into several oversize suitcases, and they were all right here in Baltimore. She flopped onto the bed and let out a sigh.

Comfortable at least. She planned on sleeping as long as her body would let her.

Assuming she could get to sleep with the memories of Deke rampaging around her head and stirring physical responses that were very hard to ignore.

CHAPTER 3

The bell jangled and the shuffle of papers and bags began, punctuated by the scraping back of chairs as a classroom full of teens filed out of their last class of the day.

"Do not forget to check the portal for any missing work. Tomorrow is the last day to upload it."

A collective groan rose as the students left and Deke settled at his laptop. He'd never understand why the school didn't extend winter break to Friday. No one was happy coming back on January second, and getting work done with only two days before the weekend was almost a joke.

"Mr. Wallace?"

Audra Pennington leaned on the edge of his desk; her lips curled into a smile in any other circumstances he might have found seductive. Even if messing around with the parent of one of his students wasn't off limits in his book, this one would be doubly so. She was trouble on two legs.

"Is there some emergency?" Deke had learned early on to

36

set firm boundaries about his time. Most parents were understanding, but many seemed to believe a teacher should be available around the clock. Audra Pennington took it to whole new levels.

She was divorced, and very vocal about it, and just as vocal about the fact that her ex was an alum and major donor to the school. For the first month, Deke had only seen her in passing. She hadn't attended freshman orientation with her son, Toby, but had come to parent-teacher night and had been showing up at regular intervals ever since.

"I really want to talk to you about Toby."

Deke bit his tongue. That was always her opening line, and she never had any real concern. If pressed, she would come up with some vague thing like 'I just want to make sure he's doing okay' but mostly, she wanted to flirt. Not something he wanted to entertain. Ever.

"You can call the office or go on the portal and set an appointment for a parent-teacher conference. It's easy to see my schedule online."

He turned back to his laptop but Ms. Pennington laid her hand on his arm.

"It won't take long. I'm sure we can chat today. Maybe after you're done here."

Deke smiled, gently pulled his arm away and snapped his laptop closed. He couldn't be rude, but from experience, he knew she'd only get pushier unless he put a stop to it.

"I'm afraid that's not possible. If you go on the portal, you'll see that my schedule is not open this afternoon. You'll also see my available hours. If you have an emergency, you can contact the office."

He rose and stuffed his laptop in his bag, then shrugged into his jacket. He'd reported her behavior once already but not that much could be done. Parents flirting wasn't exactly new territory. One thing he knew for sure, there was no way he'd have Toby in his classes next year. Which was a shame because he was brilliant and an outstanding student.

"If you'll excuse me." Deke gestured toward the door and waited for her to take the hint. She straightened slowly, ran her hands down her sides and gave him a little pout as she looked up from under lowered eyelashes.

Yeah, I know those moves. If a woman in a club gave him that look, it'd be game on. *Like Charlie.* He'd caught her looking at him more than once. To be fair, he'd been checking her out just as often. Deke shook his head and shouldered his bag. The last thing he needed to be thinking about was what had come next.

And why the fuck hasn't she called?

"Your loss." Ms. Pennington spun around and made her way to the open classroom door. Deke pulled in a slow breath and counted to ten before following her out. He got lucky and didn't run into her in the parking lot. Deke tossed his things in his back seat and set off for Cold Bottom Brewing.

He'd promised his friend Zach Muir he'd help with the post-holiday cleaning. Back in college, discovering his roommate's family owned a local brewery felt like winning the lottery. Deke hadn't minded being put to work when he was getting money and free beer. These days, he helped because of friendship.

The free beer doesn't hurt.

Deke parked, grabbed his tote bag, and headed inside. One of the things Zach's mother and stepfather established early on was closing the place on the first weekday after a big holiday. Any staff who had worked the holiday got a paid day off. They'd post signups for a short shift to clean and restock and it always filled up within an hour. Throughout college, Deke, and their other friend, Ty Lake, were part of that crew.

He pushed through the door and Zach whistled.

"Damn. Be careful teach. Don't wanna mess up the nice duds."

Deke flipped his friend off as he continued on to the bathroom where he could change clothes. Once back on the floor, he said hello to Zach's folks before checking the duty list.

Nobody liked cleaning the keg lines—it was tedious work at best, but to Deke, it was just the thing to switch gears. He grabbed the cleaning keg and supplies, then shut off the CO2 and regulator. He'd done this job enough times he could do it in his sleep.

The one thing he hadn't considered—tedious and routine meant his mind was free to wander. Of course it went straight to Charlie. He didn't know why it kept bugging him. He'd been down for a one-night stand. You didn't exactly exchange numbers with casual hookups.

Except he had left his number. The entire night replayed in his head as he unscrewed the coupling, took apart the taps, and ran cleaning solution through the lines, then rinsed them.

For real. Why hasn't she called? He'd tried telling himself it had only been a couple days. Made no difference.

"That's a fucking sour face. Who pissed in your cereal?"

Zach maneuvered a cart filled with fresh kegs into the narrow space and leaned against the bar. Deke whipped the bar towel out and caught his friend on the thigh. He went back to reassembling the system, saying nothing. The last thing he wanted to do was admit to Zach that he was stressing over a woman. Zach's approach to dating rubbed Deke the wrong way.

It was one thing to be casual, with no strings and no promises, but Zach wasn't up front about it. He never lied, that Deke knew of, but he never came out and said he was dating other people, or wanted nothing serious or exclusive. When the women he dated found out, things often got ugly.

He couldn't tell Zach he'd walked out of a beautiful woman's hotel room after she'd passed out—before anything had happened—and gone back to his own hotel and jacked off rather than hooking up with some random woman still roaming around. Hell, there were plenty of women still out and the bars had been nowhere near ready to shut down. He could've found someone.

"Flirty parent." Deke grabbed a coupler and bent over the first keg. "She actually said 'your loss' when she walked away."

"Still think you oughta go for that." Zach held up his hands like he was surrendering. "I know, I know. Work. Ethics. All that shit. Go for it and be selfish. Bet she stops."

Deke tapped the lever on the coupler as he seated it and beer erupted. He managed to get himself out of the way, but Zach got sprayed from the waist down before Deke flipped the lever all the way up and got the coupler in properly.

"Dude!" Zach laughed and swiped at his soaked pants. "That's a rookie mistake."

"Nah, that was for being gross." Deke tossed another towel at Zach and went on to the next keg. "Are you serious? You'd do that shit?"

"Me? Fuck no. I've got a reputation to uphold. But you've got a hot mom trying to climb your frame and it sounds like she's not taking subtle hints. So get unsubtle."

Deke tuned out whatever his friend said next. Didn't matter. Underneath all the bluster, Zach was a genuinely nice guy who cared for his family and friends and took artsy black and white photos in and around Baltimore. On the surface? He could be an asshole.

"Man, you need to fix whatever hit you on New Year's Eve.

There's a concert at the Metro Gallery Saturday night. You should come."

"Yeah, maybe." Deke had no desire to go out. Which was weird. Even though he'd usually be the one giving the same advice—shake it off. Go do something cool. Or wild. Or fun. "Depends on how much work I've got."

Zach looked down at his sodden pants and tossed the towel on the counter. "Now I've gotta go change. Did you have to hit me with the fucking sour red? You know I hate the way that smells."

Zach stalked off, shaking his head and Deke went back to finishing his task. The Metro Gallery could be a good distraction. It would be a night of loud music, basic drinks, and a crowd of people who were just there to have some fun.

He needed something to take his mind off of wishing he could go back in time to New Year's Eve, before they got in the car, and get Charlie's number.

CHARLIE—THURSDAY, JANUARY 2

An icy wind tore at Charlie's scarf as she stepped through the hotel doors and into the street. At least it wasn't snowing. Besides, a little wintery air wasn't going to ruin her mood. Within ten minutes of starting the interview, she'd been offered the job. Thirty minutes later, she'd signed the papers, shaken hands with the general manager, and practically floated to the elevator.

My life has become a whirlwind.

One week ago, she'd walked away from the dream job that had turned into a nightmare because of Noah. In the end, they'd paid out her vacation time and included a generous severance package even though she hadn't been terminated.

Hush money that wouldn't last long. Now, she could breathe and start planning her next steps.

Starting with an Uber, because no way was she walking. Her phone buzzed with a text from Ryan before she could open the rideshare app.

> I hear congrats are in order. Meet me in the lobby. This deserves a celebratory lunch.

Charlie thumbs up'd the message and went back inside. Ryan was down within minutes, and she managed to resist the urge to grab him and jump up and down with joy. He linked her arm into his, steered her to the garage and to his car. As soon as he was in the driver's seat, with the door closed, he broke into a big grin.

"I knew you'd nail the interview. Yay! We're getting away from here for lunch so we can gossip."

Charlie didn't bother to ask where they were going. They'd grown up south of the city, then left for college, and she had rarely visited—she'd spent the last several years working in resort towns. It was more fun for Ryan to visit her than the other way around. She settled into the seat and lost herself in the scenery. Baltimore had changed, and yet still looked the same in many ways.

Ryan found an open spot on the street and she followed him to a shawarma place near Hopkins. They placed their orders and took a table by the window. Ryan leaned in and raised his eyebrows.

"C'mon, you already know I got it," she said. His eyeroll was so big it was comedic. Or maybe she was just giddy. "I start Monday. Goes till late March. Which is perfect."

Ryan reached across the table and squeezed her hand. "I guess the universe meant for you to come home."

Charlie wasn't too sure about that, but her life had made a series of rapid twists and turns in the last week.

"Maybe. And it keeps me on the active employee rolls. Now I just have to cross my fingers something permanent comes up."

The smile Ryan gave her wasn't as bright as earlier, and she was pretty sure she knew why. He knew the hotel business as well as she did—there was no guarantee that something would come up in Baltimore.

"I'm thrilled for you, of course. But I hope you find something here. I miss my bestie."

She cupped his hand in both of hers and nodded. "I miss you too, but you've got Bradly. This job bought me time, and I need it because right now, I'm living on savings."

"Or you could start your own event planning business."

It wasn't a terrible idea, but Charlie had never had the desire to do all of this on her own. Sure, the ability to do different events and locations had its appeal, but she wasn't the hustle type. She'd struggled enough dealing with the sales end of things when she'd first started working at a hotel. She couldn't imagine running the whole business.

Their food arrived and Ryan started talking about their wedding plans, and how, in the interest of extending an olive branch, they'd invited his folks, but it was likely just going to be Bradly's family plus close friends and some work colleagues. Seeing weddings where one person had no family with them on their big day always tore at Charlie's heart.

Maybe because my own family is so shitty, and Ryan's isn't any better.

Sure, she'd seen couples bristling over the bickering and squabbles and the family politics—balancing the traditions of the older generation with the changes of the younger. More often than not, love won in the end.

Giving couples their dream moment—the public expression of their love and commitment—always made her feel like she was, in some small way, part of their family. Even if it was just for that day, and she cherished those memories.

A loving family was not something she'd ever known. The romantic in her craved finding her own family some day while the realist scoffed at the idea, knowing it was better to stick to a handful of dear friends and the vicarious joy she got in helping others have that bliss.

Ryan pushed his plate away and sat back with a wicked grin on his face. "I've taken the rest of the afternoon off. Would you like to check out the upstairs apartment?"

Oh shit. She'd forgotten about that place. Okay, maybe there was something to Ryan's assertion that the universe meant for her to come home. At least for a bit.

Back at the brownstone, Charlie followed Ryan up to the fourth floor. He opened the door to a space that was virtually identical to his and Bradly's, except it was a one bedroom, one bath. And even in January, flooded with light. The furniture was sleek and modern, and colorful art dotted the walls.

"Why is there a little framed card next to some paintings?"

Ryan plucked a frame off the wall and handed it to her. "Glenda and Michael own a small gallery and event space for local artists. They occasionally buy pieces for their home or to put in here. Several renters asked about some of the art, so now, most of the stuff is for sale. There's one that's not. C'mon."

He went through the short hall into the bedroom and pointed at the wall opposite the bed. A large canvas hung on the exposed brick—a woman's body in swirling shades of orange and red, and behind her, a masculine shape in blues and greens. The pose spoke passion.

Or maybe that was just her brain thinking about Deke.

She kicked herself again for not giving him her contact info. Someone like that was just what she needed to get over Noah. Well, she'd just have to find someone local instead.

"I haven't even done my budget yet, but assuming this is in my price range, when can I move in? I love y'all but..."

Ryan looked up from his phone and rolled his eyes. "I get it. You want your own space. Texting you the details from Glenda now, and her phone number. But she says you can move in tomorrow."

Charlie strolled through the apartment. It was bigger than most of the places she'd been in recently—but she'd always prioritized living near work, and that meant pricy real estate. Three months in this bright, airy space would be a dream.

She didn't even glance at her phone when the text came in. It didn't matter the cost—this place was amazing and the proximity to work and Ryan made it perfect.

"Guess I'm moving in tomorrow."

CHAPTER 4

DEKE—SATURDAY, JANUARY 11

The outdoor patio at Cold Bottom Brewing was deserted—big surprise. Early January and it was chilly despite the zipped shut plastic windows, a big patio heater on one end and a gas fireplace on the other. Deke sat with his friends, Zach and Ty. All three of them had spent plenty of hours helping out during their college years, and it was still a favorite place to go after their regular basketball games.

Inside, it was a crowded Saturday night. All the more reason for them to sit outside where they could be loud and cuss without disturbing other patrons. Which was a good thing, as they were on their second pitcher of beer and getting a little unfiltered.

"All I'm saying is you've been a punk since you got back from New Orleans." Zach downed the last swallow of beer, then topped all their glasses to finish the pitcher. "If I didn't know better, I'd think you met someone."

Deke shrugged and took a swallow of beer. They'd both

given Ty enough shit when he'd met Nicky. Now the two of them were living together, happily engaged, and probably planning their wedding.

"Nope," Deke replied. "You know the drill."

"Not till thirty," both Ty and Zach chorused.

"Exactly. I just turned twenty-nine, so this is my last year of freedom. I'm gonna enjoy it."

Except he hadn't been. He'd been feeling pretty damn good with Charlie on New Year's Eve, then she'd fallen asleep on him. It might've bruised his ego if he hadn't known they'd been on the bar crawl for a couple hours before he'd managed to meet her.

The trouble was, he couldn't get her out of his head. The memory of her kisses and the way she responded to his touch seemed burned in his brain. He told himself it was because they hadn't had sex. That was the only reason he was still so focused on her.

She sure as shit hadn't called him, even though he'd left his number. Yeah, fine, he'd said "if you're ever in Baltimore" so maybe she took that too literally.

Laughter from the patio entrance had all three of them turning their heads. Two impeccably dressed men followed the same server who'd waved them through to the outside dining once she recognized Zach.

"Sorry guys, you're getting company." She led the men to a table on the far side and as she turned away, Deke caught sight of a head of dark red curls and did a double take.

Oh no way in hell.

There she was. The killer smile and the curves that haunted his dreams. It was Charlie.

"Hey, earth to Deke. Yo!" Zach snapped his fingers in Deke's face. Ty turned back to their table, looking confused.

"You kinda went blank there for a moment. She someone you want to avoid or something?"

Deke shook his head, not trusting his voice yet. He hadn't told them much about Charlie. No details anyway. He'd never been the type to brag about his bedroom antics—that was more Zach's style—so no one expected him to come back and tell all. He said he'd had a good time, and that was that.

The trio settled into their menus, and Deke couldn't tear his eyes away from her. She tucked a lock of hair behind her ear. She was every bit as gorgeous as he remembered.

"Hey, you're staring." Ty nudged Deke's elbow.

"Was I? Shit. Yeah."

He should get up and go over there and say hello. There was no reason not to. Except she was with two men. One of them might be her boyfriend. They hadn't exchanged a lot of personal information.

"I get it. She's hot. But you're usually a lot more chill than that. What the fuck."

Ty shifted at the table, so Deke had to turn away from Charlie and her friends. Zach leaned around and took a long look before turning back and shaking his head.

"She's pretty, just not my type."

Ty rolled his eyes and Deke flipped his friend off. Technically, Zach wasn't choosy—he'd go for any pretty woman who caught his attention and seemed open to his advances. It just happened that his attention leaned toward tall, trim blondes with big boobs. Luckily for him, they seemed equally interested in him. At least until they discovered he was only in it for the sex.

The big difference between Deke and Zach was that Deke was always honest about his lack of interest in a traditional relationship.

Ty tossed a few bills on the table and Deke fished out his

wallet to do the same. Zach scooped everything up, then disappeared to go pay. Ty scraped his chair back and stood as well.

"Nicky's out with Sabrina and Anne tonight, and you seem weird. Come by if you want to hang or something."

"Thanks, but I'll finish this and head home. First week back after break is kicking my ass."

"What? Lightweight. What the fuck got into you? Guess I'm on my own for the Metro Gallery." Zach snagged his jacket from the chair and followed Ty out.

Laughter carried across the patio as Deke finished his beer and he snuck another look as the server came to take their order. Something clicked and he realized the two men were a couple.

So she's not dating either of them. I can go say hello.

The server moved away and Charlie glanced up. Even across the room, those beautiful blue eyes caught his attention. She blinked and her eyebrows raised, then her lips parted in a look of shock.

Fuck it.

Deke rose, shrugged into his jacket and crossed the patio. He didn't expect Charlie to stand to greet him. He was even more surprised when his body moved before his brain did and he wrapped his arms around her in a big hug and it was the same feeling from New Year's Eve all over again— holding her just felt good. He released her before he wanted to.

Charlie bit her lip and confusion painted her face.

"I um... wow... Smalltimore is living up to its reputation, I guess. What are you doing here? I mean, I'm thrilled to see you again."

Something she said didn't sit right. She was acting like he'd disappeared without saying anything.

"I've lived here all my life. I left my number. Didn't you see my note?"

The look of confusion on her face deepened.

"I left a note under a water bottle on the nightstand." He spoke quietly, so her companions couldn't hear.

"Oh! That explains the water bottle. I knocked it over when I woke up. I never saw a note, just my uh... yeah. I'm sorry. I figured... well..."

She bit her lip again and Deke could only imagine what had been going through her mind when she woke up, still in the dress from the night before and him nowhere in sight.

"Guess the powers that be figured we needed a second chance." He hoped she agreed with him. Maybe a quick hookup would get her out of his system and kick off a year of fun. Charlie tipped her head to the side and smiled—the expression took him right back to being on the rooftop with her, and had his cock waking up.

"I'd like that. Hang on." She turned to the table, said something to her friends and fished her phone from her purse before turning back to him.

"Deke, this my best friend Ryan Grant and his fiancé Bradly Simon." She pointed to the two men. He was fairly certain the sandy haired one was Ryan and the guy who looked like the Duke from some show his sister used to watch was Bradly. "This is Deke. We met down in New Orleans."

"Is he..." Probably Ryan snapped his mouth shut when Charlie glared at him.

Oh great. What the hell did she tell him? It couldn't have been too bad. The look on Probably Ryan's face had been happy. They all shook hands. Likely Bradly invited Deke to join them.

"Thanks, but I was just headed out. Umm..." He turned

to Charlie, intent on asking for her number. She handed him her phone with a new contact form open.

"Put your number in."

"Perfect." He tapped in his info then leaned close when he handed her phone back. "Maybe we can take up where we left off. Text me so I have your number," he whispered in her ear. He straightened to find a broad smile on Charlie's face.

"I'm here for a few months for work and their wedding. I'm sure I can find the time." She winked at him, then turned back to her friends.

Deke left the brewery in a much better mood, feeling like all was right in his world again.

CHARLIE

"You said he was hot. You didn't say he was that hot." Ryan fanned himself as he leaned over to watch Deke walking away.

Charlie smacked his arm. "You're a taken man. Behave."

"Taken doesn't mean dead," Bradly chimed in. "Nothing wrong with admiring. Besides, I think I know him. Sort of. He's a teacher at my nephew's school. All the single moms, and a lot of the not-single ones, drool over him."

Ryan tore his attention back to the table and scowled at his fiancé. "That's Mr. Wallace? Wow."

Charlie was pretty sure they hadn't shared last names when they'd introduced themselves. She did recall that he'd said he was a math teacher. Bradly held his phone up and there was a picture of Deke.

"Patapsco Academy?"

Bradly nodded. Charlie took the phone and zoomed in. Even in a basic headshot, he looked like a god. She closed the page and handed the phone back.

"What're the odds of you meeting some hot guy on New Year's Eve, in another state no less, then running into him again in Baltimore?" Ryan snagged her hand and gave her his puppy dog eyes. "It's like it's fate."

She didn't believe in fate. It was just a word people threw around for whatever purpose served them. Like destiny. Her mother had been convinced she and Ryan were destined to be together. *In a way, it's true—just not the way she thought.* On the other hand, she'd been dreading the idea of trying to meet someone new and running into Deke saved her from that process.

A group of laughing women came in and were seated a few tables over. Charlie didn't miss the frequent glances their way. Not that she could blame them. Both Ryan and Bradly were sinfully good looking and the two of them together was a guaranteed head turner.

Ryan was keenly aware that he'd morphed into a swan, while from what she'd seen of Bradly so far, he went through life unaware of his own near-impossible beauty. He also seemed like a genuinely nice man and clearly doted on her bestie, who returned the adulation in equal measure.

They were perfect for each other and it warmed her heart to see Ryan happy and able to be his authentic self.

"So, not to talk business, but I sent you both some dates for cake tastings and you need to let me know what works." Charlie pulled out her phone, determined to nail them both down now while she had them together and sitting still.

Ryan heaved a theatrical sigh and snagged his phone while Bradly thumbed his back on.

"Okay, Madam Drill Sergeant. The troops await your command."

Charlie rolled her eyes at Bradly. She could see why Ryan liked him so much.

"Your schedules have coinciding free times on Tuesday afternoon, Thursday evening, and this coming Friday afternoon. The baker has availability on all three of those dates, but the florist is only available Tuesday."

Five minutes of back-and-forth logistics later, Charlie was sending emails to confirm with the florist for Tuesday, and the baker for Friday.

Their meals came and the conversation and laughter flowed easily. It had been years since Charlie felt this relaxed.

"I have a sensitive question." Ryan tapped the table, a sure sign he was nervous. "Should we invite your folks? Bradly brought it up and well, I mean, we invited my family, so it makes sense, but it's up to you."

Hayley Jones had pointedly ignored Ryan at their college graduation ceremony. She'd assumed for years that Charlie and Ryan were a thing, only to be stunned when Charlie started dating someone else. When her mother learned Ryan was gay, she blamed him for Charlie's relationship with Jonathan.

It made no sense to Charlie then, and even less sense now.

"You think I've talked to her?" She sat back and laughed, then looked over at Bradly. "Sorry, I don't have the healthiest relationship with my parents. I was over at Ryan's more than I was home, to be honest. They weren't as awful during high school. That came later."

"Families are complicated," he replied. "My folks took a while to come around to my sexuality, but they've been supportive and they love Ryan. We're lucky there. His folks? Well, that's a less than rosy picture, but we're trying and they said they'd come to the wedding."

"Don't invite my folks on my account," Charlie said. "It's your day and it should be about the people who love and support you. Period."

Ryan and Bradly exchanged quiet smiles, then Ryan reached out and took Charlie's hands.

"I believe in giving people a chance. I know she wasn't the greatest, but your folks were so much a part of my life, our lives, as kids. Have you tried reaching out to her?"

Charlie swallowed hard. She didn't have the heart to tell Ryan the horrible things her mother had said.

"It's your wedding," she said. "I'll be on my best behavior no matter what. You know I'll do anything for you."

"If you're truly comfortable." Ryan's tone said it all. He'd put enough together to understand. "Because if you're not, I'll scratch them from the guest list without a second thought."

Bradly leaned in with a wicked smile. "We should send an announcement at least. And make sure it's a picture card."

"I like the way he thinks!" Charlie dissolved into laughter and the weird tension was broken.

"I'm sorry for bringing up an ugly subject." Ryan shook his head as if clearing cobwebs. "I won't do anything unless you say so."

And that was the end of it. No questions about details. Just quiet understanding and support. She reached across the table and squeezed his hand.

"I'll reach out. See how it goes and let you know."

Less than two weeks back home and Charlie felt like she'd gained a second bestie in Bradly, plus she'd secured a financial reprieve with the job and her rent was downright affordable. Now she had another chance with Deke, who was definitely an ideal way to move on from Noah.

Later, her phone buzzed as she climbed the steps to her temporary home. She forced herself to wait until she was in the door before opening the message from Deke.

> Hey, it was great to run into you. Think I could talk you into dinner next Saturday?

She tried not to think about the way her stomach clenched at the message. The night they'd met would have been a just a hookup. Maybe this would be the same. Or maybe not. She'd always preferred an ongoing friends-with-benefits type thing, but Deke had said something about that blowing up on him. Maybe all he did was hookups.

Either way, the man was hot as fuck and from what she remembered, was pretty damn skilled, and easy, fun sex would be the icing on her cake.

> Possibly. Start talking.

> Someplace quiet. A little get to know you time. Some good food. See where things go—but I'm thinking late night dessert at your place or mine?

Well, he was direct. That was a good thing. It made it easy to keep him firmly in the safe zone. The last thing she wanted to do was get emotionally involved with anyone ever again.

> I like that plan.

She had no doubt the night would end with them in bed together, and that was fine by her. She was looking forward to discovering the extent of his skills.

> Pick you up at seven?

That brought a laugh. Charlie was used to meeting a man some place. She liked having the easy out of her own transportation. Meh. She could always call a car.

Looking forward to it. Just give me an idea of dress code and I'll text you the address.

Will do, beautiful.

She smiled as she rose to get showered and tried to tell herself it had nothing to do with her weekend plans with Deke.

Except it had everything to do with that, and she knew it.

CHAPTER 5

CHARLIE—FRIDAY, JANUARY 17

One look at the world outside the hotel and Charlie ordered an Uber. It was only a mile and a half walk, but some intersections were dicey on good days, never mind in snow and after dark. It hadn't taken long to learn that Baltimore public transit was unreliable at best.

She slid into the car as her phone buzzed with an incoming text from Deke.

> Hey beautiful. About to hit the gym. Maybe I'll send a pic later.

Once inside the apartment, Charlie got out of her clothes and into a silky robe that made her feel like a goddess and contemplated whether to fix dinner first, or shower. When her phone buzzed again and she saw Deke's name, she crossed her fingers he hadn't sent a dick pic. Not that she minded them, but dammit, ask a girl first. She scrolled down and gasped. No dick pic—she should have known that a man who asked if he could touch her while dancing wouldn't send unsolicited nudes.

Deke had sent a gym shot—and not a mirror selfie. He must've propped his phone up on something and used a timer. He stood with his back to the camera. Shirt off and snug fitting shorts that highlighted a perfect ass.

> Tease.

He hadn't been kidding when he said he worked out to be fit, but not too fit. His back tapered from broad shoulders down to a narrow waist and well-muscled ass and legs. Either he was blessed by the gods with the perfect metabolism, or he worked harder at maintaining that physique than he admitted.

> I am in public. For now. Any requests?

> Surprise me. Nothing's off limits.

Three dots appeared. Then disappeared. Then appeared again. Had she broken his brain?

> Careful what you ask for. I'm all about reciprocity.

A smiling devil emoji followed. Charlie didn't think twice. She opened the camera app, propped her phone up and turned her back to it, then let her robe fall as the timer counted down. She snatched up the phone and checked the pic.

Perfect.

Light from the alley shone in through the windows, casting the bedroom in shadow and light. The picture showed some hair, her shoulder, a little of her back and a blur of soft gold satin from the robe. She hit send without editing.

> There you go. Your turn.

She laid her phone down, checked that her vibrator was charged—she suspected she'd be wanting that later—and headed for the shower.

When she came out, wrapped in a thick, fluffy towel, and flipped her phone over, she wasn't disappointed.

Deke had sent a series of images of him in the shower. Careful body angles, lots of steam, and soap bubbles meant he wasn't showing any naughty bits, but everything else was on delicious, wet, sudsy display. It was tempting to ask for his address and head straight over there.

Instead, she sent a drooling emoji, then looked around for inspiration of what she could send back. Before she could decide, Deke's name popped up on her phone and she swiped to answer.

"I want to ask you to do something for me."

His voice was raspy and low and it sent pleasant shivers all over Charlie's skin. She swallowed hard. He hit all the right buttons for her. This was going to be fun.

"I'm listening."

She tried to keep her voice steady, but something about him took her from mildly aroused to wanting the kind of primal sex where you weren't sure you could look your partner in the eye afterward.

"Don't come tonight."

What? Did he just...

Charlie's stomach knotted and her breath caught. Her body ached for touch, for release. And now her mind whirled with the idea of denial.

"It's a request, Charlie. You're free to do whatever you want. But I'm asking if you masturbate, stop before you reach orgasm."

This wasn't a new game. Hell, he'd teased her like this on New Year's Eve. She'd played it before, but she'd never felt the level of eager anticipation she experienced now.

"Okay, but tell me why."

A rich chuckle vibrated through her phone. "We have a date tomorrow night. Maybe I'm assuming too much, but I don't imagine that's going to end with a chaste kiss goodnight. Am I wrong?"

With just a few words, he'd wound her up so tight that she felt ready to explode.

"You're not wrong."

A soft growl sounded in her ears and Charlie pulled in a shuddering breath.

"Good. I like the idea of taking you to dinner tomorrow, knowing the whole time that you're aching to come."

"What about you? Are you going to wait, too?"

He let out a harsh breath that turned into another low growl. "You sure you want that? I've got a pretty high sex drive already."

It was Charlie's turn to laugh. "Bring it on. If I'm not coming tonight, neither should you. Fair's fair. In fact, we should make a game of it. Whoever asks for sex first loses."

She had no idea why that thought had popped into her head, or why she'd let it out of her mouth, but there it was. Too late to take it back.

Well, let's see where he goes with it.

"Sounds like a win-win," he replied. "If I remember right, you enjoyed being teased."

She'd already figured out that Deke had some interests beyond vanilla, and she was all for it. Now she just needed to find out how far beyond vanilla, but that could wait for tomorrow.

"And you don't?" She shot the question at him, unable to resist being a little bratty.

"I never said that. But that could lead to things that need more than a discussion of sexual history and condoms."

That was a veiled reference to negotiations and safe words if she'd ever heard one.

"That's a conversation for in person," he continued. "I have reservations for dinner. You okay if we talk in the car?"

"I like that plan."

"See you tomorrow, beautiful."

Charlie laid the phone down then stuffed her vibrator back in the nightstand drawer. She'd have to skip that tonight if she was going to abide by his request. She could still use her fingers and it would be easier to keep herself on edge than with a toy.

She sprawled on the bed and scrolled through the pictures again, recalling the night they'd met. The end of the evening might have been a blur, but the memory of his hands all over her body were clear as a bell. As was the memory of her hand down his pants.

And his girth.

She closed her eyes and sucked in a breath.

He'd said he wanted her aching to come tomorrow. Like she wasn't already. Deke had been playing a starring role in her fantasies ever since they'd met. At this rate, she'd be ready to sit in his lap at dinner and who gave a shit who saw.

DEKE—SATURDAY, JANUARY 18

Deke pulled up and found Charlie waiting on the steps for him. The streetlights turned her hair into a halo of red against a dark brown coat open over a sleek dress that seemed molded to her curves. He hopped out to open her car door and smiled.

"You look amazing. I really want to kiss you."

She crooked her finger at him and Deke stepped closer. He slid an arm around her waist and Charlie leaned into him.

The moment their lips touched, it was like a fire ignited in his veins. She was like inhaling every delicious thing he'd ever experienced. Her lips parted and she moaned softly. At this rate, they'd be going back upstairs. Screw dinner. He wanted to spend the next several hours mapping every inch of her body.

Charlie coiled her hands into his hair and somehow brought him closer. She was all softness and welcoming warmth. Deke slid his hand down and cupped her ass. When she gasped and arched against him, breaking the kiss as her head tipped back, exposing her neck, his brain flashed back to the night they'd met.

It didn't matter that they were standing on the curb as people walked by in the park behind them. Deke trailed kisses along her jaw, then under her ear and down her neck. She smelled of roses and citrus and something mysterious and spicy.

A horn honked on the street and Deke raised his head. Charlie's eyelids fluttered open and her lips curled up in a smile. Deke cupped her face and used his thumb to wipe a smudge of lipstick off.

"You're going to have to fix that," he said. "Good to see you again."

He didn't let go of her. They should get in the car. Have the conversation they needed to have. Drive to dinner. They should do lots of things, but he didn't want to take his hands off of her.

"Hang on." Charlie shifted, pulled a pack of tissues from somewhere and handed him one. "Nude Now is not your color."

She slid into the car and Deke closed the door, then went around, wiping off the lipstick as he settled into the driver's seat. Charlie had pulled out a mirror and a slim tube of lipstick.

Every fiber of his being was screaming at him to suggest they go straight inside to her apartment. Which would be great if this was a one-time thing like New Orleans was supposed to be. Now? Bumping into her again felt like maybe it was something more. He took a slow breath and tried to calm the raging desire pounding in his body. As if the physical attraction wasn't enough, their text messages over the past week had him keyed up. It had been a long time since he'd felt so much anticipation for a date.

"I think we're both in for an interesting night." He reached over and brushed a curl of hair from her face. "Should we have that conversation now?"

Charlie tossed her lipstick into a bag he hadn't realized she was carrying and nodded.

"I'm going out on a limb and saying you lean toward the dominant side."

Deke put the car in gear and pulled onto the road. "Yes and no. More pleasure dom, really. Maybe a side of not-quite primal, if I had to put labels on things. I prefer to keep it more flexible than that and figure out what dynamic works with my partner."

Never mind that his reasons were that too many past partners were a little freaked out by his kinkier side. He'd learned to hold back and let their comfort determine things. If their encounter in New Orleans was any indicator, he didn't have to worry about that with Charlie.

"We're very alike, then," she replied. "I'm less about predator-prey and more about just... uninhibited.

Unrestrained. I don't want to limit myself by putting things in a box."

That explained so much about her. The night just got infinitely more interesting. He couldn't recall the last time he'd had a full negotiation with someone who knew their own kinks.

"I figured you'd done this before." For the rest of the drive, they went back and forth, discussing sexual history and recent STI test results. Things they had not gotten to the night they met.

"I'm on birth control, but condoms are still a must," Charlie said as Deke pulled into a parking space half a block from the restaurant. "If you're particular about them, that's on you."

Deke hit the parking brake, undid his seatbelt and turned to face her. "I am. And I always have them."

He figured protection was his responsibility, so he made sure he was prepared. That and he'd made the mistake of not bringing his own only to find the ones the woman had on hand were uncomfortable as fuck.

"Now that we've gotten all of that out of the way, did you masturbate last night? And did you finish?"

Charlie whipped her head around to look at him. Her mouth popped into a perfect 'O' then she broke into a wide grin.

"I did masturbate, but no, I didn't orgasm. What about you?"

"Same," he replied. He wasn't going to tell her that he stroked his cock for an hour, imagining what he was going to do with her tonight. Right now, he was so on edge, he was surprised he hadn't come in his pants when they kissed.

"So what's the goal with this game of yours?" Deke had a feeling he knew the answer, but he wanted to hear her say it.

She arched an eyebrow at him. "I thought I made that clear. If you want to be in control, you're going to have to take it."

Exactly what he'd imagined. *Time to make sure I win.*

"Are you sure you're up for that?"

Charlie threw her head back and laughed, then leveled him with the sexiest gaze he'd ever seen. "Are you?"

"Game on."

Deke came around and opened her door. She slipped her hand into the crook of his arm and walked with him like they'd done this hundreds of times.

The meal passed in a blur of pleasant conversation that was very different from the matter-of-fact discussion they'd had during the drive. Over dinner, Charlie was light and funny, charming and warm and flirtatious. She sparkled with life and joy. Her blue eyes danced in the candlelight as she leaned forward to tell a slightly dirty joke, then again when he made a not-so-subtle innuendo.

She touched him frequently—the brush of her fingers against the back of his hand as they ordered after dinner coffee sent his pulse racing.

He crooked a finger and beckoned her closer. She leaned into him, her leg pressing against his.

"I'd like you to go to the ladies', take off your panties, then come slip them into my jacket pocket."

Charlie sat back and smiled. "You'll have to work harder than that."

She had turned fully to face him. Her arms relaxed by her sides and her head tipped at an angle. The expression on her face made it clear. She might as well have said 'make me'.

Deke laid one arm over the back of her chair and slid his hand up the nape of her neck. He curled his fingers into her hair and clenched. Not enough to be obvious to anyone watching, but enough that Charlie caught her breath and sat up straighter.

He leaned close and placed his lips against her ear. "Go to the ladies' room and take off your panties. You did it for me in New Orleans, but you didn't get to enjoy the reward. Show me you want it now."

He released his grip on her hair but stayed close to her. Charlie tossed her napkin on the table and rose, never taking her eyes off his.

"I'll be right back."

The sway of her hips in the slim-fitting dress was magnificent, and several other diners followed her progress.

Look all you'd like, tonight, that is all mine.

He took care of the check and stood when Charlie came back. He caught her wrist and tipped his head toward the door. She nodded and leaned in to him. Her hand slipped into his jacket pocket and she winked.

Back in the car, he started the engine and caught her gaze. "Before we go any further down this road, I need to ask if you're okay with everything so far, and if you're comfortable with everything we've talked about."

Charlie chuckled, her shoulders shaking slightly. "We're good. I am very capable of communicating if I have a problem."

Deke nodded. Tension coiled in his gut and his cock throbbed at the thought of what could come next. He swallowed hard and laid a hand on Charlie's thigh, pinched the hem of her dress and dragged it up her leg.

Charlie didn't hesitate. She lifted her hips a little and shimmied in the seat. He hiked her skirt until it sat high on her legs and he had a glimpse of red hair at the juncture of her thighs.

"Spread your legs."

Deke put the car in gear and got onto the road as Charlie complied. Not as wide as he'd have liked, but this was the fight for control that she said she liked. He put his hand on her leg and pulled until she opened wider.

The screen on his dash lit up and a loud ring filled the car. *Sarah. What the fuck?* He swore and tapped the ignore button. No sooner had he returned his hand to Charlie's leg than the phone rang again. He ignored the call only to have his phone buzz with an incoming text. Deke sighed and fished his phone from his pocket and handed it to Charlie.

"I'm sorry, but that's my sister and two calls, then a text? Something's up. Can you check the message." He rattled off the unlock code, something he'd never given anyone before and Charlie hissed in a breath, and not in a sexy way.

"Just says 'Emergency. Call now.'" Charlie held the phone out to him.

Deke shook his head and tapped the screen. Sarah picked up halfway through the first ring. The sound of crying children pierced the air and Charlie's face scrunched up. He couldn't blame her. The noise was horrible in the small car.

"Jacob took a tumble and he cut his head and there's blood everywhere and he and Olivia won't stop screaming and I've been on the phone with an on-call and they say to bring him in but I don't have anyone to watch Olivia because Chris is out of town and Lizzie and Rick are on vacation and I don't know where Marisol is and just get here."

She'd rattled through everything so fast he wasn't sure she'd had a chance to breathe. Deke glanced at Charlie. She'd tugged her skirt back into place and her face bore a concerned expression. This was not how he'd pictured their evening.

"I'm not alone," he said. He reached over and took Charlie's hand. She squeezed his fingers and he wasn't sure if it was meant to encourage him to take care of family business, or to hang up and turn off his ringer. "Why didn't you call Mom and Dad?"

Deke loved being an uncle. So much so that he didn't entirely hate the idea of settling down and having a kid of his own someday, but he liked things planned, not this 'drop everything and get over here now' kind of shit. *Which is kinda what parenting is, come to think of it.*

"They're with Lizzie and Rick and the kids. Come on, Deke! Jacob is bleeding all over the place."

Fuck. No matter how much he wanted to, he couldn't ignore this.

"There in five. Bye."

He hung up and took the next right, then glanced at Charlie.

"I'm sorry. This is..."

He stopped when her hand landed on his thigh.

"It's family," she replied. "I'll call a car to get me home."

He'd been planning to suggest she could hang around, but that wasn't the kind of thing you did with a fuck buddy. That was relationship kind of stuff.

"Can we raincheck? I promise I will more than make up for this."

She narrowed her eyes as if weighing the options, then smiled. "Yeah. I think that can be arranged."

When he pulled up to his sister's house, he leaned over and gave Charlie a quick kiss.

"You are welcome to come in..." He didn't finish. Charlie shook her head and patted his hand.

"Get in there and take care of business. You don't need a stranger cluttering up things."

He didn't like the sound of that, but Sarah was standing on her front porch, cradling both kids and looking desperate.

"I'll leave the keys in the car so you're not standing around on the curb. Just turn it off when you get out and I'll come get them later."

He kissed her again and got out before she could tell him no. The second he opened the car door, the high-pitch crying of both kids assaulted his ears. He took the porch steps two at a time and scooped Olivia from Sarah's arms. His sister was smeared with blood and Jacob had a big gash across his forehead that was still bleeding.

"Do you need me to drive?"

Sarah picked up a bag from the bench next to the door and shook her head. "It'll take too long to get them both in car seats. The doctor called ahead so they're expecting us. You're not making your date wait in the car, are you? Don't be rude!"

She went down the stairs and hauled open the door of her SUV right as a small sedan pulled up and Charlie exited his car. She waved at him and slid into the Uber and they were off seconds before Sarah backed out of the drive.

His niece's tears turned into sniffles and hiccups, then she laid her head on his shoulder and by the shift in weight, fell right asleep.

"Figures." It took about two seconds to decide he was better off carrying Olivia to his car to get his keys rather than trying to lay her down inside first. He didn't want to risk waking her up.

His phone buzzed as he closed and locked the car door. *Fuck.* Whoever it was would have to wait. Olivia was a thirty-pound sack of potatoes with a lolling head and arms. He nearly tripped on a toy going up the porch steps and Olivia's foot caught him square in the groin.

Once inside, he tucked his niece onto the couch and headed for the kitchen. He'd take care of cleaning her up later. For now, he was crossing his fingers his sister kept beer in her fridge.

Score! He snagged a can of a local IPA, cracked it open and rummaged in his pocket for his phone. Something caught his finger and the phone tumbled from his hand before skittering across the floor.

What the hell?

His phone seemed none the worse for wear and he checked his pocket for whatever had caused the fumble, then groaned as he pulled out a scrap of thin, stretchy fabric.

Charlie's panties.

He tucked them back in his pocket before stripping off his jacket and hanging it up, then thumbed his screen.

> It was a good start to an evening. If you'd like a raincheck, here are my free times.

A short list of dates followed. Deke settled on the couch with Olivia curled up next to him and pulled up his calendar. He'd make time for Charlie.

CHAPTER 6

CHARLIE—SUNDAY, JANUARY 19

The clink of silverware and the hum of excited conversation filled the air. Charlie's job was done. The brunch itself was in the capable hands of one of the event coordinators, but these were the moments Charlie lived for. When everything came together and the guests got to relax and enjoy their special day. In this case, it was particularly rewarding.

The engagement brunch had been scheduled for twelve guests, then increased to thirty, and down to two dozen just before the cut off for changes. The whole thing was almost canceled late Saturday night when the groom-to-be's parents got delayed with the weather. But now, everyone was here and there were happy smiles all around.

Frantic movement down the hall caught her eye and Charlie moved away from the door of the private dining space so as not to disturb the guests with whatever crisis was coming her way in the form of the spa manager.

"I have two staff members out sick. There is no way we can

71

handle a couple's massage." Sharon stuck her hands on her hips and glared toward the room.

It had taken Charlie less than a week to figure out that Sharon was one of those people for whom everything was a catastrophe. When something went wrong, she'd immediately go worst case scenario and choose the most extreme, and inconvenient, solution. On the plus side, it was easy to talk her down and offer better options.

"So, there's no qualified staff to do a massage today?"

The trick with her was to not jump in with suggestions until you had gotten the full story. She never led with all the relevant details.

"Well, no. Or yes. We have two massage therapists who are in, but that means I'm shorthanded."

Charlie bit her lip to keep from laughing. She tried to look like she was thinking for a moment before responding.

"And there are other massages booked at the same time?"

Sharon scowled and shook her head. *There it is. The truth.*

"So, you can handle the couple's massage," Charlie said. She grabbed her tablet and tapped the screen. "They're not scheduled for that until one—that's an hour from now. They bought a whole spa package. If you get a walk in before then, shuffle their services around. Start with the sauna. Or facials. Or the mani-pedis."

She shouldn't have to be having this conversation, but Sharon was new to the job and while she was terrific at some parts of it, she didn't excel at the juggling. Combined with her tendency to be overdramatic when it came to the inevitable hiccups, Charlie imagined she wouldn't last long in the role.

"I just hate to turn away a guest."

"Then call someone in," Charlie replied. "You have time."

She, on the other hand, did not have time for this. She had a meeting scheduled for noon, which left her ten minutes to wrap this up and get back to her office. The spa was not Charlie's department. She had to coordinate with them quite a bit, but she didn't have in-depth knowledge of their inner workings.

And I don't want to.

"Yeah, I mean, I guess you're right." Sharon heaved a sigh and shook her head. "How do you stay so calm?"

That was the first time Charlie had heard her say anything that revealed she was stressed, and knew it. Maybe there was hope.

"Years of experience," Charlie replied. "And I'm sorry, but I have a couple coming in to discuss a wedding and reception. You all set?"

If the answer was no, Charlie couldn't do much to help, but she could damn well call someone higher up the food chain. Her only concern was making sure the couple celebrating their engagement would get the whole experience they had scheduled and paid for.

The spa manager nodded and thanked her, then went back down the hall much more slowly than she'd come up. Charlie took one last glance at the happy crowd in the room then headed for her office for a meeting that she hoped she could wrap up in an hour. She had late lunch plans with Ryan and Bradly.

At one on the dot, Charlie saw the new guests to the lobby then checked her phone again—no texts about a delayed or canceled couple's massage. Still, the moment she was back in her office, she confirmed the couple were checked into the spa on time. *Good.*

She set her email to her out of office reply, made sure she didn't have anyone else coming in today, then grabbed her coat and called an Uber.

Inside the Baltimore Museum of Art lobby, Ryan met Charlie at the door and grabbed her hand.

"Bradly's just over there. We ran into his new boss." He pointed across the room to where Bradly stood with an attractive couple. The man was handsome in a preppy sort of way, but the woman was a standout. She was a walking explosion of color—bright yellow chunky boots and a sweater in swirls of red, orange, and yellow that matched the wide streaks in her hair.

"Hey. Hello!" Ryan's voice was filled with laughter as he waved a hand in front of Charlie's face. She blinked, tearing her gaze away from the woman.

"I'm sorry," Charlie said. "She's stunning." She nodded toward the woman. Ryan broke into a broad grin and tugged her toward the group.

"That is Nicky Bisset. She's an amazing artist. Teaches at MICA and does some things with the Baltimore Office of Promotion and the Arts. She did that gorgeous painting that's in your bedroom."

Of course she's an artist. And of course she was the one who'd done the painting. Charlie admired it every day—and wasn't surprised it was the only one without a price tag, she wouldn't let it go either. She embraced Bradly, then he turned her attention to the couple.

"This is Ryan's best friend Charlie Jones. This is Ty Lake and Nicky Bisset. Charlie works at the Four Seasons and is also here for our wedding. Oh, and she's staying at Glenda and Michael's place."

Charlie shook hands with both. Up close, they were both even more attractive than she'd thought. *Good grief, when did Baltimore get overrun with good looking people?*

"We were about to have lunch at Gertrude's," Bradly said. "Want to join us?"

They crossed the lobby and somehow Ty charmed his way into a table on the enclosed patio where outdoor heaters made the space comfortable despite the January chill. They settled into low chairs and ordered their drinks.

"Bradly was telling me that you painted the piece that's in the bedroom," Charlie said. "It's gorgeous."

Nicky let out a little gasp and her cheeks turned rosy, but she smiled. "Thank you. I didn't know who bought it until recently."

Looking at Nicky and Ty, it was obvious the painting was them. The colorful forms on the canvas might be abstract, but they captured the vibe of the attractive couple. *Their sex life must be amazing.*

"Ty is the new Assistant Director at the Baltimore Museum of Art," Bradly said, pulling Charlie's mind back to the conversation. "We had a welcome reception and when I met Nicky, I recognized her name and asked her about the piece. Glenda and Michael had just bought it, and I helped them hang it. So the artist's name was fresh in my head."

The conversation ebbed and flowed between talk about the Baltimore art scene, tourism, and some local politics. Nicky asked Charlie about work and where she'd been, which led to discussions of travel.

Charlie's phone buzzed for the fourth or fifth time and she let out an exasperated sigh.

"I'm so sorry. Let me just shut this thing up." Charlie fished her phone from her bag and silenced it, but not before she caught that she had missed texts from Deke. She stuffed her phone away but couldn't wipe the smile from her face. They'd been texting every day since they reconnected, and he was just as flirty as in person.

"Oh, must've been the hottie you met the other night." Ryan flashed a grin and winked. Nicky and Ty exchanged the sort of smile couples saved for when a friend met someone new—a sort of knowing conspiratorial grin. Bradly leaned in and gave her a 'tell us more' look.

"She met a man on New Year's Eve," Ryan explained to Ty and Nicky when Charlie didn't immediately pipe up. "In New Orleans. They never exchanged numbers. Then, who should she run into when she comes back here? It's fate."

At least he'd kept it tame and not shared all the details.

"I flirted with a guy at a holiday bar crawl," Charlie added. "Hardly groundbreaking. And yeah, it was a pleasant surprise to run into him here. I don't think my personal life is riveting lunch conversation."

"Honey, I've seen the man. He's hot," Ryan said. Charlie wanted to kick him. She'd forgotten how chatty he could be. Still, it was all in good fun and he was never hurtful.

"Mr. Wallace? Hot isn't doing him justice." Bradly fanned himself, then leaned toward Ty and Nicky. "He's my kid brother's math teacher."

Ty burst into laughter—full and throaty, then shook his head, whispered something to Nicky, who nodded and looked like she was stifling a laugh as well. When he got control of himself, he leaned forward and braced his elbows on his knees.

"If you met Deke Wallace, you should know he's a great guy, the best, but he's not the relationship type. He's pretty good about making that clear though—just believe him when he says it."

Part of Charlie bristled at this guy she had just met inserting himself into her personal life. On the other hand, it was good to know that Deke was being honest.

"Good thing there's no danger of me wanting a relationship," Charlie replied. "He does seem nice. You two are friends?"

Ty sat back and picked up his drink. "We met in college.

Him and his roommate, Zach. The three of us have been friends ever since. Welcome to Smalltimore."

"He means they're virtually inseparable," Nicky said with a laugh.

The easy laughter and friendly banter were things Charlie missed. She'd never had close friends after college—just her long-distance friendship with Ryan. For the first few years after graduation, she'd been too busy and too transient. Then it became habit.

She settled back in her chair and let the atmosphere wash over her. *I could get used to this.*

DEKE—WEDNESDAY, JANUARY 22

The classroom door clicked shut behind the last parent of the day. Deke's mentor taught him years ago to build in extra office hours at strategic points during the year. A few weeks after winter break was one of those times. No surprise, Audra Pennington was nowhere to be seen on the schedule for parent-teacher conferences, despite her repeated insistence that she wanted to talk to him about her son, and Deke's repeated insistence that she could make an appointment.

Another thing his mentor had drilled into him—set your boundaries and protect your down time. Deke closed the student information portal and turned off the Smart Board and his laptop. The buzzing of an incoming text brought a smile—it had to be Charlie. Texting with her had become a regular thing.

It was mostly flirtatious banter and borderline sexting, but had begun to include a lot of personal bits and general checking in. He swiped at his phone screen and a low moan escaped his lips when he opened the picture.

Charlie was face down on a bed and the camera angle gave

a terrific view of her cleavage and her ass. He imagined the position she had to be in to get that shot, and the thought of it sent blood flowing straight to his cock. Didn't help that yesterday, when they'd agreed on a date this Friday afternoon, he'd repeated the request for her to not orgasm until their date. She'd again insisted he do the same, then upped the ante by suggesting edging—bringing themselves right to the brink of orgasm before stopping. Repeatedly.

Except she'd started playing dirty. Leaving sexy voice notes and sending the most provocative pictures. He responded in kind, of course. Neither had sent anything that showed naked genitals, but there had been a lot of hinting.

Deke pushed his chair back and angled his phone to capture a shot of the clear outline of his cock pressing against his pants.

> That's a fucking sexy pic. You can see what you do to me.

He hit send. Her reply came in seconds.

> I like it. We still playing the little game to see who can hold out the longest?

A slow groan escaped his mouth and Deke cringed at the thought. He had no interest in denying himself longer than he had to. As far as he was concerned, Friday was time to relieve the tension that had been building up over the three weeks since he'd met her.

> I think we're past that. I'm interested in being able to let loose and enjoy, so let's see where things go.

A little heart appeared next to his message. *Good, she likes that plan.* Judging by their interactions so far, and the things they'd discussed, Deke suspected sex with Charlie was going to be off the charts good. She brought out a side of him he usually kept in tight control.

> I like it. I do recall someone promising to make me come with his mouth. I intend to hold you to that, and hopefully return the favor.

That sent another jolt to his still hard cock. Deke stuffed his laptop in his bag and gathered his things. He needed to get home if he was going to continue this conversation. He typed out a quick note to let Charlie know he was packing up and would be a few minutes, then closed his classroom and hurried to his car, thankful his bag covered the obvious bulge in his pants.

Once on the road, he tapped the button to record a voice note.

"I have every intention of making good on that promise. You will have to beg me to stop. You're welcome to return the favor if you enjoy doing it, but I have a take it or leave it attitude on getting head. I'll text when I'm back home. How was your day?"

He shifted his attention back to driving and when he got home, there were messages waiting for him.

> I like the way you think. And wait? Really? You may be the only guy I've ever heard say that.

Deke kicked off his shoes and rolled his eyes at the last part. He'd heard that before, but he really didn't care one way or the other about getting head. It was hot as fuck when a partner enjoyed doing it, and he loved the visual. Too many women went about it like it was a duty, not a pleasure, and teeth were not a good feeling.

> Day was good. A lot of folks making plans for the 14th. Gotta love romantics. And a lot of corporate planning. I won't miss that when I leave. Most places I've been were more vacation and occasion.

A little stab of something jolted through him at the mention of leaving. He'd gone from thinking one-time hookup, to casual sex, and somehow that had turned into him subconsciously thinking long term friends with benefits. *And where the hell did that come from?* He dropped his things on the small dining table then padded upstairs to change clothes, typing while he walked.

> You'd mentioned the job was temp. All the more reason to fully enjoy what time we have.

He stripped, stuffed his clothes in the hamper and settled on his bed in his shorts and undershirt.

> Are you at home?

She could have taken that pic earlier, but he suspected she was home and in a mood. Well, fuck, so was he. His cock pulsed and throbbed, demanding attention. Deke pushed his waistband down and wrapped his fingers around his cock.

> Yes. And naked. Wishing it was Friday.

So did he. The idea of having seeing Charlie at home, with

no time constraints, was intoxicating. The day couldn't come fast enough.

> I'm looking forward to exploring every inch of your body and finding out just how much you can take. I want you to make a voice note right now of you playing with yourself —I want to hear the sounds you make.

An 'OK' appeared almost immediately and Deke slid his hand up and down his cock. A drop of precum gathered at the head as he stroked.

On Friday, he'd get Charlie up here, ass on the edge of the bed and legs spread wide and see if she tasted as good as he expected her to.

Finding a woman who wanted to explore her kinkier side wasn't that difficult. Finding one who wanted the same level of intensity that he craved was. So he kept himself under control and carefully mapped out their boundaries so he could stay within them.

The steady ache of unrelieved sexual tension had him wanting to grab a bottle of lotion and let himself come. But he'd wait. And he'd hope he could let go more than usual with Charlie.

His phone buzzed and he tapped the screen, then hit play on the voice note.

There was a rustle of what sounded like sheets, a little giggle, a sigh. The sounds painted a picture.

Charlie settling back on the bed, a little self-conscious maybe, then getting comfortable. A soft moan made his cock jump. Deke closed his eyes at the hissing intake of breath and a whispered 'oh fuck'. She'd be spread out, head thrown back as she fingered her pussy.

The drop of precum grew, spreading over the head of his

cock as he stroked in time to Charlie's gasps and moans. Her tempo sped up and he could almost feel the tension in her from the sounds she was making.

A sharp gasp and a louder moan had him thinking she'd pushed herself over the edge, but the next sounds were softer. Then more sheet rustling.

"I'd better stop and cool off." Her voice was full of smoke and sticky honey. Sultry. The stuff of fantasies. Then the recording ended.

Deke grabbed his phone and typed.

> That was beautiful, thank you. What were you imagining?

He hit send and went back to long slow strokes over his shaft. He played the voice note again, loving the rise and fall of her breathing, feeling the changes in her pace by the sounds she made. Was she imagining what they'd do Friday? He snatched his phone up at the first hint of vibration.

> The rooftop. When my back was to you and you were fingering me and pinching my nipples. I almost came right then. That's what I was imagining.

Deke hit the call button and waited for her to pick up.

"Hey." Her voice still had that sultry note and Deke closed his eyes, willing himself not to come.

"We've touched on this, but I get the feeling you like it a bit rough."

Her soft sigh felt like confirmation, but he wanted to hear her say it.

"It's more about passion. Intensity. That's the primal thing, I guess. I don't want to think about should or shouldn't."

She paused and made a humming sound, then chuckled. "But yeah, okay, if I'm being honest. I like it a bit rough at times. Never mind feeling it the next morning, I want to feel it for the next couple of days."

Oh fucking hell. Deke stopped stroking. If he kept it up after what she'd just said, he'd explode.

"I can guarantee you will," he replied. He was not prepared for her low moan in response. Nor was he ready for the little gasp that followed.

"Yes, please." It was barely a whisper, but it echoed in Deke's soul like the loudest shout.

"Charlie, did you like being pinned against me and finger fucked on a rooftop? Did you like me pinching your nipples until your whole body clenched up? You looked so amazing that night—your skin flushed, your hair getting all messed up. Tell me something, before we bumped into each other again, had you made yourself come thinking about that night?"

Something like a whimper sounded through the phone and Deke knew—she had.

"Tell me," he said.

"Yes." She cleared her throat and let out a sigh. "Yes. I did."

"Good girl. I like that. I did too. I stroked my cock thinking about how good you felt. I wanted to fuck you right on that rooftop. Just push your skirt up and pin you against the wall. I think you'd like that. What's your safe word?"

"Café." Her response was so instant he knew she'd not only done this before, but this was her normal. *She just keeps getting better.*

"Good girl. I want you to listen to my voice and touch yourself—one hand on your pussy and one hand on those magnificent tits. Don't come. Not until Friday. If you are on the edge and need to stop, tell me. But do not come. Understood?"

Her low moan sent prickles of pleasure straight to his pounding cock.

"Yes."

Deke kept his hands off himself. One stroke right now and it'd be all over.

"You know what I wanted on that rooftop? When I pinned you in that corner and you wrapped your legs around me. Your bare pussy right against my crotch. All it would have taken was a couple of tugs of fabric, slip on a condom, and I'd have been inside you."

She let out a shuddering breath.

"You were so wet," he continued. "How wet are you right now, Charlie? Tell me. Is your pussy wet and ready to be fucked?"

"Oh my god. Yes. I'm gonna have to change the sheets."

There was still too much thinking going on in her brain if she could concern herself with a wet spot on the sheets.

"Pinch your nipples, baby."

The little gasp and moan combination was a delicious reward.

"Good. Don't stop. Keep it up just like I touched you that night. You liked being finger fucked. You really liked it when it was multiple fingers. You said you liked intensity, well good. So do I. And I want to see how hard we can go together."

Deke paused and reveled in the sounds coming through the phone. Charlie's breathing was ragged and fast, peppered with little moans. She was closer to where he wanted her.

"Harder, baby. Just like you asked me that night when I was sucking on your nipples, with my fingers buried in your pussy, and my thumb on your clit. You begged for harder."

Charlie cried out, but didn't say stop.

"That's it. Keep it up, baby. Finger yourself while you remember the things I did to your body on that rooftop.

Come on, you can go harder. You can take it. Harder, baby. You said you wanted to feel it for days."

Whatever words might have come out of her mouth, they made no sense.

"You liked my teeth on your nipples. And you liked it when I pushed the hood back and stroked right on your clit. So imagine, Charlie. Imagine when I have you on my bed, spread wide open so I can see and touch all of you. Imagine when I treat your clit just like I did your nipples. When my lips, and tongue, and even my teeth, are sucking your pussy like I sucked those gorgeous tits."

Charlie let out a strangled cry.

"I think you're ready to stop," Deke said. "Catch your breath. Maybe take a shower. Do you have a toy? Not an external vibrator. I mean something for penetration."

"Yes. A couple, actually. Why?"

An idea was forming in Deke's head and he liked where it was going.

"Pick the biggest one you have. Tomorrow, before you go to bed, get that toy and your lube. I want you to call me. Then you're going to fuck yourself with that toy while you tell me about all the things you've wanted to do with me. Or more accurately, that you've wanted me to do to you. But do not, under any circumstances, have an orgasm."

He ignored her sputtering non-response. He wasn't about to tell her that his goal was all about keeping her going long enough without coming that she'd spend all Friday morning very aware of her pussy. Which was just the way he liked it.

"And you expect me not to come while doing that?"

Deke laughed. "I do expect that. If you're a good girl and can manage not coming, I'll more than make it up to you Friday."

"You'd better," she muttered.

He might be ready to explode the moment he kissed her on Friday, but they'd have all the time in the world that afternoon and he planned to make it memorable.

CHAPTER 7

DEKE—THURSDAY, JANUARY 23

"What's got you grinning ear-to-ear?" Zach shifted an empty keg from under the counter. He'd roped Deke into helping when a few of the staff called out sick.

"Oh, wait... the hot redhead." Zach hefted the new keg into place and connected the lines. "I haven't had to work the floor in ages. Fucking flu bug." He straightened up, wiped his hands on a cloth and surveyed the empty bar.

"Joy of being the owner. Well, owner's kid." Deke stacked the empties on the dolly without being told. "And yeah, but it wasn't that kind of a good time. Not yet, anyway."

Zach scoffed as he collected up the trash while Deke wheeled the dolly into the storeroom. The regular crew could deal with them from there. Zach tossed the garbage into the dumpster and locked up the back. They went through the taproom, making sure the lights were off, windows closed and locked, and all the normal end of night shit. Except it was late afternoon.

Deke went to hit the last set of lights over the bar but Zach stopped him. He took down glasses and pulled two pints of the citrus IPA. Deke's favorite. Zach perched on a stool and took a sip before fixing Deke with an amused look.

"You're telling me you didn't get laid on a date? For real? That may be a first."

"Blame Sarah and the kids," Deke replied.

"And you want a kid some day?" Zach downed half his beer and shook his head. "Man, why?"

Deke threw a wadded-up bar rag at his friend.

"First Ty, now you. Fuck. I figured Mr. I'm Not Settling Down Till Thirty would spend his last free year partying even harder. Guess I'm gonna have to make up for you two going soft."

"Fuck off." Not that his friend was wrong. Deke was keenly aware that instead of going hard in what he saw as his last year of freedom, he'd slowed down. Even more keenly aware that for years, he'd kept his parents' nagging to a minimum by telling them he'd be happy to settle down, get married, and have a kid once he tuned thirty, and that was looming closer.

"So, what's she like and when are you seeing her again?"

"Tomorrow. School's closed." Deke said. While he didn't brag, he wasn't above a little locker room chat with his best friends. Except, he didn't want to talk about Charlie that way. Maybe he'd feel differently if they'd slept together, but he doubted it.

"She's only here for a few months. Far as I know, she's gone after her best friend's wedding in March."

Zach leaned over the bar and refilled his glass. "Shit. You can't get better than that. Built in end date."

"Yeah, right?" But Deke wasn't feeling the joy over an existing expiration date. Hell, between New Year's Eve and their abbreviated date, he'd spent all of a few hours with Charlie, plus a shit ton of text conversations and a few phone calls. There was no reason for him to be this into her. Except, he was.

"Huh." Zach tapped Deke's half empty glass. "Refill?"

"Nah. And what the fuck are you looking at me like that for?"

Zach's eyes were narrowed and he was looking like Deke had sprouted horns or something. Deke ignored him and took another swallow of cold beer.

"I dunno, something tells me another one's about to bite the dust." He started mouthing the bass line of the Queen song and Deke wished he had another towel to toss.

"Yeah, whatever. Fuck off, man."

They finished their beers in silence, cleaned up and completed the lock up process. Deke made it home and realized he had fuck all to make for dinner. He debated texting Charlie but he'd told her to call before bed. He was looking forward to that conversation. Hell, he might have to insist on a video chat instead.

Fuck it. He'd walk over to R. House and grab something.

He nearly turned around and left the second he walked through the doors. If his sister hadn't seen him and waved him over, he would have.

"Marisol." Deke slid onto the barstool next to his sister. "Where's Jaime?"

The second oldest of his sisters and four years older than Deke, Marisol was also the only divorced sister. A bitter pill for their parents to swallow.

"With his dad and his...whatever." She waved at the bartender and pointed to Deke, then pushed a pizza box toward him. "Dig in."

"Aw man. You and your weird ass pizzas."

"I like my pineapple and bacon. If you don't want it, go get yourself something else. But I know you..."

She trailed off as Deke picked up a slice and stuffed a bite into his mouth.

"I didn't feel like cooking."

The bartender delivered two beers and whisked Marisol's empty glass away.

"Sorry, I didn't realize he was spending this week with Gene. How many is that?" Deke pointed at her full glass. She'd made it through discovering her husband was cheating, the church refusing to grant an annulment, and Gene filing for divorce then moving in with his mistress.

Everyone thought she was holding it together until she showed up to the family's Christmas Eve dinner already tipsy, then proceeded to get so drunk she couldn't go to midnight mass.

"I'm being good. This is my second, and it will be my last tonight." She took a small sip and shook her head. "Yeah. My first Christmas after divorce and finding out that Gene got remarried as soon as it was final. It was a little rough and I didn't handle it well. But uh... lesson learned. Thanks for standing up for me that night."

Deke couldn't respond around the mouthful of pizza that he'd never in a million years admit was pretty damn good, so he waved his hand like it had been nothing. Which was the truth.

"You might not be so blasé when you realize that Mom and Dad switched from fussing about my lifestyle choices to yours."

The bite he'd just swallowed stuck in his throat and he coughed, slugged a gulp of beer, then looked at his sister through watery eyes. "What?"

"You don't see them as often as I do, so you've missed that

transition. Especially after you showed up at Sarah's with a date in the car. Prepare for the third degree on when you're planning to bring the nice young lady around and get serious." Marisol eyed him over the rim of her beer glass. Even that couldn't hide her smirk. She was enjoying torturing her kid brother.

"I'm not thirty yet," he replied. Not that he needed to tell her that. "I'm not even..."

"Thinking about marriage until you're thirty," she finished for him. "Yeah, we all know. You say it often enough. But that's barely a year away and if they can't harp on me, you're the next target. Lord knows our sisters are above reproach on the relationship front."

"Don't fucking remind me," he replied. "I know, and it's on my mind, and yeah, I get it. Time to grow up."

He and Marisol had always been the closest. Lizzie, the oldest, was serious and driven, but enjoyed playing the martyr. Sarah, between Marisol and Deke, seemed happy, at least on the surface. She somehow maintained a career as a marketing consultant, had active and successful social media pages, a house that looked like a Pinterest board, and was a proud mom of the twins, Jacob and Olivia.

When her kids were born, she described herself as a boy-mom, a term that made Deke want to vomit. Then one day Deke had asked her if she ever considered how that might make Olivia feel once she was old enough to realize Mom favored Jacob, just because he had a penis.

That had earned him a stern talking to from his parents as Sarah had dissolved into crocodile tears. Worth it as far as Deke was concerned, because she stopped using that damn term.

To their parents, Lizzie and Sarah were perfect, while Deke was an intractable son who spent too much of college partying and despite his job, wasn't taking life seriously enough. And

Marisol was just a failure—a divorce in a Catholic family was a source of embarrassment.

The joys of Catholicism.

Marisol reached over and grabbed another slice of pizza. "Whatever. They're gonna bitch at someone. Aren't you off tomorrow? How are you not getting into mischief? Or do I not want to know?"

Deke didn't talk about his personal life with his family. He didn't tell his parents because opening that door meant listening to them berate him for not being married yet, or worse, trying to set him up. He'd accepted his duty as the only son, but that didn't mean he had to rush into shit, or that he couldn't be at least a little picky. He'd long ago given up on the idea of a romantic and loving marriage—his sisters were enough evidence that didn't exist.

Yeah, but look at Ty and Nicky.

Deke shook his head. Lizzie was all about responsibility— as far as she was concerned, Deke had a role to fulfill. Sarah always pointed out how empty her life was until she had kids. The moment he mentioned seeing a woman, they'd all be nagging him to bring her around. Is she Catholic? Does she want kids? And on it would go until he was ready to scream.

All except Marisol. She was different. She knew how he lived his life, and she rarely asked questions.

"I've got a date tomorrow. Attempt two, after being cockblocked by our sister and Jacob's head wound. Not that it's any of your business."

"Thanks for oversharing. Man, I'm glad I missed that." She laughed, then stopped and looked at him, her eyes wide. "Wait, you're actually going back when the first date didn't work out well? Who are you and what did you do with my baby brother?"

"Meh. Wasn't her fault."

Marisol narrowed her eyes and glared at him. "You like her."

Deke wanted to deny it, but knew better. No matter what he said, Marisol would give him shit because that's what she did. Plus, the moment he opened his mouth about Charlie, she'd see something different. He sure as hell felt something different when he thought about her.

He couldn't shake the image of her soft curves, bouncy curls, and pale blue eyes.

Like Ty when he met Nicky. And I gave him shit about it.

"Holy shit. I was teasing, but fuck. You do. You met someone and you really like her. Whoa!"

Deke flipped her off and stuffed another bite of pizza in his mouth. The less he said, the better. Besides, he had to get home. He had a phone date with an amazing woman.

CHAPTER 8

CHARLIE—FRIDAY, JANUARY 24

Charlie breathed a sigh of relief as she hurried out of the hotel. Since she was the newbie and stepping in as manager for a short stint, she couldn't miss the big monthly meeting of all the event staff. Meetings were never her favorite things to begin with and this morning, she'd had a hard time sitting still. The fact was, she was still feeling the hour and half she'd spent on the phone with Deke last night—most of it fucking herself with a good-sized toy.

She had hoped to make it home in time for a light lunch before heading to Deke's. The anticipation of that was like a live thing. Her skin prickled at the thought of him and every time she saw a text, her breath caught and her nipples stiffened. She'd have to settle for a smoothie because the meeting went longer than expected and she was damn well going to shower.

Once home, she stripped and headed straight for the bathroom. A text buzzed as she was about to step in and she spotted Deke's name. She tapped the screen to find he'd sent his address and a picture of him in a very low-slung towel.

After three days of teasing herself and their phone calls, she was so on edge she might explode, or jump him the moment he opened the door. Still, she needed an everything shower. At least that might distract her from the maddening urge. Forty-five minutes later, she called an Uber, texted that she was on the way and shared the ride with him.

The car dropped her in front of a small brick row home. The glass storm door swung open and Deke waved her over, all smiles and sweetness.

He surprised her with a quick hug and kiss as she reached the top step, then moved aside to let her by. He latched the storm door, but stood with his hand on the wooden door, eying her with a devilish look.

"Can I take your jacket?"

Maybe he was stuck in work mode, but the perfectly calm and polite manner was not what she had expected. She peeled off her heavy wool coat, revealing the soft wrap dress she'd decided on. Deke whistled soft and low, then cleared his throat.

"I prefer no shoes in the house as well." He took her coat and hung it on a peg next to others, then pointed at a bench with shoes underneath. Charlie sat and stripped off her boots and socks. In light of the afternoon plans, she'd skipped tights.

Just like she'd skipped a bra and opted for a silky thong. Everything about her outfit was about looking good and easy access.

Judging by the casual charcoal gray pants and lighter gray button-up shirt he wore, she'd guess he had a similar plan. She stashed her boots next to the bench and stood.

"You ready?" His voice dipped into a soft, sultry purr that pooled all the buildup of the last few days into a hard, hot pulsing that settled low in her abdomen. She nodded and Deke closed the door.

Charlie didn't have a chance to look around before he had her pinned to the wall with both hands on her shoulders and one of his legs pressing between hers.

"I just want to check that we're on the same page here."

The hard bulge against her hip left little room for doubt what page he was on. Not like she wasn't right there with him.

"Worried I changed my mind on the ride over, or something?" She reached forward, grabbed Deke's shirt and pulled him closer. "What was the plan? Let's see where things go?"

The slow smile that curled his lips was flat out hypnotic. He tipped his head and brushed his lips over her ear, then down her neck, and her nipples tightened in response. She still had her hands fisted in his shirt. She splayed her fingers on his chest, relishing the bunching of tight muscles and the fact that he was almost vibrating with tension.

He cupped her chin in his hand as he leaned in closer until his lips hovered a mere breath above hers.

"Your safe word is café, right? I use red if I need to stop. We clear?"

Charlie nodded. The fact that he had a safe word spoke volumes, and she liked it. His calm demeanor when she came in was making more sense—Deke kept himself under tight control. Even now, it was obvious he was taking care of business before he let whatever beast out of its cage.

He surprised her again by dropping his hand, stepping back and gesturing to the open living room.

Oh hell no.

Instead of going past him, Charlie stepped closer, wrapped her hands in his shirt and tugged him forward, then spun them until his back thudded into the wall. Deke let out a laugh that sounded more like a growl. His hands snaked around her waist and he hauled her against his body.

Their mouths collided in a demanding kiss that erased any pretense of calm and polite. He tangled his hands in her hair and angled her head back as he traced kisses down her throat. Charlie tugged his shirt from his belt and worked her hands between them to undo buttons.

However things had started no longer mattered. All she cared about what getting Deke out of his clothes. The last button came undone and she pulled back to lock eyes with him and sank to her knees.

Deke's hands stayed clenched in her hair as she hit the floor in front of him. Hard ridges of muscles strained against the white undershirt he wore, but Charlie's attention was focused on what was right in front of her face.

She undid his belt and popped the button on his pants. She'd had her hand around him before, admittedly, she was drunk at the time and it hadn't been a great angle, and he'd teased in pictures—showing her the outline of his hard dick through his pants, or a shot of him in bed with the sheets tented over him—now she wanted unfettered access.

His zipper whisked down with a soft burr of sound and Charlie hooked a finger into the waistband of his gray shorts. She expected him to pop free as she pulled down, but he didn't. She understood why the moment she dipped her hand into his shorts and wrapped her fingers around the base of his shaft.

She'd known he was girthy, but not this. Deke was hung. His take it or leave it attitude about receiving oral made a lot more sense—she imagined all he got was teeth. She pulled in a deep breath. Well, she was never one to back down from a challenge.

She licked the tip then slid him into her mouth and worked her way slowly down.

"Oh, holy fuck, that's hot." Deke groaned as she took another inch of him in. To his credit, he kept his hands loose, not holding her head still or anything, but letting her have control as she adjusted her angle to keep going.

Charlie's eyes watered as she pulled back to breathe, then slid down on him again. One more deep breath through her nose and she relaxed, angled her head back and made it the last bit. Deke let out a strangled sound and his hands clenched in her hair.

"Oh my fucking... you just..." His words trailed off as she moved. He took in a shuddering breath and moaned on the exhale. She wrapped a hand around the base of his dick and sped up until he started pumping his hips in rhythm.

His dick twitched and Charlie tasted precum. Deke's hands clenched again and he pulled away from her.

"I'm not ready to finish yet," he said. "My turn."

He grabbed Charlie's hands, hauled her up and without warning, bent and scooped her over his shoulder then turned for the stairs. Nothing in her life prepared Charlie to be carried upstairs like she was some conquering hero's prize. If anyone had told her she'd like it, she would have laughed.

Upstairs, he turned and dropped her onto a soft mattress. He didn't even seem out of breath and his dick was still raging hard. Deke pulled her to the edge of the bed and knelt in front of her. He didn't bother pulling down her thong. Instead, he hooked his fingers along the sides and tugged until it tore.

After days of teasing, the last thing Charlie wanted was slow and gentle, and Deke seemed to understand her need. He wrapped his arms around her hips and lowered his head. The first touch of his tongue on her labia was a tease, encouraging her to spread her legs wide. Then he pulled her already swollen clit between his lips and sucked.

Charlie cried out and arched against him and was rewarded with him slipping fingers into her wetness and curling into her g-spot. Everything was hypersensitive after days of teasing and last night's dildo escapades. Some distant part of her brain figured that had been his plan. That part shut up as Deke thrust his fingers in a slow, intense rhythm.

She'd had partners who enjoyed going down, but Deke turned it into an art form, bringing her to the edge of orgasm, then backing off before ramping her back up again.

He slipped another finger into her as he flicked his tongue over her sensitive clit. All the tease and denial and anticipation of this moment built up, then Deke stopped abruptly and Charlie gasped. He lifted his head and slid his fingers from her. Charlie went to sit up, but Deke moved in a flash, somehow getting straddle her hips and pinning her hands over her head with one hand.

"Did you want something?" He reached down and loosened the tie on her dress, tugging until the bow came undone. He pushed the neckline open, exposing her breasts. "Magnificent."

Deke caressed her nipples, rubbing his thumb over the tight buds. Somewhere along the way, he'd pulled off the button-up shirt and was wearing just the white a-shirt and his pants.

"I've replayed the night we met so many times. I didn't get to taste you then, so I want to savor this. Your pussy tastes amazing, by the way. Stay there."

He slid off her and peeled off his pants and underwear as he stood. Charlie was too mesmerized by his body on display to think about moving. He tugged his undershirt over his head and she sucked in a breath. The man really was a god. A soft dusting of dark hair covered his chest then got thicker in a trail from his bellybutton down to... that.

Deke rolled a condom down, and so much for any guy who'd ever claimed condoms were too tight. Deke didn't seem to have any problem. She shook her head and rose to her knees, intent on getting him into bed and straddling him.

"Didn't I say stay there?"

"Who said I had to listen?"

Again, Deke moved faster than she expected, and in an instant, he'd hauled her off the bed and had her pinned against him with her back to his body. Rough play was one of her favorite things, but she'd never known a man who felt like he could actually overpower her if he wanted to.

"How much do you care about this dress?"

Charlie tried to pull away, but he had her around the waist and high enough her toes barely touched the floor. She struggled, but his grip was like steel. *Fucking hot.*

"The dress, baby. How much do you care what happens to it?"

"No trashing the dress," she replied.

"Okay, fair." He let go of her and tugged the fabric down her shoulders. In seconds, she was standing there naked. Then Deke's grip closed on throat and he backed her against the wall.

"Don't come," he instructed as he slid his other hand between her thighs. "Spread your legs."

Charlie did as told and found herself stretching because Deke held her neck tight against the wall. His fingers grazed her labia and teased lightly. He lowered his head and pulled a nipple between his lips. Charlie gasped and reached to tangle her hands in his hair, then he changed his grip on her neck, forcing her chin higher and she switched to wrapping both hands around the wrist pinning her to the wall. Deke lifted his head and smiled at her.

"Much better. Stay just like that." He sucked her nipple back into his mouth, then his teeth grazed her skin and Charlie whimpered. His fingers on her clit mimicked what his mouth was doing and soon Charlie was panting and arching against him, ready to come. He lifted his head and leaned in close.

"Not yet, baby," he whispered. "I know you want to. You're on the edge and you're aching for release, but not yet. Remember, we're gonna see how hard we can go."

His thumb stroked over her clit and she clamped her hands over her mouth, willing herself to ride it out. The strokes came faster and harder and she rocked her hips in time.

A quiet click caught her attention and she looked down. At some point, he'd moved the hand from her throat and was stroking lube over his hard dick.

Deke caught her looking and winked, then stepped closer, hooked her leg into the crook of his elbow and lifted. The head of his dick pressed against her pussy and Charlie let out a sigh as he pushed forward.

"Oh my god." The words tore from her at the intense pressure as Deke slid into her. He took his time, his fingers still stroking her clit as he eased further in. She braced her hands on his shoulders to push herself up and Deke lifted her other leg as he settled himself into her and pinned Charlie against the wall.

"Oh fuck yes," Deke groaned. "This is what I've been dreaming of for weeks."

Charlie felt like she was stuffed full and ready to split in two, but fuck it was good. Then Deke rolled his hips, pushing deeper and grinding against her clit and her body trembled.

"Oh! Just like that!"

Deke repeated the move and Charlie felt like the heavens

opened up. Her entire body was in tune with whatever he was doing and she wanted more of it. Deke sped up and Charlie threw her head back, crying out his name.

"That's it baby, ride that wave," he said. Another hard thrust and heat spread through her. Again and the trembles turned to full-body shakes. A few more deep strokes and she was incoherent.

"Come for me, baby."

Whether good timing or her body subconsciously obeying, the dam broke and Charlie saw stars as an intense orgasm raged through her. She clung to Deke's shoulders, her nails biting into his skin, as he continued to drive himself into her, over and over again.

She was dimly aware of him grabbing her hips and peeling her away from the wall. Then he laid her back on his bed and settled himself between her thighs. His kiss was an all-consuming fire that left Charlie gasping for more and harder.

And Deke delivered, giving her everything she begged for and then some. She lost count of the number of orgasms. When she thought he was done, he flipped her over, pushed her legs wide apart and ate her from behind until she came again, pushing herself back against his face and hands. Before the tremors stopped, he was on his knees, sliding his dick back into her and taking her to new heights.

He rolled onto his back so she could straddle him. But instead of expecting her to take control, he caught her hands and held them behind her back. Then Deke sucked and nibbled her nipples as he lifted his hips to grind into her from below.

As impossible as it seemed, she came again. Charlie's legs shook as she collapsed against his chest, but Deke didn't stop. He wrapped his arms around her and rolled her to her back and his strokes turned hard and deep. He entwined his fingers in hers and held her hands over her head. They were nose to nose and she lifted her legs to wrap them around him. The move took him even deeper and Charlie gasped at the sensation.

Just when she thought she couldn't take any more, Deke's jaw clenched and his lips pursed. He held her gaze for another few strokes then his body went rigid and he dropped his forehead to hers with a soft moan. He shifted off of her but still held one of her hands.

So much for my theory that guys who look like walking gods are terrible in bed.

She'd expected Deke would be good. She didn't expect him to be mind blowing.

"Holy shit," he breathed. "Gimme a minute then we can shower and grab some food. You think you can handle a round two later?"

Charlie sat bolt upright and stared at him, her mouth hanging open.

"After that? You can..."

She was usually the one suggesting a second round.

"I did warn you. But only if you're up for it. I understand if you're not. Doesn't change anything else."

She wasn't sure she could handle more of Deke, but she sure as shit wanted to try.

DEKE—SATURDAY, JANUARY 25

Pale sunlight streamed through the bedroom window and Deke turned, reaching his arm out to snag Charlie, only to find an empty bed. He sat up and blinked. She'd slept over— that wasn't his imagination, and it wasn't his normal, but it had felt right. The torn remnant of her panties on the floor and the curly red hair on the pillow were evidence of her presence.

In the bathroom, a damp towel hung on the hook. His phone vibrated on the nightstand and Deke went back to scoop it up.

> Good morning. Thank you for a wonderful time. Sorry I had to run out this morning. Had wedding business to deal with. Let me know when you're free again.

It was the kind of note he was usually sending and it left him feeling a little flat. *What the fuck?* Charlie was perfect and Zach was right—an automatic end date was the ideal thing. So why was he moping over the note? He didn't catch feelings. It wasn't his way.

> I had a great time, too. Friday is another half day but I have admin work. I could be free by four at the latest.

He hit send and tossed his phone on the bed. Halfway back to the bathroom, he turned around and snatched up the phone again.

> Most weeknights are free for dinner, but my first class is at eight, so it's an early morning.

Deke hovered his finger over the button, debating. This wasn't like him. He kept his life separate. His whole thing was all about if it happens, it happens. He didn't go about making time. Except, for Charlie, he wanted to. He hit send.

Any other time, facing a Saturday afternoon free, he'd be hitting the gym. Or calling a fuck buddy. Today, he had no desire to call anyone else. He told himself it was because he was a little worn out from the night with Charlie. His eyes landed on the empty condom wrappers in his bedside trash.

Wrappers, plural.

Yeah, and I was ready to start the day with morning sex—with her.

Fine, he wasn't worn out. He just wasn't interested in anyone but Charlie. What the actual fuck? Maybe he should find someone anyway.

Nope. Fuck that.

Deke didn't play those kinds of games. Detested them, in fact.

His doorbell rang and *fuck. Ty.* He'd forgotten it was game day. He never forgot game day. Deke tossed the phone down and padded downstairs in nothing but his shorts. He threw open the door and waved a hand toward his kitchen, then turned for the stairs.

"Whoa. Someone have a shitty night?"

Deke flipped his friend off and went to put on clothes. He changed plans and headed to the shower when he walked in his bedroom and smelled Charlie—an unmistakable combination of roses and who knew what else, but if someone asked what angels smelled like, it would be this.

Freshly showered and in gym clothes, he headed downstairs and found Ty sipping a coffee and twirling a dangly earring on one finger.

"My turn to give you shit about forgetting we're playing ball. I'd expect you to be in a good mood. I brewed a pot—figured you hadn't had any yet. And did I see bite marks on your shoulder?"

Deke poured a coffee and glared at his friend. He'd given Ty the same kind of shit, and worse, when he'd fallen for Nicky. *And oh no, not going there. Not even thinking about it.*

Except he was. He was barely a year away from his self-imposed limit on playing the field. One night with Charlie and he was ready to rethink that plan. *What the hell?*

He snatched the earring from Ty and tossed it on the kitchen counter. He'd text Charlie about it later.

"It was a good night," he said, finally. "So good I overslept. What's your point?"

The bravado might work with Zach, but Ty had always been the more preceptive one. For once, he seemed willing to let it go. He nodded and took another sip of coffee.

"You better hope someone doesn't suggest shirts and skins. You'll catch some hell."

Deke took a swallow of too-hot coffee to keep from cussing. He'd forgotten today wasn't just one-on-one with Ty, but all the fraternity brothers gathering. They'd never let him live it down if they caught bites and scratches on him. Ty would never suggest shirts and skins, but it wasn't beyond him to text Zach and put a bug in his ear. After the shower, Deke knew damn good and well there was more than a couple bite marks on his shoulder. Charlie had left a scratch or two on his back. He wasn't complaining at the time. He might've left a few marks on her as well.

"Yeah, whatever." He'd catch hell, but it wouldn't be the first time he'd had marks on him. And it likely wouldn't be the last. "Let's go."

Someone did wind up calling shirts and skins, and Deke got lucky when Ty claimed shirts. Their team won three out of five, but Deke was feeling it by the end. Most of the crowd took off after the game, but a few landed at Cold Bottom Brewing where Deke caught some ribbing for being off his stride.

"Man, you are usually an animal on the court. What the fuck was that? Fucking Ty was outplaying your ass, and even Zach was picking up the slack."

Remy had been a year ahead of Ty in college and now worked in research at Hopkins. He tossed a few bills on the table as he stood.

"It's been real. See you fucks next month."

As usual, that started the exodus. The older, married members would leave early and the younger, single guys were quickly off to shower and hit the clubs. It was the universal signal to wrap it up.

"Never thought I'd see the day you weren't itching to take your shirt off." Zach poured the last of the pitcher into their glasses and arched an eyebrow at Deke. "You're all about showing off the abs."

Zach was the tallest of the three and because of his height and build was frequently asked whether he played basketball or football, but his sport of choice had been swimming. That and rolling kegs around at the family brewery. He didn't have any room to talk about showing off the abs.

"Yeah, well. Didn't feel like catching shit, okay? I'm outta here. Promised Sarah I'd take the twins tonight since hubby's back in town."

Zach cringed. It was no secret that he'd had a thing for Deke's sister during college. Deke had threatened Zach with serious bodily harm if he so much as flirted with her. Even back then, Zach was a player, and Sarah was still grieving the boyfriend who cheated on her. Instead, Zach became her second kid brother.

"Man, fuck you. I did not need that image of your damn sister. For real?"

Ty gathered up the cash and started counting. "You going there or taking them out?"

"They're going out, so it's Disney movie night with Olivia and Jacob."

"Gotta get your Daddy practice in." Zach swiped the cash

from Ty and tossed about half of it down as a tip. "Start cramming now. Clock's tickin'."

He took the rest of the cash to the register and Deke hooked a thumb after him and looked at Ty. "What crawled up his ass?"

"If I had to guess? He doesn't have plans for tonight, no wingman, and the girl he's been with since Thanksgiving just dumped him." He stood and waved a hand at Zach. "C'mon, I'll drop you. Nicky's got some event and if I don't get my ass home and showered, I'm gonna be late."

Later, sitting on the couch with two sleeping toddlers curled against him, Deke had to admit it was kinda nice. He didn't mind being Uncle Deke. In fact, he enjoyed it. Sarah and Lizzie both had stable lives, unlike Marisol. They both also had marriages that were more about companionship than love. Well, who knew with Lizzie and Rick. Sarah and Chris, though? It was security.

He couldn't imagine a life without wild passion and uninhibited sex, but as far as he could see, that was marriage. You got married, you had kids, and you didn't just settle down. You settled.

Maybe though, with someone like Charlie, it wouldn't be like that.

CHAPTER 9

CHARLIE—WEDNESDAY, JANUARY 29

A glossy postcard landed on Charlie's desk—bright red hearts and lip prints framing an invitation to a Galentine's celebration at the hotel.

"Did you approve this?" Billy, the day supervisor of guest services, crossed his arms and scowled at her. He'd been a pill from day one and she was tiring of it.

Charlie picked up the card, then opened the event calendar. Sure enough, there was a Galentine's cocktail party scheduled on February fourteenth. She tossed the card back to her desk.

"It's been on the books since mid-December. Looks like it was Cheryl who scheduled it, and DeeDee approved it. That?" She pointed at the card and laughed.

"The RSVP info is not the hotel. That isn't from us. It's from the organizer, and per their contract, they're free to promote their event. What do you find objectionable here?"

"It's lurid." Billy's nose scrunched as if he'd smelled something distasteful.

Charlie took a deep breath and leaned back in her chair. She'd known that being the event manager, even temporarily, meant doing more of this and less of the part of the job she loved—dealing with people and helping them make their dreams a reality. Still, it didn't mean she had to like it, especially when it meant playing these little power trip games.

Welcome to management, yay.

"Really? Did you see the materials the hotel put out for the last Bygone Ball? That looked like a nightclub promo. This is tame."

"In the future, I will approve all promotional materials."

Charlie grabbed her tablet, pulled up the event contract, scrolled to the relevant section and tapped her finger on the screen to highlight the text, even though she could have quoted it chapter and verse from memory. She needed time to collect herself so she didn't bite Billy's head off. After a moment, she nodded, put the tablet down and looked up at the man.

"Is this a new policy from Stewart?"

She knew the general manager would do nothing of the sort and Billy's lack of response was telling.

"You'll have to take it up with him or corporate. Not me. I go by what's outlined in the current contracts. I can't add a layer of approval that is not spelled out. You're welcome to re-familiarize yourself with the event contract."

She nudged the tablet toward him, but he made no move to look at it. Charlie had no idea where this was coming from —maybe Billy found the idea of Galentine's offensive, or maybe he was using the fact that DeeDee was gone to exert some control. Whatever it was, he was out of line.

"It doesn't need to be in the contract. It's an internal process."

Billy loomed over her desk. His feet planted wide and his

arms over his chest. His body language screamed aggression. It also screamed insecurity. Charlie counted to ten and gave professionalism one last shot.

"That goes directly against the terms that we are contractually obligated to uphold. I will not do it, and I will instruct the event staff not to do it unless we hear otherwise from Stewart or corporate and see an updated contract from legal." *Okay, semi-professional.*

Billy opened his mouth, but she'd had enough. After years in this industry, and what she'd been through at her last post, a manager on an ego trip didn't scare her in the least. Charlie rose, laid her hands on the desk and leaned forward.

"You even asking that of me is inappropriate and I will be taking it up with Stewart. That's who I, and this department, report to. As do you."

She sat down, opened an email and started typing. Power plays were a sure-fire way to piss her off, and she suspected that's exactly what this was. People like Billy thrived on silence and others not wanting to rock the boat. *Just like Noah.* But the best way to deal with that kind of bullshit was to meet it head on and call it out. Force that person to defend their actions. She'd made the mistake of being too quiet about Noah and wouldn't fall into that again. *Screw rocking Billy's boat. I'll capsize that thing.*

After being ignored for several minutes, he snatched the card from her desk and stormed out of her office, swinging the door open so hard it hit the wall and bounced back.

Good grief, save me from grown men who act like children.

The spa manager popped into her head and she amended that thought to just grown people. She finished the email and logged out. Her work was done for the day and after that little surprise meeting, she was ready to leave.

Too bad Deke isn't free.

She could use the stress relief. Her phone buzzed and she snatched it up, hoping maybe it was Deke. Ryan's name popped up on her screen. And a summons to his office. Not the same kind of distraction as Deke, but just as effective. *Well, almost as effective.* She made her way upstairs and to her bestie's office.

"Close the door," he greeted and waved her to a chair while he frantically typed away. Charlie had just settled into the cushy seat when he closed his computer with a flourish and steepled his fingers in front of his chin.

"I still say you should branch out on your own as a wedding and event planner. You can do the part you love and stay in Baltimore."

He'd been at this as soon as she knew she'd landed the job. Charlie sighed and shook her head.

"It's not a bad idea, but I can't make that happen between now and the end of March."

In the wake of the whole Noah thing, she'd considered it. Even in Geneva, where she had contacts and had been running events for over a year, she didn't have enough to make it work. Ryan's heart was in the right place, but people outside the industry didn't realize the amount of work self-employment took.

"That's a hustle I've never wanted," she continued. "I don't even like upselling folks. Plus, I need to be focused on what happens in April, and branching out on my own has too many unknowns attached."

Ryan's face fell and though she hated to disappoint him, the simple fact was, she was stressed about what would come next.

"It's not that I don't want to stay," she continued. "Ten years of my life, of building a solid career, was almost flushed down the toilet because some asshole lied to me, and everyone else. I got fucked. It could have been worse, but I'm not in a place where I can consider going freelance."

She leaned forward and took Ryan's hand.

"I miss you, too. And I love Bradly. I'm not pinning all my hopes on anything at this point. I'm already looking at other opportunities—some of them local."

Ryan squeezed her fingers and the shy smile he offered made him look like her high school bestie—the young man who still hadn't quite found himself.

"You're right. I want you to stay. I also know you have to do what's right for you. I get it. Doesn't mean I'm not gonna suggest things and try to sway you to stick around."

He let go and leaned back and his expression turned mischievous.

"Besides, are you really telling me that incredibly hot man you're seeing doesn't tempt you to stay?"

The laugh came automatically. So did the wave of her hand, as if brushing away the thought. Charlie didn't do relationships. She'd tried twice and both had been failures of the epic variety.

Deke was a great distraction. And definitely the most fun she'd ever had in bed. Which was the only reason she couldn't keep her mind off of him. He was a spectacular boy toy and nothing more.

"A romantic relationship is the last thing I need," she replied. "Been there, done that, and I'm over it."

"You never know. Third time's the charm, right? I'm just saying I have a feeling about you two. Okay. Real reason I asked you to stop by—juicy gossip."

He braced his elbows on the desk and leaned in.

"So, you know Billy? He's always been a bit of a pill, but lately he's been even worse than usual."

Charlie schooled her face into a passive expression and

waited for him to continue. She'd tell him about the Galentine's thing later. For now, she wanted to hear the rest of the dirt. And Ryan could usually be counted on to know all the politics.

"Well, there have been complaints about some folks he hired—like the spa manager—and the gossip is he's setting his sights on the folks who made those complaints."

Ryan pointed a finger at Charlie. *Fuck.* She had sent a note regarding the spa manager, but it hadn't been a complaint, more an observation that she'd seemed stressed and maybe needed help. And sure, she'd copied Stewart, the general manager—because she reported directly to him, not to Billy. *Whatever.*

"What the hell game is he playing?"

"No clue. Best guess is he's working to cover his ass. He's either looking to shift blame, dredge up some dirt, or be the golden boy who finds some major problem that's someone else's fault."

Yeah, that's how it works. Never mind whatever issues someone caused, that can all be swept under the rug with the right motivation.

Charlie shook herself. That was a road she didn't need to go down.

"And he needs to cover his ass. Housekeeping is constantly complaining about being behind during day shift because they're understaffed. The evening supervisor has bitched about things being left a mess and there have been numerous guest complaints about scheduling with the spa."

Well, that explained Sharon's attitude of not wanting to turn away guests. Not like her solution was any better.

"Great. And now I'm on his shit list."

"Apparently, he wanted event services, but it's always been

under the general manager. Billy has tried for DeeDee before. I didn't know about it or I would have warned you."

Charlie waved a hand, dismissing the concern. Sure, the heads up would have been nice, but it wouldn't have changed things.

"On to more pleasant topics," Ryan continued. "I also got an email from the dress shop—they got samples in. Wanna take a run over and choose yours? We'll pick up Bradly on the way."

"Oh hell yes. Let's go!"

Ryan and Bradly had a mixed wedding party and they'd decided that instead of matching suits or dresses, they'd ask their attendants to choose from several options. They had already picked out three suit options, including more feminine cuts and the option to choose a skirt or pants. When they hadn't loved the options at the dress shop, the owner had pulled out a sample book and let the couple select a handful of dresses.

Trying on fabulous clothes while being plied with champagne sounded like a great end to an otherwise stress-filled day.

CHAPTER 10

DEKE—FRIDAY, JANUARY 31

The creak of the door opening carried up the stairs and Deke tipped his head, waiting. The muffled thud of something hitting the floor made him laugh—she remembered to take off her shoes. He bent and lit the last candle just before Charlie walked into the bedroom door.

He was stuck again by how stunning she was. Dressed today in slim fitting rust-colored pants and a soft gold silky top. She looked like a sunset. She looked good enough to eat. She glanced around the room then at him and cocked her head to the side.

"Wow. What's all this?"

Deke crossed to her and wrapped his arms around her from behind. She leaned back into him and he breathed in her scent. *Delicious.* He guided her to the foot of the bed and stopped.

"I make no assumptions and have no expectations. We can sit and talk. Or cuddle and kiss. Or you can find out exactly what I mean when I say pleasure dom. All of this—" he gestured around at the candles "—is atmosphere."

For a moment, he worried he'd miscalculated, then Charlie chuckled and turned to face him. She wound her arms around his neck and kissed him lightly.

"I thought you had to be up early for some weekend event?"

"That would be another reason for this," he said. "Easier for me to control the night. You're welcome to stay over if that works for you. You don't even have to get up in the morning when I do. The door will lock behind you when you leave."

There he went again, doing something he never did. Not just inviting her to stay over, but not telling her she had to be up and out when he was.

"I didn't bring a change of clothes." She leaned in and kissed his neck, and if she kept that up, he'd be tossing her on the bed and skipping his plans. Part of him was disappointed at the thought of not sleeping next to her again. He'd enjoyed that. Maybe too much.

"Your call. Just letting you know the options." He caught her hands in his and stepped back. Charlie craned her head and looked around the room, then back at him, her eyes bright and curious.

"Good to know, thanks. So, show me what you got."

Deke smiled and walked backward, taking her with him to the bathroom. She gasped as she came into the room. He'd filled the tub when she said she was on the way and the bubbles in the tub danced in the flickering candlelight.

"I don't want to mess up your hair."

Her curls were piled on her head in some complicated-looking thing. Charlie laughed, reached up and pulled out what looked like a short, two-pronged chopstick and it all tumbled loose.

"Nice." He made short work of getting her out of her clothes, neatly folding them and stacking them nearby. "You wanna put it back up?"

She did something to twist her hair and stuck the chopstick-thing back into it. Deke gestured toward the tub and Charlie stepped into the frothy water. She sucked in her breath, then let out a sigh as she sank into the heat.

Deke pulled up a stool and grabbed a washcloth.

"Oh, you're serious?"

"Shh." Deke started with her back, then down her arms and her fingers. He moved on to her chest, and yeah, he lingered a bit over her nipples.

"The whole idea is for you to relax and enjoy being pampered," he said as he pulled one leg out of the water and scrubbed the washcloth down her skin. "Instead of rushing into the shower to wash off the day, just sit back in the bath and let someone care for you."

He'd discovered long ago that most women were overworked and stressed out. They couldn't turn their brains off enough to relax and enjoy sex. Put it in terms of kink instead, and for some women, it might take a bit for them to let go, but eventually they did.

It was the fastest way to get them into a good headspace for play. Bonus, he got to fondle a little. But only a little. He deliberately kept the bath sensual as opposed to overtly sexual. He'd had partners in the past who fell asleep while he was bathing them, and he was fine with that.

Charlie didn't fall asleep. No real surprise there. It was clear she had some major trust issues. Instead, she watched him with eagle-eyed curiosity. When he was done, he drained the tub and used the handheld shower head to rinse her off. Then he wrapped her in a giant fluffy towel and helped her from the tub. Once she was dried off, he pointed her to the bed.

"Lie down, face up, arms and legs spread wide."

Charlie complied and Deke took a moment to fluff the pillow behind her.

"I would like to tie your wrists and ankles to the bed. It's just soft ties, and you can easily get out of them. Are you okay with that?"

She nodded and Deke pulled out the lengths of thick, satiny rope from the box under his bed. He tied her ankles first, making sure there was space between the ropes and her skin before securing them to the bed posts. Then her left hand, and finally her right.

"Comfortable?"

Charlie nodded. She looked intrigued, but relaxed. Deke stepped back to admire her lush body. She was tan for a redhead. Her skin glowed in light golden shades with a smattering of brownish freckles over her shoulders that matched the ones on the bridge of her nose. Faded tan lines showed off that she wore a bikini in summer, though the tan lines were less noticeable on her top. Coppery curls over her mons said the red hair was all natural.

He stroked his finger along the petal-soft skin under her breasts. "You go topless at the beach."

Charlie laughed and Deke could watch the effect on her body for hours. "Usually on vacation."

He leaned down and kissed her lips gently. She tried to reach for him, but the ropes kept her hands close to the bed and Deke chuckled.

"Your entire job is to lie back and enjoy."

He kissed his way down her neck, taking his time and savoring the way her skin felt under his lips. Then he lavished attention on her breasts and nipples until she was gasping at each swipe of his tongue. He made his way down the curve of her belly, then each hipbone and down the inside of one leg before going back up the other.

By the time he got back to her hips, Charlie was trembling. He slid between her wide-spread legs and traced his tongue along her labia. As much as he enjoyed wild, uninhibited sex, he loved moments like this when he could take his time and savor a woman's body at his leisure.

And Charlie was worth savoring.

She tasted as good as she smelled—like heaven on a plate. Last time, he'd been all about bringing her to the brink and building intensity before taking her over the edge. This time, he intended to push her over that brink as many times as he could. But it would start gently.

His tongue parted the folds of her pussy until he found her clit. He kept his touch soft, barely caressing her until she was panting and arching against him. Then he pulled her clit between his lips and sucked.

Charlie exploded almost instantly and Deke kept going, still gentle, just insistent. Her orgasm rolled on and still he didn't stop. He licked and sucked as she went from gentle trembles to hard shakes and soft moans turned into loud cries.

She tugged on the ropes and her hands clenched into fists. Her head tossed back and her body arched. Deke slipped two fingers into her pussy and curled up.

"Oh my god!" Charlie's toes clenched tightly and still Deke didn't stop. He did go a little lighter, letting her come down a bit. Once she'd relaxed, he added a third finger and sucked harder.

Charlie opened her legs wider and lifted her hips.

That was the moment he was waiting for—when she gave herself over to the experience. He reached for the lube and got some on his hand, then gently circled her asshole with one finger.

"Oh, yes." It came out as a soft sigh and Deke pressed the finger against the tight ring, slowly easing inside her ass as he kept paying attention to her pussy. It only took a few strokes before he added a second finger in her ass, then a third.

Charlie ground herself down on him and Deke pulled her clit more firmly into his mouth, then flicked with his tongue until she was crying out again. When she came again, she drenched his hands and face.

He slowly pulled his fingers out and wiped off, then leaned down to whisper in her ear.

"We're not done yet, baby. I'm going to untie you and flip you over."

Charlie seemed like she was in a haze of pleasure as he undid the ropes and rolled her over. He stretched her arms and legs out again and tied her back to the bed.

"I love playing with your ass, but since I'm not sure you can take my cock yet, this will have to do." He lubed up a slim butt plug and worked it into Charlie's waiting ass. She lifted up for it and it popped in with little effort.

"You've done this before."

"Maybe." She giggled a little and wriggled her ass. Deke slipped on a condom and reached for a small vibrator that fit in the palm of his hand.

When he positioned himself between her thighs and pressed the head of his cock against her pussy, Charlie hissed in a breath.

"Both? Um... Are you sure?"

"I'll go slow," he replied. Pushing into her was tight as fuck and for a moment, he thought it would not happen. Then Charlie let out a slow breath, tipped her hips and on the next thrust, he slid into the warmth and wetness of her pussy.

He turned on the vibe and brought his hand around, cupping it over her clit.

"Oh! What the..."

Charlie's body twitched and she writhed under him, but between the ropes and the weight of his body, she couldn't go anywhere. All she could do was take what he was about to give her—or tap out.

Deke ground against her, keeping his strokes deep and smooth, aiming to hit her g-spot with every thrust. She came again almost instantly, but he didn't stop. He kept going, faster, then slower, then faster, until she came again, and again.

The only downside of this game was that his partner often reached their limit before he was ready to come, so he'd finish with his hand. Worth it, as far as he was concerned. But Charlie didn't seem ready to call it quits.

He rose to his knees, slid the small plug from her ass and wrapped it in a towel to deal with later.

"Let's up the ante here." He found a thicker, vibrating plug. It took a little more effort to get that in her ass and holy shit, what a fucking view. Then he thumbed the palm vibe to a higher setting and leaned over Charlie's tied up body.

"You ready?"

She was already panting from the vibe in her ass and lifting her hips to him.

"Yes, please."

If he'd thought she was tight before, that was nothing. He added lube and changed his angle. Charlie brought her hips up higher. When he finally pushed into her, it was like his cock was in a warm velvet vise. He would not last long like this.

He brought the palm vibe around and slid it over her labia.

"Oh fuck. I don't think I can come again."

She hadn't said no, and she hadn't used her safe word.

Deke brought the little vibe closer to her clit. "You can, baby. And you will. What did you think I meant when I told you I was a pleasure dom?"

The vibe touched her clit and the reaction was instant. Charlie's entire body clenched, squeezing around Deke's cock. He closed his eyes and counted backwards from a hundred as he started rocking in her. The vibrations from the butt plug felt amazing on him as well, and Charlie's hips were moving between his cock and the vibrator in his palm.

She was gone to the world. Every bit of her focus was on what was going on with her pussy and ass. Just how he liked it. She ground against the vibe, then back against his cock, then back to the vibe again.

Deke felt his own orgasm rushing forward, so he switched tactics and held the vibe tightly in place on her clit and shifted to pound into her with hard, deep strokes.

"Deke! Oh my fucking god!" The last word turned into a high pitch wail as she came again, clenching around him so tightly he couldn't move. Deke came so hard he nearly saw stars. Then Charlie was wriggling and tugging on the ropes as if she was trying to crawl away from him and the vibrator and chanting something that sounded like "off."

Deke switched off both vibes, eased himself from her and untied the ropes. He cradled Charlie as aftershocks wracked her body. Then he stroked the hair from her forehead and covered her face with tender kisses.

"When you're ready, we'll go shower and take care of that butt plug."

She said something, but it was incoherent, then she let her head drop to his chest and curled against him.

Mission accomplished.

Deke wrapped his arms around her and let her come down

at her own pace. Charlie took in a shuddering breath and Deke tightened his embrace.

"I've got you," he said. What he didn't say was that she had him.

What the fuck. I think I'm falling for Charlie.

CHARLIE—SATURDAY, FEBRUARY 1

Waking up in a man's bed with him already gone was not in Charlie's usual routine. Then again, nothing about Deke was in her usual either. She had some vague memory of him kissing her this morning and saying something about coffee downstairs. Then she'd fallen back asleep.

She'd thought they were done after round one last night. Then she'd felt Deke's hard dick pressing against her thigh in the middle of the night. Sleepy kisses turned into fumbles in the nightstand to find a condom and her sliding on top of him.

Charlie stretched and rolled out of bed, padding into the bathroom where she found the two butt plugs laying neatly out on a clean towel next to the sink. She picked up the larger, vibrating one—about as big around as an average dick, but shorter. She couldn't believe she'd handled that and Deke at the same time.

Get your mind outta the gutter.

If she didn't turn off those thoughts, she'd be using Deke's handheld shower for something other than getting cleaned up. She imagined he wouldn't complain about the idea. More likely, he'd complain that she didn't share pictures.

Speaking of which...

She found a good angle for her phone and set it to record while she stepped into the shower. When she was done, she dressed and made her way downstairs to find the coffee pot already set up with a sticky note on it.

Enjoy—D

Charlie snagged a brief clip from the shower video while waiting for the coffee to brew and sent that to Deke. Hopefully, he had the good sense to not check his messages while at a school event. Come to think of it, she should probably ask him about that.

She rinsed her empty mug, then rummaged around until she found the pad of sticky notes and a pen in a kitchen drawer.

Back upstairs, she scrawled a note and stuck it next to the butt plugs.

This was fun. More please—C

She liked ass play, hell; she liked anal sex. Whether or not she could handle Deke was another question, but damn she wanted to try. She just wasn't going to come right out and say that yet. Charlie made a quick pass upstairs to make sure she wasn't forgetting anything then did the same downstairs. She found her earring on the kitchen counter and dropped it into her purse.

Once back at the apartment, she changed clothes and figured she'd make good on her promise to Ryan. It had been years since she'd been back home, but she'd bet her mother's routine was the same as always.

I'm in town for work and thought I should say hi. Are you free for coffee this afternoon?

Charlie pocketed her phone. It was unlikely her mother would respond right away. Meanwhile, she could enjoy some sightseeing on her day off and aim to be in Annapolis around the time her mother was usually done with afternoon Pilates.

Sure enough, she got a text just after three, suggesting they meet at a local coffee shop. Charlie found the place with no problem, ordered a lavender latte that sounded good, then found a table by the window to enjoy the view over the water while she waited.

Ryan's suggestion that she go freelance was tempting, but Charlie had no illusions. She didn't have connections in the area, and successful event coordination meant building relationships, and that would take time.

Ridiculously low rent for the next few months was a surprise bonus, but that wouldn't last forever. The reality was, she'd have to have regular work and build her business on the side.

She might be able to stay on at the hotel, but the big question was—did she want to stay.

"Charlotte? I was surprised to get your text. Are you moving back to Maryland?"

Hayley Jones—Charlie's mother—stood with her mouth pressed into a thin line, one hand resting on her hip and the other clutching what was almost certainly some vegan decaf thing with whatever the latest superfood was blended into it.

She looked exactly the same as always—perfect highlights in her sandy hair, pressed straight and sleek. A golden tan—meticulously maintained with weekly spray visits. If anything, her already glowing white teeth were even more perfect, though Charlie had no idea how that was possible. Botox ensured there wasn't a wrinkle to be found on her face and years of Pilates and good genes kept her body long and lean, not that she'd ever admit to the Botox or the good genes. Just as she never admitted to spray tanning.

Charlie had gotten her mother's blue eyes and that was about it. Everything else, she got from her dad's side of the family. Sure, the red hair had to come from both sides, but it had skipped both of her parents.

"Mom." They'd always had a strained relationship at best. When her parents learned Ryan was gay, it had not gone over well. They were even less thrilled when Charlie announced she'd accepted a job overseas and made that clear at her graduation ceremony.

What Charlie had never told Ryan was that her parents blamed him for her moving away. He already knew they disapproved, he didn't deserve to be hurt by them again.

Her mother settled into a chair and tapped her fingers on her cup. If "live, laugh, love" were a person, it would look like Hayley Jones.

"I'm here for a few months for work." Charlie saw no reason to explain anything else to her mother. "And Ryan's wedding."

"You know, I always believed you two would work things out. Good for you for supporting him even when he's marrying another girl."

The swallow of coffee in Charlie's mouth felt like dry sand as she choked it down. She willed herself to maintain eye contact and took in a slow breath before responding.

"There was nothing to work out. The man he's marrying is amazing."

Her mother's grin turned hard and fake, like the world's worst customer service face. "You know, you shouldn't be having those sugary drinks with a wedding coming up. You need to watch your figure. You've gotten far too plump.

Weddings are great places to meet attractive men. Will there be straight people at the reception, do you think?"

Maybe it was the fact that she'd been away from her mother's toxic bullshit for so long, or maybe it was that she'd just spent the night with a man who had made it clear how much he loved every inch of her body. And maybe she'd grown up and gotten a sense of self. Whatever. Charlie was done.

She shook her head and looked across the table at her mother. "Wow. Just wow. There was a point when that crap would have hurt me. Now? Wake up. It's gross. The whole anti-gay bit? It's gross. Food shaming? Body shaming? All of it? Gross."

She gathered her things and stood. "After years away from it, I'm finally seeing it for what it is."

Charlie shoved her chair back and turned away, then stopped and faced her mother again. She could tell her mother that the constant criticism that she considered love was abusive, but she wouldn't be believed. Nothing she could say would change her mother's mind or heart, but she could at least be clear about how she felt.

"I took work overseas partly to get away from you and Dad and your ridiculous and unrealistic expectations and constant judgement."

Charlie spread her arms wide. "I'm a size fourteen. That's not fat. Even if it were, so what? Fat is not a bad word. You think you're perfect and maybe on the outside, you've got a pretty package, but inside, you're ugly. And I don't need that in my life."

She turned, tossed her cup in the trash and walked away. She didn't turn around when her mother called her name as she exited the shop. Whatever her mother had to say, Charlie didn't care. She fumbled the door to Ryan's car open and slid behind the wheel, breathing hard and trying not to throw up.

Any sliver of hope she'd ever had for reconciliation with her family was dead. Her dad was as bad as her mother, he was just quieter about it. His entire practice was boob jobs and tummy tucks. Not that there was anything wrong with those, but he'd been right there encouraging Charlie to diet even as a teen so she wouldn't get "too big" and could avoid having a tummy tuck and breast lift when she was older.

Gross. They're gross.

They were both only children, so there were no aunts or uncles, and her mother's parents were even worse than she was.

Charlie thumped her head against the seat and groaned. Too bad there wasn't some way to divorce your parents as an adult.

Well, at least I can tell Ryan I tried.

CHAPTER 11

DEKE—MONDAY, FEBRUARY 2

Finally.

Deke hit save after entering the last test results. *Caught up on grading.* Between testing and getting everything ready for progress reports, he'd been busy all day. It didn't help that he kept getting distracted by memories of Friday night with Charlie.

He'd come close to telling her to stay Saturday morning. They'd go have lunch when he got back. Now he was torn between wanting to spend more time with her and being more than a little freaked out that he wanted to.

"Deke, you got a minute?" Frank Cooper, the school administrator, stood in the classroom doorway. Deke waved him in and waited. If Frank was coming to the classroom and not closing the door, whatever he had to say wasn't terrible. For that, he'd have called Deke into the office, and called him Mr. Wallace.

Frank pulled a chair up to Deke's desk and sat. "Audra Pennington."

Oh fuck. What now? He took a slow breath and braced himself.

"She's complained that she can't get time with you to discuss her son's progress. Seems she's very concerned."

Something in his tone dialed Deke's stress level down a notch or two. That and the fact that Frank was sitting with one ankle propped on the opposite knee and leaning back in the chair in a way that made him look like one of Deke's students instead of a fifty-something year old school administrator.

"Oddly, she didn't come to parent-teacher night and has failed to schedule anything during my office hours." Deke opened the portal and pulled up his schedule, then flipped to his emails. "No messages in the portal or via email either."

Frank put a hand out as if to say enough. "I noted you'd filed a report that she was being intrusive. We sent out a general advisory to parents that all of our faculty have office hours and that is strictly scheduled online or by calling the office. Is she continuing to corner you in person?"

"Last time was about a month ago," Deke replied. "I'm kind of surprised it took her this long."

He double checked his messages, even looking in the spam folder. There was nothing from her. Not that he expected there to be.

"Doesn't surprise me at all. She heard some juicy gossip and funny thing, a day later, came in to file the complaint."

Again, there was something in his tone that hinted at more and Deke shook his head. "I can't imagine what."

He was careful about how he presented himself. Kept his ink covered and didn't wear earrings on campus, or at school events. He drew the line at curtailing his social life, but even then, he was fairly circumspect.

"Oh relax. Ms. Pennington came into the office while a

couple of the admin staff were talking, and one of them mentioned seeing you on a date. You know you're the topic of... well... let's just say a lot of match making and wishful thinking."

Yeah, Deke knew. It had taken almost an entire year before things settled down and he wasn't getting goo-goo eyes from half the women on staff.

"On a date?" The only thing he could think of was his dinner with Charlie. "Yeah, um, two weeks ago, I went out to dinner."

"Your personal life is yours to live," Frank said. "This isn't the Victorian era. I admonished the office staff about gossiping in places parents might overhear. It's not a good look."

Frank rose from the chair and tapped Deke's desk. "According to the staff, the lady you were with was quite attractive. As for Ms. Pennington, I'll remind her to use the portal or call the office. That's what faculty hours are for. It may be time to remind parents that our faculty has personal lives and to please respect those boundaries."

Frank headed toward the door, then paused and turned back to Deke.

"Though you being in a relationship might make your life easier." He laughed as he continued into the hall.

Nothing like awkward work conversations to round out your Monday. Deke powered down his laptop. Even if he wanted to get more done now, he couldn't.

What the hell does that woman want?

The idea that the office staff had been chatting about his dating life was the least of his concerns. He'd been the topic of speculation from day one. Frank's parting comment about a relationship making his life easier was probably not too far off base.

Nope. Not going there.

Except he sort of wanted to with Charlie. Or at least, some small part of him did.

Fuck it.

He stopped packing up his things and pulled out his phone.

> Hey, this is out of the blue, but are you free this Saturday? The school does an annual carnival and it's hokey, but fun. Thought we could spend some time there then head back to my place.

It was Monday. They'd just spent the night together. Setting up the next date just a few days after the last was not his norm. He went back to packing up. His phone didn't make a sound until he was in the car and headed home. He thumbed the screen as soon as he'd parked.

> Sounds fun. Particularly the second half. Send me the details.

That brought a smile to Deke's face.

> FaceTime later?

He needed to make dinner. He needed to do a lesson plan. He needed to do laundry. *I need to talk to Charlie.*

> Sure. I'll be free after 8.

For the next two hours, Deke kept himself busy. He wasn't the type to get all caught up in a woman, but here he was, barely a month into knowing her, only a couple of dates, and he couldn't get her out of his head.

He was sitting down to fold his laundry when his phone

rang and he snatched it up. Charlie's face appeared on the screen, looking radiant as ever, in front of some bright orange backdrop.

"Where are you at? The art looks interesting."

She smiled, then spun and did something with the camera so he had a view of a huge painting. *Oh, that one. Holy fuck that's hot.* Ty had mentioned it, but Deke had never seen it.

"Painting by Nicky," Charlie replied. "Nobody's said anything but I'm pretty sure the woman is her—like it looks like she painted herself and then laid on the canvas."

The image of his best friend's fiancée naked and covered in paint was not something Deke cared to think about.

"Oh, shit, that's probably weird for you. I'm sorry." Charlie laughed and turned the phone back to her. She moved so the painting was no longer in the background.

"Maybe just a little, but it's not a big deal." He'd seen Nicky's work and he liked it, but he felt like some creepy voyeur looking at what he knew damn good and well was exactly what Charlie had thought.

"So, this carnival. What is it?"

Deke didn't want to talk about the carnival. He wanted to get to know Charlie.

"It's a fundraiser. You'll see on Saturday. So, tell me how you discovered you were, ah… not vanilla."

Her laughter was musical, light and bouncing. "That's a little complicated. I didn't date in high school—everyone assumed Ryan and I were a thing."

Deke nodded. That wasn't surprising. Then the implication hit him. She hadn't dated. So she likely hadn't had sex. *Oh.*

"I got swept off my feet in college and thought I was in love. It was not a healthy relationship and the breakup was pretty bad. Y'know, first love and all that."

She shook herself as if to clear out that memory. "I moved to Europe right after college, and made friends with a woman who introduced me to a nightclub—dancing, drinks, just hanging out kind of stuff. But it was a fetish club. And since I'd given up on love, I was open to experimenting."

The image of a 20-something Charlie at the club was stirring, to stay the least. Still, he was certain this version of Charlie—older and wiser—was preferable.

"So, I experimented and discovered that the sex I'd had before was boring. I found things I liked. Things I didn't like. Found a lot depends on the other person. What about you?"

She stretched and he got a glimpse of smooth skin as her shirt rose up, exposing the waistband of her yoga pants.

"I think I always knew there was something more. I tried fooling around in high school. It never went anywhere."

"Can't imagine why." Charlie winked.

"Yeah. Exactly. A lot of hand jobs and a couple of blowjobs full of teeth and gagging. You have some impressive skills in that area, by the way."

She gave him an innocent smile and fanned herself with her hand, batting her eyelashes. The fact that she could be silly was a big bonus.

"So, college, had about a fifty-fifty experience. Half the time, making out led to sex. The other half it led to more hand jobs and slightly better head. Still a lot of teeth. Kinda where I started not caring about it and started learning to focus on my partner."

He'd never really talked about how he got into kink. Not in detail. If a partner asked, he just said he was introduced to it by a former partner.

"Larissa was two years ahead of me and she was my first real exposure to the primal side of things. Except, she was the one doing the chasing."

"Oh, she was dominant?"

"Not really. Just demanding. Aggressive about getting what she wanted. That shaped a lot of my attitudes—both in things I do, and in things I don't do. After that, like you, I experimented. A lot."

Deke moved to the kitchen and poured himself water. He hadn't thought about college in years. Larissa was the first woman who'd put marks on his body. Ty and Zach had teased him mercilessly about it, until he'd shut them up by reminding them that he was getting laid regularly.

"Do you have any fantasies you haven't fulfilled? Or things you love but don't get to do often?" Charlie had sprawled on the bed and it took everything in him to not suggest he just drive over there. He took his time thinking about her question.

"Hard to answer."

It wasn't. Not really. But it was hard to explain to someone who didn't know him. Plus, he didn't want to create some bar that she felt she had to meet, when really what he wanted was to find her desires and fantasies.

"I've accepted some things are best left as fantasies. I guess the only thing I can really say is it takes a lot of trust to let go, so that's rare for me to do."

That was as close as he was willing to come to discussing the whole truth. If he told her he wanted to figure out what she liked, and craved, and needed, then give her all of those things, but at his pleasure, in his time, and at his command, she might understand. If he added that he wanted to keep doing that until she was an incoherent puddle, and then keep going, she might run.

"I can see that," she replied. "There's a lot of trust both ways. And it's hard."

"Exactly. How about you?"

Her face colored pink and she shook her head, then laughed. "Should've known you'd ask that right back."

Charlie bit her lip and looked away. "I've always wanted to do double penetration. I mean, with a toy. I guess two guys sounds fun but there's logistics, and... y'know what? Skip that. Forget I said any of it."

"Like hell I will," Deke replied. "That's fucking hot."

She had no way of knowing, but with a toy was something he could make happen. Assuming they could build the trust to do that. He wasn't opposed to two guys, either. He'd done threesomes, just never double penetration. She was right, the logistics were a thing, but...

He stopped himself from going too far down that line of thinking.

"Anyway..." Charlie drew the word out. "What drew you to teaching?"

It was everything he could do not to laugh. He didn't get the impression that Charlie was all that inhibited, and she was usually right there with him, jumping into sexy talk. Then again, that was mostly physical intimacy. Revealing secrets and talking fantasies was different.

"I was a bit of a math whiz kid, but wasn't into programming and tech. Wasn't all that into the sciences, either. And wasn't a good enough athlete to land a scholarship with sports. So, I focused on math and figured it out as I went."

Her hearty laugh brought a smile to his face. She was easy to talk to and he liked it.

"Since we're trading info here—it's your turn."

CHAPTER 12

DEKE—SATURDAY, FEBRUARY 8

The sound of laughter and squeals of delight floated through the air and brought a smile to Deke's face. His first year at the academy, he'd thought the annual fundraiser Sweetheart Carnival was a silly idea. Why did people need an event to donate money? After seeing how much fun everyone had, and how much it helped build a sense of family, he changed his tune.

"So, carnival like there are rides? Or what?" Charlie looked amazing, as always. She had on tight jeans with a wide belt that showed off her curves. The dark brown knee boots and a matching leather jacket had him drooling, but it was the soft gold scarf that made him want to wrap his hands in it and pull her closer. Everything she wore made him want to touch. Okay, maybe it was her, not what she wore—he wanted his hands all over her. Always.

Deke cleared his throat and shoved those thoughts from his head. The last thing he needed to be doing was walking into a school event with a fucking hard on.

"There are some small things but no big carnival rides," he replied as he grabbed her hand and walked toward the gym entrance. "Usually some fun activities, lots of food. And there's a local company that does those midway type games. Their owner is an alum, so..."

He shrugged. That was the way it was with private schools. Students grew up, moved on, and those with fond memories tended to pay it forward to the next generation.

"Games in the gym. Food vendors in a big tent outside. Supposed to be some new stuff this year."

"I'm still surprised we're going to a work event."

Deke didn't want to think too deeply about that. He'd never brought a woman to anything at work. Just like he'd never introduced a woman to his family. Not since high school. It wasn't his style. You didn't take fuck buddies to things like this, or take them to meet your parents.

Things with Charlie felt different. Even though he knew she'd be leaving in a couple months, something about her didn't feel temporary. The scary part was, he liked that feeling.

He wasn't working today, so he thought nothing of walking into the gym that had been transformed into a carnival midway with her hand in his. *Hell, maybe Frank was right about looking like I'm in a relationship. Might shut people up.*

They got tickets and headed for the games. Charlie turned out to be an expert at getting ping-pong balls into the little cups, a game Deke failed at. She passed on the stuffed animal prize. They both bombed at the basketball toss, then she tugged him to the pitching booth.

"Let's see your arm." Charlie handed over tickets and the attendant gave her a basket with five balls.

"Ladies first." If he was being honest, the idea of watching her wind up and pitch sounded more fun than doing it himself.

She handed him her jacket and scarf, then palmed a ball. Her first throw was wide, but she had good form. She knocked down two bottles with the remaining four. And he was right, watching her move was a delight.

"Never was much good at softball. Your turn."

Deke returned her things, produced more tickets and hefted a ball. He'd done this enough times to know the backdrop was visually disorienting. The bottles were often weighted as well. He focused on the table, not the bottles and fired off the first ball, knocking all three down.

Charlie clapped and laughed, then squealed when he did the same thing with the next two balls.

"See, I knew you were an athlete." She elbowed him gently.

"Gimme your jacket." He held out his hand for her coat, then laid it carefully on the counter next to the basket and two balls. He took her hand and pulled her to stand in front of the target.

"You have good form, but you're thinking softball, and this is a carnival game."

He reached an arm over her left shoulder and pointed. "Follow my finger out and aim there. Throw harder than you think you need to."

"That'll hit the table."

"Trust me," he whispered in her ear and stepped back.

Charlie grabbed a ball and threw. All three bottles tipped over.

"What the..." She gave him a wide-eyed smile and offered the last ball. Deke shook his head and gestured for her to try again, this time without his help.

"Here goes nothing." She tipped her head to the side and squinted. After a moment, her shoulders relaxed and she let out a soft chuckle. Her next pitch was smooth and fluid and smacked into the bottom two bottles, sending all three tumbling.

"You're sneaky." She shrugged back into her jacket and looped her arm through his. "You said there was food here. Ready to eat?"

After walking around the food tent, they settled on pit beef sandwiches, then took their orders to the picnic tables that were surrounded by heaters to ward off the chill.

Deke straddled the bench next to Charlie as she stuffed a bite of sandwich into her mouth. Her eyebrows raised and she made a humming sound that went straight to his cock.

Yeah, knock that shit off.

Charlie swallowed and took a sip of soda. "Okay. That's damn good. So, explain a carnival in February. What gives?"

He'd had the same reaction when he first started at the school. "I guess it used to be over spring break, but that conflicted with Easter. Then they tried May, but there's Mother's Day and the Mount Vernon Flower Mart. It kept getting moved earlier and earlier until it landed on the weekend before Valentine's Day. So, it got renamed the Sweetheart Carnival."

"Dates can be so complicated," she replied. He supposed she'd know, her entire career hinged on schedules.

"Hey, Mr. Wallace!" A group of students waved as they passed by. Deke raised his hand and waved back. *Well, that'll start the student gossip chain.* One of many reasons he'd never brought dates to school events, except here he was with Charlie, and he didn't care about the gossip.

After food, they tried their hands at a few more games. Charlie beat him soundly at skee-ball, a game she claimed she hadn't played since high school. She shook her head at yet another neon-colored stuffed animal prize.

"What do you think? Darts? Or should we try the Velcro obstacle course?"

He turned to point out the side doors toward the towering structure that was a new addition this year and came face to face with Audra Pennington, mom to Toby, and a constant pain in his ass.

"Oh! Hello. You look so different not dressed for class."

"Ms. Pennington."

"I really want to talk to you about Toby."

Deke nodded and took a slow breath.

"As I've said before, you can call the office or go on the portal and set an appointment for a parent-teacher conference. It's easy to see my schedule online."

He turned back to Charlie but Ms. Pennington laid her hand on his arm.

"It won't take long. I'm sure we can go somewhere and chat today."

Deke smiled as he stepped back. Apparently, Frank hadn't talked to her yet, or he had and she hadn't listened. Deke couldn't be rude, but from experience, he knew she'd only get pushier unless he put a stop to it.

"I'm afraid I'm not working today. I'm here supporting the school. Also, I wouldn't want to be rude to my friend. This is Charlie Jones."

He extended his hand to Charlie and was relieved when she stepped next to him and slid her hand into his.

"Ms. Pennington's son Toby is a freshman here."

"Just friends?" Ms. Pennington's tone made it sound like she was implying something inappropriate. Deke was stuck— he wouldn't lie, but had no intention of discussing his dating practices with a parent.

"Oh, Deke, you didn't tell me the school required faculty to divulge their personal lives." Charlie turned a bright and concerned looking smile on Ms. Pennington. "Or is it that the faculty is expected to be single? It was a pleasure to meet you."

She arched an eyebrow at Deke. "C'mon, we've got some balloons to pop."

"Darts it is," he said to her, then turned back to a frustrated-looking Audra Pennington. "Set an appointment. We can discuss your concerns about Toby during my office hours, but he's doing fine."

He held in his laugh until they were far enough away that it wouldn't be obvious. At least he hoped it wouldn't. It started as a chuckle, then grew to a full laugh until he had to stop walking and catch his breath.

"I'd kiss you right now if it wouldn't make a scene." He grabbed Charlie's hand again and kissed her knuckles instead.

"In my business, you get very good at deflecting people—and knowing when a polite 'no thank you' will work, and when you have to be a little firmer. That one—" she gestured back the way they'd come "—is not going to get subtle. Or nice. And I'm willing to bet will be the first one to complain if you get brusk. However, you can't be held responsible for my attitude. Do you have to put up with that from a lot of parents?"

Deke resumed walking and shrugged. "It goes with the territory. Most parents are well meaning. Sure, there are occasional pills—either they're entitled and think their child merits special treatment, or they're fine as a parent but can be personally intrusive."

"Or both," she suggested, and Deke nodded.

"Nailed it in one. And yeah, she'd complain. She already has and probably will again, but..." He gave Charlie a quick outline of the ongoing Audra Pennington drama.

"Ugh, nothing like a little sexual harassment in the workplace. Enough of that garbage. Let's have some fun."

Deke couldn't agree more. "Okay. Darts. How about a friendly bet?"

"Yeah? What stakes?" She handed tickets to the booth attendant, then smiled at Deke, batting her eyes.

"Someone left an interesting note."

Charlie made a face and Deke wondered if he'd stepped in it somehow. Then she shook her head with a sad grin.

"That's going to have to wait. Kinda bad timing."

It took no time at all for that to process. He hadn't grown up with three sisters to have learned nothing.

"Your call. But doesn't bother me if it doesn't bother you."

She narrowed her eyes at him. "It depends, but I'm going to have to pass this time. So what else might you have in mind?"

Deke gathered up the darts the attendant laid out. "Who said the prize has to be claimed tonight? Bubble bath, back rubs, and a movie sound like a great night to me. But for stakes? Hmmm..."

He threw the first dart and popped a balloon, then he leaned over to put his lips against Charlie's ear.

"If I get all five, next date, when you're up for it, I get to claim all of you," he said. "I want every hole, Charlie. I want to fill your mouth, your tight little pussy, and that gorgeous, round ass with my cock."

Her skin prickled with goosebumps, and a pink flush crept up her neck. She swallowed hard and her mouth curled into a smile, then she bit her lip and regarded him with narrowed eyes.

"And what if you don't? Or what if I get all five as well?"

Deke fired off two more darts, popping balloons both times. "You can ask for whatever you'd like."

They'd exchanged lists of hard limits and he knew their interests were compatible, so he wasn't worried about what she might choose.

"I'm game. Just to be clear, if we tie or I get more than you, I get to ask for whatever I want?"

"That's the deal." Deke offered his hand to shake on it. Charlie's laughter filled the air as she took his hand and gave it a single, business-like pump. Deke turned, unleashed the last two darts and two more balloons popped. "Guess you'd better get five balloons."

Charlie stuck her tongue out at him and stepped up.

"You should've placed this bet on the baseball throw." She took her time throwing the first dart and popped a balloon. "Ryan and I played a lot of darts in college. Just pub games. Nothing serious." The next three went in fast succession and each time another pop followed.

"Four out of five," he said. "One more for the tie."

Charlie took aim and tossed but the dart hit the balloon stem. She gave him a wide-eyed innocent look and lifted her shoulders. "Guess you get to claim all of me."

Nothing would ever convince him she hadn't intentionally missed on that last throw. He slung his arm over her shoulders, not caring who might see.

"I don't know about you, but I need to burn off a little pent-up energy. You up for the Velcro obstacle course?"

Charlie leaned into him and nodded, then laced her fingers in his as they walked away from the darts.

CHAPTER 13

The smell of roses filled the air and the usual happy hum of people having a good time was punctuated by the regular popping of champagne corks and occasional excited squeals.

Like that one.

Charlie turned her head to follow the high-pitched happy sound and sure enough, there was a man in a suit, kneeling in front of a woman who had her hands clapped over her mouth. Another Valentine's Day engagement.

She should have been on her way home by now, but the Galentine's event was scheduled to start soon and she wanted to be available just in case. One of the junior event planners was on staff for the event itself and Charlie wouldn't put it past Billy to make the woman's job more difficult.

As if summoned by her thoughts, the man himself appeared at her elbow, pointing into the lobby as the young event planner met a trio of women, each holding a giant bundle of bright red lip print ballons and towing a wheelie suitcase.

"This is what you consider tasteful?" Billy spoke loudly enough that several guests turned to look at him as he crossed his arms and glared at the women across the lobby.

They were out in the open. Where guests could see him. *Nope. Not gonna ignore that.*

Charlie tapped his shoulder and nodded toward the hallway leading to staff spaces, then marched that direction, fully expecting him to follow. Luckily, he didn't argue. Her patience was beyond paper thin, but no way in hell would she call Billy out in front of everyone.

Once they were out of sight, Charlie whirled on the man.

"I do not know what your issue is, nor do I care. If you cannot maintain a professional attitude in public, then you need to remove yourself from the space."

She didn't care if she was overstepping her role. When Billy started berating her for lecturing him on professionalism, she pulled out her cell and hit Stewart's contact number. He wouldn't be thrilled about being called on his day off, and on Valentine's no less, but she was done.

"You're not even listening to me." Billy threw his hands in the air and paced the hall. The line connected and she turned her back on him.

"Charlotte, I'm five minutes from leaving. It had better be good."

As she outlined the situation, Billy figured out who she was talking to and his ranting died down, replaced with a murderous glare.

Whatever.

"Kindly remind him of our policies," Stewart replied. Charlie didn't have to know him well to recognize the exasperation in his tone. "And I'll see him in my office Monday morning."

She thanked him and was about to hang up when he cleared his throat as if he had more to add.

"If you are free, please consider staying to ensure there are no further issues. If not, just let your staff know to document any problems. Thank you."

The line went dead and Charlie turned back to Billy with the sweetest smile she could muster.

"I should not have to tell you this. Those were guests who are hosting an event here. Your opinions on the matter are irrelevant and standing in a public space, pointing, raising your voice, and scowling at them is not acceptable."

She glanced at her watch. His shift had been over for half an hour—Billy was the day supervisor. "Go home. Stewart expects you in his office first thing Monday morning."

Where was this fuck-it attitude when Noah pulled his shit?

Not that she imagined pushing back would have saved her job there. No. Noah had seniority. He and the regional manager were childhood friends. His wife was from a powerful and wealthy local family. She'd done the best thing she could do then. None of that applied here. Besides, she wasn't sticking around Baltimore.

But I could.

It would be nice being near Ryan again. And Bradly was pretty cool. And then there was Deke. He was definitely an attractive bonus.

A door slammed down the hall as Billy headed for who knew where. So long as he wasn't storming around where guests could see, she did not care. Charlie sent a text to the night shift supervisor, giving her a heads up. She hit send, then added that she was sticking around until the end of the last event and could handle any issues. The reply came back almost instantly.

> I hope this means you gave Billy hell.
> Please tell me I can see security footage.
> Thanks. You know what a shit show VDay can be.

Charlie replied with a laughing emoji then pocketed her phone. She hadn't thought of security footage, but safe bet there was. Equally safe bet someone would pull it up. Billy was not well liked. Valentine's wasn't as big outside the US, but she'd spent her entire career at destination resorts—which meant a lot of American tourists. And a lot of Valentine's proposals. Or weddings. Or anniversaries. She imagined things were even more hectic here, where folks turned the day into a commercial explosion of all things love and romance.

She hadn't celebrated Valentine's Day since college. Not since Jonathan—who took her out to dinner, then criticized everything she ate and questioned whether she should be eating dessert. She avoided it with her more casual relationships. Then came Noah. He had skiing plans on Valentine's Day—claimed it was tradition. She'd thought nothing of it, since it wasn't a big holiday in Geneva. Later, she learned he'd been with his other girlfriend—the one he later married.

Nope. Put that shit out of your head. Now.

Charlie closed her eyes, took a deep breath and held it for a count of four, then blew it out as slowly as she could. She pulled her phone out again and sent a message to the event staff on duty that she would be here until the end of the night and they could route all issues and questions through her. She tucked it away, put a smile on her face and headed back to the lobby.

Time to check on everything.

The sight of a tall, dark-haired man with tattoos up his forearms walking in with an attractive brunette had her stopping in her tracks and doing a double take. It took no more than a second glance to know it wasn't Deke.

And what if it had been?

They didn't have any promises beyond their conversations about safety. She had no expectations and she'd told him she was likely working tonight. There was no reason he couldn't or shouldn't be here with someone else.

So, why does that idea make me feel like shit?

That was another thought she didn't want to entertain right now. She popped over to the room with the Galentine's event—they'd gone all out with the decor. Red hearts and lip prints everywhere. The trio had changed clothes and were now decked out in sparkly cocktail attire. Sultry music filled the room and several of the party attendees walked past Charlie as she strolled by the door.

The junior event planner hovered in the hall, looking a little like a scared rabbit. Charlie stood next to her and gave her a gentle nudge with her elbow.

"You've got this," she whispered. "You're working with Cheryl, and she's good. She wouldn't have you here if she didn't think you could do it."

The woman's shoulders dropped about an inch as she let out a long sigh. Charlie had met the handful of senior planners one on one, but had been introduced to the rest of the event staff in a group meeting. She hadn't felt the need to do more—she was the stand in, after all. Still, she recalled her own nervousness when running her first events.

"What's your name?"

"Lucille," the woman replied. "Lucille Perkins."

Her eyes were wide like she was worried she was in trouble.

Charlie nodded toward a pair of women entering—both dressed to the nines, but one carried a large, puffy tote bag.

"Those two have been pre-gaming and probably have extra booze. Hopefully they don't get too wild. I'll be around all night. Call me if you need anything. But seriously, you'll do just fine."

Lucille smiled and nodded as Charlie walked away, confident Galentine's was in good hands. She doubted the two partiers would get out of hand, but if they did, Lucille had backup.

For now, Charlie had very little to do. Which meant she could grab a coffee and find a behind-the-scenes spot to settle. Maybe text Deke. Or not. What if he didn't text back?

She made a stop for coffee then opted for an employee break room rather than returning to her office. She thumbed open her phone and snapped a quick selfie, then sent it to Deke.

Her phone buzzed less than a minute later.

> Hello, beautiful. I was just thinking about you. Wanna see? Warning. Adult rated.

She sent the smiling devil emoji. Like she'd say no to pictures of that gorgeous man. They'd shared more than a few not safe for work pics. Her phone buzzed again, and she clicked the message and gasped.

Deke's hand wrapped around his hard dick.

> Thinking about the deal we made at the carnival.

She nearly choked on the mouthful of coffee as her entire body clenched up in anticipation. She'd been thinking about that deal all week, and it was a damn good thing they had a date scheduled tomorrow night.

CHAPTER 14

CHARLIE—SATURDAY, FEBRUARY 15

Bright sunlight slanted into her face and Charlie sat bolt upright, grabbing for her phone. *Fuck.* She'd overslept. She didn't have anything pressing to do today—just laundry—but she tried to maintain a normal schedule. She and Deke had texted off and on until she left work, then FaceTimed late into the wee hours. Tension vibrated through her at the thought of tonight. She needed the stress relief after dealing with Billy. The buzz of a text had her swiping without looking, assuming it was Deke.

It was Bradly.

> Can you come down? Ryan's folks are being assholes and he's locked himself in the bedroom.

She was out of bed in a flash, rapid texting that she'd be down ASAP and rushing through brushing her teeth. She'd make coffee at Ryan and Bradly's, if they hadn't already. One look at her laundry pile and she grabbed yoga pants and a hoodie, then padded downstairs in her socks, trying to remember what was up on the wedding schedule this weekend.

Oh shit. The parents.

Bradly's parents wanted to meet Ryan's family, and considering how unpredictable Ryan's folks were, the couple had wisely chosen to host a breakfast at home. If Bradly's text was anything to go by, it was not going well.

The smell of burnt bacon wafted from the open door and a layer of smoke hung in the air. Charlie walked in to find Ryan's parents shrugging into their coats and Bradly banging on the bedroom door. Sounds from the kitchen meant his folks were probably in there.

"Oh. Charlie. Can't you talk some sense into these two?" Natalie Grant waved a hand toward the bedroom. "You're a wedding planner. There are traditions."

Charlie had no idea what all the fuss was about, but if the Grants expected her to insist on tradition at the expense of the couple's wishes, they were sadly mistaken.

"I'm not sure what you mean," she replied, using the same tone she'd take with difficult guests. "Weddings today are often about the couple expressing their commitment in ways that best suit them. What seems to be the issue?"

Larry Grant shook his head and paced the small living room with his hands shoved in his pockets while his wife seemed on the verge of tears and unable to speak.

"They're upset that we're having a secular officiant instead of a minister." Bradly stood in the hall, his arms crossed, glaring at his soon-to-be in-laws.

Oh.

She'd forgotten that Ryan's folks went to church every week. They weren't super conservative Christians, but they'd struggled when he came out and weren't exactly understanding. A tall and stunningly gorgeous light-skinned black woman came out of the kitchen, a soapy sponge clenched in one hand. She crossed to the Grants, shook her head and pointed a finger down the hall.

"That is your child in there. As a parent, you love your child no matter what. How can you not see that you're hurting him?"

She turned, then spotted Charlie and smiled. "I would shake your hand, but..." She waved her hands in the air. "I look forward to meeting you properly. Bradly and Ryan have said so much about you."

The woman disappeared into the kitchen. Well, now she knew where Bradly got his good looks. She took in a slow breath and faced the Grants.

"I'm afraid I'm with Mrs. Simon. This is Ryan and Bradly's wedding and it should be meaningful to them. The guests, and family, are there to show love and support."

Mrs. Grant burst into tears and her husband wrapped an arm around her, glared at Bradly, then shook his head at Charlie before leading his wife out the door. Bradly came into the room and sank to a chair, shaking his head.

"This is why we did this at home." He looked up as his mother came back in, wiping her hands on a towel. A tall, handsome, dark-skinned man followed her. *Okay, two gorgeous parents equal an impossibly gorgeous child.*

Bradly made the introductions and his parents settled on the couch.

"We knew Ryan's parents were less than supportive, but never imagined they were so..." Robert Simon paused as if searching for the right word.

"Stubborn," Kayla Simon finished his thought and he nodded.

Bradly made fresh coffee and it came out that Ryan had

been cooking while Bradly poured coffee and the four parents sat at the table. Within minutes, the conversation devolved into the Grants getting upset, then the emotional manipulation started.

Yelling ensued. The bacon started smoking. Mr. Grant made some comment that it never would have happened had Ryan been straight. Which opened up all the old wounds and eventually, Ryan had apologized to Bradly and his folks, told his own parents to fuck off, and stormed out of the room.

That's when Bradly had texted Charlie.

"I should go check on him." Bradly sat his coffee down and Charlie shook her head.

"I've got this. Not my first rodeo with him and his folks." She stood and went down the short hall to the bedroom and scratched on the door, same as she'd done when they were kids. The door cracked open and she slipped inside, closing it behind her.

All her work stresses faded. Her best friend sat on the bed and hugged his knees, his misery painted all over his face. She sat next to him and rubbed his back. Ryan tipped his head to rest on her shoulder.

"You have an amazing man, there." She ruffled Ryan's hair and laughed. "And fucking hell his parents are beautiful people—inside and out. No wonder he's so awesome."

She didn't have to see his face to know he was smiling. Fucked up family aside, Ryan had lucked into something remarkable with Bradly. And his parents.

"Your folks? That was nothing new. Nothing unexpected. And I know it sucks. And it hurts. You always hope it will be different. Bradly's mom had it right—parents are supposed to love their children."

Somebody needed to tell her parents that, but she'd come to grips with that fact long ago.

"Guess we should go out for..." Ryan shifted to look at the watch on his wrist. "Brunch, at this point. Fuck. I'm sorry you got dragged into this."

Charlie ruffled his hair again. "Please, like we haven't been through worse together. And like you haven't seen me through some shit."

She got Ryan out of the room and they discovered the Simons had ordered food. The rest of the morning was filled with love and laughter, and Ryan's reddened face and the lingering smell of bacon were the only reminders of the rocky start.

Charlie headed back upstairs after helping clean up. Safe behind her closed door, she sank to the floor and cried for the family she didn't have.

Bradly's parents were everything she wished her family, and Ryan's, could have been. Yeah, maybe that was surface, and every family had issues, but there was genuine love and respect there. It left her feeling needy and emotional and she hated herself for it.

She considered canceling her evening plans with Deke because she was in such a grumpy mood, but shook herself. No, she would not give in to that shit. Besides, she needed to get laid. She needed orgasms.

Instead of canceling, she closed herself in the bathroom and indulged in the joys of virtually endless hot water—a quick shower to rinse off, followed by a long, very hot bath, then the shower to wash her hair, shave, and everything.

After scrubbing, then lotioning, and wrapping herself in her favorite fluffy robe, she was feeling much better. And very, very eager to see Deke.

She grabbed her phone and texted.

> On top of yesterday's shit, today started even worse. I need to forget my name. Can you do that tonight?

She hadn't even put the phone down before the little dots appeared, indicating he was typing.

> Absolutely beautiful. Whatever you need. Come on over now if you're ready. How hard do you want to go? And anything in particular you do or don't want?

Charlie responded with a thumbs up then went in search of something to wear, letting her brain roll his question around. Once she got dressed, she called an Uber and texted Deke.

> I need to not think. I need to just feel. To be consumed and filled and taken past the edge. I don't know what that looks like.

She hit send as the car arrived and shared her ride with him. When they pulled up in front of Deke's, she got out and climbed the four steps up his front stoop. Deke threw open the door, his face an unreadable mask.

Inside, he closed the door behind them and in an instant, had her pinned against the wall with his hand on her throat.

"What's your safe word?" His voice was a dangerous, low growl that sent heat flooding through her body.

"Café."

"Good girl."

He pushed harder with his hand, forcing her to tip her chin up as he stepped closer and used his body to press her against the wall.

"As of right now, you're mine. Your entire body is mine for the taking. And I plan on taking everything."

He stepped back and pulled her forward so her body collided with his, then picked up her hand and put it over his crotch. His hard dick throbbed and pulsed under her fingers.

"That's going in your ass today." He cupped her chin in his hand and pressed his lips to her ear. "Every single fucking inch. Now let's go."

He shifted his grip into her hair and turned for the stairs. Charlie didn't have time to even kick her shoes off. She followed him up, her body already clenching with desire.

Upstairs, she barely registered the dim lights before Deke pushed her to her knees. The sound of his belt buckle coming undone, then the leather whisking through his belt loops had her trembling in anticipation.

He clutched his hand in her hair again as he pressed his dick against her lips.

"Open."

There was no denying that command. Charlie opened her mouth and tried to relax as Deke shoved his dick between her lips. He took a few short pumps until he was wet with saliva, then he held her head tightly in his hands.

"Keep it open," he growled as he thrust forward, gagging her a little. "That's it. Take that cock like a good girl."

Her eyes watered and she gagged again when Deke went deeper than before. Her jaw started to ache, but Deke kept going until drool was dripping from her chin. Then he pulled out and hauled her to stand.

He tangled his fingers in her hair and reached his other hand under her skirt. In seconds, he'd yanked her panties off and tossed them aside. He tugged on the buttons of her blouse and shoved it off her shoulders then unhooked her bra and pushed it off as well. His touch was rough as he hiked her skirt and thrust his fingers between her legs.

"You're wet. You like this. Seems like it's just what you craved. Well, I'm happy to oblige. So here's what's going to happen. I'm going to bend you over the foot of my bed and then I'm going to fuck that tight ass of yours until you beg me to stop."

He thrust two fingers into her pussy and pumped hard. This was exactly what she needed—pure physical desire. No thinking needed.

"Do not come." He kept thrusting and Charlie bit her lip as he hit her g-spot.

"Stop doesn't mean shit tonight, baby. You are mine and I plan on fucking you until you can't see or walk straight for a few days. Only your safe word matters."

He pulled his fingers out and thrust them between her lips. "See how good you taste?"

In a flash, he had her on her knees on the floor; her face pressed into the bed and her hands tied behind her back. He hitched her skirt around her waist, and Charlie felt the warmth of lube hitting her ass. There was a crinkle of a condom wrapper and she braced herself to feel his dick pressing into her.

Instead, he worked a finger into her ass, then a second. His other hand brushed her clit, teasing lightly until she was pushing back against his fingers. Then he added a third finger in her ass.

"That's it. Fuck yourself on my fingers. Gotta get you loosened up."

The fingers on her clit sped up, keeping her right on the edge of orgasm, but not pushing her over. She was ready to beg him to fuck her already when his touch changed and the heavy head of his dick pressed into her asshole.

"Take a deep breath, baby," he growled. "We're gonna go slow until you get used to it."

The pressure was intense as his head pushed in and Charlie sucked in air and tried not to clench up.

"That's it. You can take it. Take another deep breath."

As she blew it out, Deke pushed in again and holy shit, the man was huge. Inch by inch, he worked his dick into her ass.

"Almost there, beautiful. Fuck, that's a sight."

Another push. Charlie already felt stuffed full and stretched more than she'd ever felt before.

"You asked for this," he said. "You said you didn't want to think. You wanted to just feel and be taken past the edge. I told you I'd claim all of you and fuck all your holes. So that's what we're going to do."

He pushed again and she felt the brush of his pubic hair against her ass.

"Good girl. You took every bit. Show me how much you like it. Fuck yourself on my cock."

Charlie was afraid to move, then his hand landed on her ass cheek with a resounding smack. She inched up slowly, then back down. Deke poured more lube on and she did it again. In a few strokes, her muscles unclenched and she was bouncing on Deke's hard dick.

"That's my girl. Brace yourself."

He wrapped his hands around her bound wrists and leaned into her. If she'd thought she'd taken all of him, she was wrong. He thrust forward hard and deep and Charlie cried out. It was intense but felt so good.

Deke gave her a few slow strokes, then sped up until he was pounding into her and holy shit she loved it.

"Let me hear it," Deke commanded.

Charlie moaned as he hammered into her. "Fuck that's good."

"You like my cock in your ass, baby? Tell me."

She wasn't a shy woman and had no problem talking as dirty as a man liked. Deke wanted to hear her say she loved it? Okay.

"Fuck my ass," she said. "That feels so fucking good."

He pulled out and Charlie pouted until he hauled her up on the bed, then pushed a hand between her shoulder blades and bent her over till her ass was in the air. He slammed back into her and his next stroke hit hard and the sound of skin slapping echoed in the room.

"God yes! Don't stop!"

Deke shifted positions, grabbed her hair and hauled her up against his body. He shoved her knees wider apart and suddenly he felt even bigger. He let go of her hair and wrapped one hand around her throat, then trailed the other down to cup her pussy.

His fingers splayed over her, then slid between her labia and trapped her clit between two fingers. He stroked and squeezed in time with his thrusts and tension coiled in her gut.

"That's it. I can feel it in you. Ride it out, baby. I want you to come with my cock buried deep in your ass."

His fingers squeezed again, then he did something and it felt like her clit was being stroked like she'd stroke a dick. Whatever it was, it was magic and Charlie let a low moan. The hand on her neck tightened, keeping her upright.

"Open your eyes."

She did as asked, knowing what she'd see in the mirror behind his bed.

"Look at how you take my cock," Deke said into her ear. "You fucking love it. You're such a good fuck toy."

He stroked her clit harder and Charlie cried out as the orgasm ripped through her, but Deke didn't stop. Instead, he tipped her forward so she was face down on his mattress, pushed her legs as far apart as they would go and pounded into her, hard and fast until she came again and the world went a little gray around the edges.

"Deke..."

Oh fuck. Another orgasm was already barreling after the last and Charlie screamed as it hit. Deke's hand cupped over her mouth and his pace slowed.

"That's what I wanted to hear. I want you so fucking cock drunk you can't think straight."

He ground into her ass, rolling his hips as his free hand stroked her clit until she was crying out his name, then begging him to stop.

Deke withdrew and Charlie didn't know whether to breathe a sigh of relief or plead with him to come back. He untied her hands and rolled her over then helped her to stand.

"Let's get cleaned up," he said, his voice soft and gentle. "Then I'm going to eat your pussy and ass until you're begging me to fuck you again. After that, we'll see how much fucking your pussy can take. Ready?"

DEKE

Charlie's dazed look as he helped her into the shower was exactly what Deke liked seeing. The idea of getting her so overwhelmed with pleasure that her brain shut off was his happy place, especially since she'd specifically asked for exactly that. He took his time washing her and himself, then toweled them both off and led her back to the bed. He sat her on the edge of his bed then went to his knees between her legs.

"Lie back, baby."

She laid back and Deke parted her thighs. Even from this angle, in the soft lighting, he could see her ass was puffy and dark from their fucking. If he had his way, her pussy would look the same by the time they were done.

But first...

He pushed her legs apart and ran his tongue along her asshole. Charlie yelped as he buried his face in her ass. He hadn't shaved today, so he was sure the prickles of his beard were interesting on her tender, freshly fucked skin.

She didn't seem to mind, and soon was panting and rocking against him. He moved up and licked along the folds of her labia, starting gently and teasing her open. When she started grinding down on him, he gave up on gentle.

He sucked her clit between his teeth and she cried out but widened her legs. Deke reached for the big, vibrating butt plug, lubed it up and pressed it against her ass.

"What? Oh my god. Really? I don't think I can."

Deke lifted his head and chuckled. "That wasn't a no. I believe you can."

He pushed and Charlie took a deep breath, then blew it out hard. When she did, he slid the big plug home.

"See? I knew you could take it."

He lowered his mouth back to her pussy and thrust two fingers into her while he switched on the vibe. Charlie's entire body twitched. He wrapped one arm around her hips as his fingers curled into her g-spot, and sucked her clit like a mini cock.

She came hard and fast, like he expected, and before she stopped shaking from it, he'd slipped on a condom, pulled her legs up and back and positioned the head of his cock at her pussy entrance.

"Oh god, I can't." Her words said one thing, but her hips rocked against him. This was a dangerous game. He had to rely on her being able to use her safe word, and how well he could judge her body and mental state.

"You can," he whispered. "Your pussy is dripping wet and ready. I've fucked your mouth. I've fucked your ass. And I've eaten your ass and pussy. Unless you tell me stop, for real, I'm going to shove my cock in your pussy and I'm going to fuck you good and hard."

She cupped her hands under her knees and tucked them up by her shoulders, spreading herself wide. The vibrator in her ass was slick with her pussy juices.

"Fuck me, Deke."

Deke groaned as he pushed his cock into her tightness. Charlie clenched around him and she threw her head back as he inched his way in.

"That's it, baby. You can take it. Nice and easy to start."

He thumbed her clit and waited for her to unclench, then he shoved home in one hard thrust. He didn't give her time to catch her breath. She wanted her brain shut off, that's what she was going to get.

Deke leaned forward, pushed her legs farther apart and sucked a nipple into his mouth, then pumped his hips. Forget gentle. He fucked Charlie hard—going deep and fast, while his teeth grazed her nipples.

The harder he went, the more she moaned and writhed against him. He worked a hand between them, caught her clit between his fingers and squeezed.

"God you are so fucking amazing," he panted as Charlie shook beneath him. "I fucking love the way you take my cock. I want you to see me fucking you. I want you to see us."

He pulled out and turned her so she could see in the mirror, then got on his knees behind her and pulled her to straddle his thighs as he thrust up into her.

The effect was electric—Charlie gasped and her hands flew to her body, fingers squeezing her nipples hard. In the mirror, his cock disappeared into her soaking pussy.

"Look at us," he commanded. "Look at your pussy taking my cock."

Charlie's gaze was glued to their reflection in the mirror.

"Finger your clit, baby. Make yourself come for me."

Her hand snaked down her belly and her fingers circled her clit. She stroked and slid, then pinched and rolled.

Holy shit. She likes it rougher than I thought. Nice.

He wrapped both hands around her neck and thrust into her as she fingered herself. She came in a sudden burst of wetness and Deke slid out, flipped her onto her back and sank into her to grind his body against hers as she continued coming.

As her tremors died down, he ramped up his thrusts, pushing her legs back as far as he could.

"Oh god, right there! Don't stop! Don't stop!"

Charlie's fingers clenched on his shoulders. He'd have scratch marks again, and he didn't care. Her body arched under him, every muscle drawing tight as a bowstring.

Deke finally allowed himself to let go of his own control. He came with a rush and his hands clenched into her thighs as Charlie cried out his name and came one last time.

Her body twitched and jittered as Deke eased himself from her and turned off the butt plug. He pulled the blanket up and held her, letting her come down. When her shakes stopped and her breathing returned to normal, he slid the plug out and got a warm wet cloth to clean her up then wrapped her back in the blanket and curled up next to her.

He'd clean up in the morning. For now, his only concern was making sure Charlie was okay. She snaked her arms out and wrapped them around his waist, buried her face in his chest and sighed. She mumbled something that sounded like 'I needed that' then her breathing got deep and slow and the weight of her against him changed.

She was asleep.

Deke shifted her a bit so he could get more comfortable. She mumbled in her sleep and threw off the blanket, draping an arm and leg over him.

I could get used to this.

That wasn't a thought he needed right now, but it was the truth.

He'd had plenty of partners, explored his kinks and theirs with pleasure, but he'd never felt the kind of abandon he experienced with Charlie.

And he'd never felt the deep ache that now settled in his gut any time he thought about her leaving.

CHAPTER 15

CHARLIE—MONDAY, FEBRUARY 17

Charlie closed her laptop in a daze. She hadn't known what to expect when she'd gotten a call from a recruiter representing a small group of luxury hotels. Nothing had prepared her for being offered a role as the event services manager at their resort in France. Even better, it started in early April, so she could see Ryan and Bradly off on their honeymoon, then get packed and move.

She had the offer already in her email. It was the best thing she could hope for and solved all her problems. Sure, it meant even less client contact than she had now, but the money was good and she'd not only be back in Europe, but she'd be on the French Riviera.

It was her dream come true.

A twinge of guilt stabbed at her gut. She couldn't tell Ryan. Not yet. With barely a month to go before the wedding, he didn't need that stress.

I should tell Deke.

She reached for her phone then stopped. She didn't need

to say anything. He'd known from the get-go that they were temporary. His best friend had even warned her that Deke didn't do relationships.

So call him just for fun.

It was ridiculous to be so hung up on a guy she'd known for less than two months, and fucking only half of that time. Especially one that was supposed to be a one-night stand.

Except the sex was out of this world, but more than that, she wanted to see him. To hear his laughter. See the way his eyes lit up when he smiled. Then that dark look he'd get sometimes—the look that told her she was going to enjoy whatever came next.

It wasn't like her to miss a guy. *What the fuck!*

Whatever her brain was thinking, her hand had a mind of its own. Her thumb tapped Deke's name. The line rang only twice before he picked up.

"Hey, beautiful."

Two short words and the tension that had been building in her chest loosened.

"I'm done for the day and figured I'd see what you're up to."

The low chuckle that came through the phone had her wanting to grab her favorite toy. Or better yet, him.

"I've got parent-teacher conferences tonight, but I have some time free if you wanna grab a bite. I need to eat."

The ache of the weekend hadn't faded and still food was the last thing on her mind, but she could spend that time with him, then go home and use a toy. Or catch up with him after he was done.

"Yeah, that sounds great. Should I just meet you near the school?"

This wasn't friends with benefits type stuff. This was the

kind of discussion people in relationships had. She should be proposing a quickie somewhere.

"I'm feeling burger. I'll text the address."

Ten minutes later, she was on the way to Abbey Burger near his work. Still not sure how they'd gone from fuck buddies to whatever this was. She was sure that she wanted to spend time with him, especially now that she knew when it would end.

Deke was waiting inside the nondescript brick building, but at least he'd snagged a booth and they had high backs that offered a little privacy. He surprised her by standing, wrapping an arm around her waist and kissing her.

Not just a peck, either. He breathed her in as if she were some decadent treat, then his tongue slid between her lips and Charlie lost track of time and place. When he lifted his head, she wanted to beg him to skip food. All she needed was him.

"Good to see you, too." She tried to laugh, to make it a joke, but he gave her a look that seared into her soul. Raw passion simmered under his surface, ready to overflow, and that look said he was keeping things tightly in check.

"Likewise, let's eat. I'm starved."

They settled into the booth and placed their orders. Deke chatted easily about the school, his students, and their parents. Charlie was content to let it wash over her until their food arrived. She hadn't realized she was hungry until the plate filled with a burger and fries landed in front of her.

In between bites, she told him about work events, but skipped over anything about her leaving in six weeks. No sense in bringing it up. Instead, she focused on the flex of muscles in his forearms as he reached for the ketchup, or the way his eyes crinkled at the corners when he smiled.

Like he's doing right now. What'd I miss?

Deke pushed his food across the table, then rose and slid

into the booth next to her. He draped an arm over her shoulders and leaned in close. Charlie caught her breath. He radiated warmth and the spicy scent of him called up memories of them naked in his bed.

"I asked how you're feeling," he whispered into her ear. His breath caressed her skin and set her nerves tingling in anticipation of his touch. "The weekend was pretty intense."

An involuntary clench ratcheted through her entire body at his words. It was like someone flipped a switch and cranked her arousal level up as high as it could go. Heat crept up her neck, a sure sign her face would soon be bright red. The curse of fair skin.

She'd woken up to him bringing her breakfast in bed. Then more sex. Some of it was even tender and gentle. They spent the entire day and night barely getting out of bed.

Deke brushed a lock of hair back from her ear. "Tell me, Charlie. Did you enjoy me fucking your ass?"

She managed a tiny nod. She had more than enjoyed it, and he knew it. It's not like she'd been shy about voicing her desires, and she'd played her fair share of spicy games, but Deke somehow hit all the right buttons to turn her on.

"Good girl. Would you like more ass fucking? Or would you prefer something else?"

Charlie's breath caught and her nipples tightened. He didn't even have to touch her and she was melting. She cleared her throat and forced her face into what she hoped was a neutral expression, then turned toward him.

His lips were a breath away and his scent surrounded her. *What the hell is happening here?*

"Is both an option?" She might be incapable of walking after, but oh it would be worth it.

Deke threw his head back in a hearty laugh then clenched his fingers into her hair and brought his lips back to her ear.

"I think you know by now that both is always an option."

He let go slowly and turned back to his food. "I'm off Wednesday, if you're free. And Thursday is a late start."

Charlie fumbled her phone out. Her brain was short circuiting for sure. All she could think of was what Wednesday might bring. She tapped her calendar and smiled.

"I'm done by noon, and then have Thursday off, so yes, I'd like both." He wasn't the only one who could play these games. "And then some. If you think you're up for that."

She expected him to laugh. He didn't. A slow, dangerous looking smile curled his lips and his eyes danced.

"Challenge accepted," he whispered, then went back to his fries as if they'd been talking about the weather.

DEKE—WEDNESDAY, FEBRUARY 19

The doorbell rang at half-past twelve and Deke forced himself to take his time answering it. He'd told Charlie to pack a bag so she could come straight from work. He didn't want to waste any time. The idea of her leaving at some point after her best friend's wedding tore at his gut, but he pushed those thoughts aside. Tonight, he had every intention of making her forget her own name, while ensuring she'd always remember his.

He swung the door open to see Charlie dressed for work— a dark pencil skirt, knee boots, and some silky blouse peeked out from her open jacket.

"Why don't you head straight to the shower?" He leaned in and kissed her, then plucked the bag from her hands and pointed toward the stairs. "I'll put your things in the bedroom then finish getting stuff ready down here. Come down when you're done."

Her eyebrows arched up, but she said nothing. She turned

for the steps and marched up like she had a purpose. Deke put her bag down by what he'd come to think of as her side of the bed, then went back to the living room.

He'd finished hanging the swing when he heard her squeal of delight from upstairs. *Sounds like she found her present.* It had taken him all afternoon yesterday to track down just the right thing for her. Now he just had to hope it fit. He lit the last candle and turned as Charlie came down the stairs; her face glowing with a bright smile.

"You got this for me?" She waved her hand up and down her body, then twirled. The silk shimmered in the candlelight —a tissue-thin cascade of rich amber that draped Charlie's breasts like liquid, then skimmed her waist before falling softly over her hips. He'd seen the color and knew it was the perfect thing for her. The lady at the shop called it a slip dress, but it wasn't the sort of thing to wear in public—the delicate fabric was nearly see through.

Charlie flung her arms around his neck and kissed him. He wasn't in the habit of buying lingerie for the women he dated, but he'd wanted to do something special for Charlie.

"You look amazing, as always, and that looks even better on you than I imagined." Deke took her hand and brought her to the couch. She hadn't said anything about the contraption hanging in the corner, but she looked at the boxes spread out on the coffee table with clear interest.

"This looks mysterious." She settled on the couch next to him and Deke's heart skipped a beat. Orchestrating remarkable experiences for his partners was his favorite thing to do. He had something unique in mind for Charlie and he was a little nervous about it.

"Maybe a bit. We're going to play a game. There is something I want to do with you that I've never done, never been able to do with anyone." He laid his hand on one of the boxes. A custom-made toy that had never been used.

"As always, I need to know this is what you want. If you don't like what I have in mind, you can pick one of the other boxes. And no, I won't tell you what's in any of them."

Her lips pursed and her eyes narrowed, but she leaned closer. "Then how am I supposed to consent?"

He handed her the box. "You open the box and we go from there."

She lifted the lid and her eyes went wide. "Deke, um... that looks like..." She hefted the toy, wrapping her fingers around the base. "This is your dick."

"It is," he replied. "Kind of a long story, but I had it made a few years ago with the idea of double penetration. You're not the only one who likes that idea. Never got to use this, and here it sits."

Charlie's mouth dropped open as his words sunk in. "Double... both... you and uh, you."

She hadn't said no. Deke closed his hand over hers on the dildo. "Which would you rather have in your ass?"

The little moan she let out nearly sent him over the edge. His cock was throbbing hard at the idea of taking her to new heights and satisfying both of their fantasies at the same time.

"That's a lot of dick."

Deke braced for her to refuse. It was a hot fantasy, but he understood why it would be a challenge. There were plenty of other sexy things for them to do.

"How would it work?"

Oh! Hello!

"I can hold the base in my hand, or it fits in harness, so there's basically an over-and-under thing going on."

Charlie nodded and looked back at the toy, still clutched in both their hands.

"I think this in my ass." She let go of the dildo and smiled. "If we're doing this, it's going in a harness and I want to watch you put it on. I suggest you get busy before I chicken out."

"Heard."

Deke dropped the toy and helped Charlie up. "Much as I love this on you, I think naked is better for this."

He dropped his clothes and pulled on the stretchy harness. It felt, and looked, a lot like a jock strap and allowed him to wear the dildo either above or below his own cock. He slid it into place below and looked up to see Charlie with her lips parted, watching intently.

He peeled the sliver of fabric from her and directed her to sit in the swing. It took less than a minute to get her arranged comfortably on her back, with her feet in the stirrups. He slid his hand down her belly and grazed his thumb over her pussy.

"Baby, you're wet. Really wet. I like it." Deke knelt and pushed her thighs apart. Charlie moaned as he pressed his lips against her slick folds. Then again when his tongue parted her lips to find her clit. In seconds, she was panting and grinding against his face.

"Deke, I want you." Charlie tugged at his hair until he lifted his head. He'd expected to spend extra time getting her ready, but the look on her face was pure demand. "Fuck me."

It took no time to put a condom on the toy then pump lube over it. He positioned the head of the dildo against her ass and rubbed it in circles. Charlie wriggled her hips, lifting and arching. He took it slow, pressing into her asshole then retreating. Bit by bit, he worked the silicone replica of his cock into her ass.

His own cock glistened with precum, but that would have to wait. Once she took the whole dildo, Deke stroked slowly, pumping into her ass in an easy rhythm. He rested his palm low on her belly and dipped his thumb to her clit.

He'd known the instant he saw her on New Year's Eve that he wanted to be inside her, but he'd never imagined it would be like this

"Use your legs and ride this cock, baby." He poured more lube on the dildo then stroked his cock with one hand while his other continued rubbing her clit. Charlie tensed her legs and pushed. It took a few tries, but she found the rhythm and was bouncing herself on the dildo in her ass. She gripped the swing's hand straps and shifted her weight, then sped up.

Deke slid his fingers down, pressing two into her pussy.

Fuck that's gonna be a tight fit.

"Don't stop. More!"

He added a third finger and curled into her g-spot. Fuck, if she kept this up, he'd be coming before he even got his actual cock into her.

Charlie's entire body shook and wetness flooded over his hand. Deke slid his fingers from her, rolled a condom onto himself, then positioned the head of his cock against her pussy.

"Take a deep breath, baby."

Charlie whimpered, but her legs relaxed and opened wider. Deke pushed forward. The sensation of sinking into her velvet softness was amazing on its own, but the pressure from the dildo in her ass turned her body into a tight fist around his cock.

He took a few slow strokes, watching her the whole time. She was beautiful. Her head thrown back, tension etched into the lines of her body. He cupped one luscious breast in his hand and rolled the nipple in his fingers. Her answering moan was all the encouragement he needed. He slid his other hand to her pussy and rolled her clit the same way.

"Fuck yes!"

It hadn't taken him long to figure out that Charlie liked it hard and intense. She seemed to crave almost overwhelming sensation. Which was exactly what he was hoping to deliver.

"Ready for more, baby?"

He didn't wait for an answer. Deke reached for the little palm vibe and got that wedged against Charlie's body. He leaned forward, caught those magnificent tits in his hands and swallowed the wail she let loose with his mouth.

Her nipples were like pebbles in his fingers and the vibe tickled against his body as he ground into her, pressing both cocks balls deep.

She was slippery with want and her hands clutched at his shoulders. Deke pinched her nipples and Charlie begged for more. He pulled his hips back and pounded into her until his skin stung from the contact and still she begged him not to stop.

Her body arched and she cried out. She grabbed his face and pulled him up to her.

"I want to see. I want to watch you fucking me from behind."

Fuck. She's a fantasy come to life.

Deke pulled out and helped Charlie out of the swing. She headed straight for his bedroom while Deke went to wash off. He came into the room to find her already sprawled on his bed, her fingers stroking her swollen pussy.

"Still want the dildo in your ass?"

Charlie shook her head. "Switch it up. How do you want me?"

Deke rearranged the pillows so he could prop himself up with his legs out and she could ride reverse cowgirl, facing the mirror.

"You're going to back yourself up here and fuck yourself until you come. Then I'm pushing you face down and fucking you hard and deep until I come."

It was tempting to ask if he could skip the condom. He wanted to fill her ass. *Maybe next time.* He pushed those thoughts aside as Charlie spread more lube on him then straddled his hips. Deke positioned the dildo at her pussy, then pressed the head of his cock against her ass. She was warmed up enough that it only took a few short strokes before Charlie settled on him with a sigh.

She ground her hips for a minute then started sliding up and down. Deke couldn't tear his eyes away from their reflection. Her tits bounced with her every move and the dildo disappeared into her pussy with every stroke. But it was her face that held him.

Glowing and flushed, she looked like she was in bliss. She fingered her pussy and stroked her tits, her touch hard and rough. Deke raised a hand and smacked her ass. Charlie gasped and her body tightened around his cock. He smacked again, a little harder.

"Yes!" Charlie's eyes were locked on the mirror, watching herself take two of him. He smacked her ass again and she moaned.

"Harder." It was a whisper, but he heard it. The next slap stung his hand but Charlie shivered and moaned louder. Again and again, alternating light and stinging smacks, then shifting to a steady pattern of hard slaps. Her ass turned bright red and his legs were drenched from her juices.

She started trembling and shaking and her body arched back. Deke grabbed her hips and held on as she rocked against him, crying out as she came.

He didn't let her come down. He wrapped his arm around her waist and shifted, pulling out so he could move her forward then get behind her.

Charlie arched her back, popping her ass up in the air. In the mirror, her eyes met his, fierce and determined.

"Don't be gentle."

Her words bypassed all logic and spoke to his soul. Deke leaned forward, plunging his cock and the dildo into her at the same time. She lifted to meet his thrust, their bodies coming together in a resounding clap. Deke wrapped a hand around her and caught her clit between his fingers.

She'd told him not to be gentle and he intended to give her exactly what she wanted. His teeth sank into her shoulder and his fingers closed on her clit. Then he pounded into her in a punishing beat, hard, fast, and deep.

She was coming again in less than a minute, begging him not to stop even as her body twitched and convulsed. She begged for harder. Deeper. Faster.

Deke wrapped one arm around her shoulders until he could reach her nipples. He pinched and pulled at her nipples and clit in time with his strokes.

"Spread your legs wider, baby." She complied and Deke sank in deeper. He tucked his knees under him and levered himself up to drive into her harder. She somehow spread even wider, and her asshole tightened around his cock.

"I love the way you take my cock," he growled in her ear. "Come for me."

As if on command, Charlie trembled; her mouth opened on a gasp, and her hands clutched at the sheets. Trembles grew to full body shakes and Deke teetered on his own edge. Another hard thrust and she cried out. The sounds and sensations of Charlie lost in another orgasm sent him tumbling after her.

The room faded away until there was nothing but the two of them—their gasps and moans mingling in the air and their bodies grinding together until they became one. No sense of time or space.

At some point, they wound up on their sides, spooning as

his cock went soft inside her. Deke eased himself and the toy from her and pulled a blanket around them. Charlie sighed and shifted in his embrace, her body still vibrating.

"I've got you," he whispered. *And you have me. Always.*

A few weeks ago, he'd been shaken at that thought. Now, it felt right. Like puzzle pieces clicking into place. They just fit.

He'd found a woman he could imagine spending the rest of his life with, and she wasn't planning to stick around. Maybe he could change her mind. He brushed Charlie's hair back from her face and kissed her cheek.

"I know this may be short notice, but..." Deke didn't introduce his dates to his family, but he wanted his family meet Charlie. Maybe it would scare her off, but maybe it could be the thing to convince her he was serious. "How does a weekend at a ski resort sound? Weekend after next."

CHAPTER 16

"You seem a little uptight." Charlie reached over and laid her hand on Deke's thigh. He'd been quiet the whole drive to Killington, Vermont. Deke picked up her hand and kissed her knuckles as he pulled into the drive.

"Just uh... well... last time I brought a woman to a family thing, I was in high school."

What in the hell possessed me to agree to this?

Instead of voicing her own doubts, she leaned into him and put her head on his shoulder. "We didn't have to do this. It's not like I've been nagging about when I get to meet your parents."

Deke chuckled and tapped the back of her hand. "I already said we would be here. I'm more worried that you're gonna get the third degree."

"Goes with the territory, and it's not like I think every family is as fucked up as mine." *Or Ryan's.* Never mind that she had never done the whole meet-the-family thing with a guy, so she'd never been subjected to familial interrogation. The joy of having kept her relationships casual and often with men who were only temporarily around. But she'd wanted to spend time with Deke, and he was going to some annual weekend at a ski resort. So, after an eight-hour drive, here she was in front of what looked like a cluster of townhomes connected to a ski lodge.

They hauled their bags out of the trunk and headed inside one of the townhomes. Chaos hit the moment the door opened. Two toddlers ran toward Deke, shrieking in what Charlie presumed was joy. Her suspicions were confirmed when Deke scooped both of them up and the shrieks turned to giggles. A young girl with dark hair and wide eyes came to an abrupt halt when she saw Charlie.

"Hey Mik, this is my friend Charlie." Despite having two arms full of kids, Deke somehow squatted down next to the girl. "Do you wanna say hi?"

The girl raised a hand and gave a half-hearted wave that Charlie returned. She knew enough about kids to recognize shy when she saw it, and she knew it was best to let the kid be.

"This is my niece, Mikayla, but she goes by Mik. These two—" Deke put the toddlers down "—are Olivia and Jacob."

Oh yeah. The kids who interrupted our first real date.

The younger kids went zooming out of the entry and Mikayla overcame her shyness enough to give Deke a big hug before she eyed Charlie with something like suspicion and took off after her cousins. Being ignored was far better than being bombarded by an enthusiastic and curious child as far as Charlie was concerned.

It wasn't that she disliked children, she just didn't want any of her own, and preferred to keep them at a professional distance—like at a wedding. Deke was obviously a beloved uncle. Charlie tried to recall if he'd told her how many kids there were. He had three older sisters, and all of them had children, so there was at least one more.

"Paul likely has his head buried in a game." Deke straightened up and put an arm over Charlie's shoulder. "He's eleven. Mikayla is his younger sister and she's nine. They're Lizzie's kids. Marisol isn't here yet, but she'll have Jaime, also nine. The twins are Sarah's—she was the one who...well, y'know. They're three."

Seeing the normally confident Deke turn a little uncertain almost sent Charlie into a fit of laughter. Instead, she arched an eyebrow at him and winked.

"Uncle Deke!" The voice came from behind and Charlie stepped aside in time to avoid being bowled over by a child with a head full of curls. Behind him, still pulling bags inside, was a woman who looked like a female version of Deke. She straightened and eyed Charlie, then stuck her hand out to shake.

"Hi, I'm Marisol and if anybody gets too much this weekend, come find me." She snapped her fingers at the curly-headed kid then pointed at the bags he had ditched in his haste to get to his uncle. "That's Jaime. Hey kid brother. Help a gal out, wouldya?"

She held a carryon-size suitcase out to Deke then shooed her son away and looked at Charlie and Deke's bags still sitting in the entry. "Looks like you got bombarded the second you walked in. Hell, I can carry my own."

Deke rolled his eyes, slung Charlie's tote over one shoulder and his over the other, then grabbed both of Marisol's suitcases. He tipped his head toward the stairs.

"Can you get the blue one? If we get upstairs quickly, we might have a minute of actual calm before the storm.."

Marisol held out what looked like a large purse. "Drop this

in my room for me and I'll distract everyone so you two can get settled."

She handed Charlie the purse and disappeared after the kids. Deke turned for the stairs and Charlie hurried to follow. Mariel's voice carried in from another room, talking a mile a minute. Deke hustled them up to the next level, stopping to drop Marisol's suitcases and purse off in front of one door, then going across the hall and ushering Charlie through another door.

"We've got maybe five minutes." He hefted their bags onto the bench at the foot of the bed, then tossed the blue tote into the closet. "You okay? That was a little wild."

Charlie sank to the other end of the bench and surveyed the room. Like the entry, it looked like pretty much every ski lodge she'd ever seen—wood everywhere. At least there wasn't a lot of plaid. Instead it was neutral tones and a lot of nature themes. The window commanded a view over of a snow-covered mountain.

"Honestly, this makes up for it." She pointed at the window. Deke sank to his knees in front of her and wrapped his arms around her waist.

"Thank you for coming with me. It's almost dinnertime, so I could text that we're gonna clean up and change. That'll buy us time before we have to go down."

Charlie leaned into him, took his face in her hands and kissed him. Even in a strange home, with his family all waiting to meet her, the desire to drag him into the bed and lose themselves in each other for a few hours was nearly overwhelming.

Instead of giving in, she sighed and nodded. "Nah, let's get this over with. I'm claiming dibs on the bathroom."

At least they had their own bathroom—she couldn't imagine sharing with a bunch of folks she didn't know. After freshening up and a few kisses from Deke, she figured she was as ready as she'd ever be.

Charlie almost had second thoughts as they descended the staircase and the sounds of a lively conversation drifted up to them. Deke cringed and took her hand.

They stepped through the door into a huge, vaulted great room and Charlie wasn't sure where to look first. Floor to ceiling windows looked out on the same mountain she'd seen from the room they were staying in, and a fire burned in a gigantic fireplace. The toddlers were both running around the middle of the room while the older kids were playing some tabletop game and being loud.

Adult conversation came to an abrupt halt as the seven grownups all turned to look at Charlie and Deke. His hand clenched on hers and she squeezed back. A middle-aged woman who looked like everyone's idea of the mom next door stood and crossed the room.

"You must be Charlie." She extended her hand and Charlie plastered a warm smile on her face and let go of Deke to shake hands. She kept telling herself this was no different than meeting the family of a bridal couple.

"I'm Susan. It's so good to meet you. I was beginning to think Deke would never settle down."

She released Charlie's hand then moved to hug her son. Then she held him at arm's length as if inspecting him for damages.

"You're looking well," she pronounced. "It's about time you brought a lady friend to meet us."

Charlie could almost hear Deke's eyeroll and she stifled a laugh. Families were all the same. Susan grabbed Charlie's arm and circled the room making introductions. By the time Charlie settled next to Deke on a small loveseat near the fire, her head was buzzing with a dozen names.

Treat it like work. You've got this.

The difference was, at work, no one thought anything of her making notes on her tablet the whole time. She didn't imagine it would go over well here. But she could still go through the mental process, hoping to keep everything straight and herself sane.

"I don't know if Deke told you the history." Susan handed Charlie a large photo album then sat in the chair next to her. Charlie dutifully opened the album to see a wedding photo of Deke's parents. The style was firmly in the '80s, which made sense.

"Thomas and I met in college. He was a year ahead of me and we were going to wait until after my graduation in June. That January, he was offered a job overseas and could only take a wife, not a fiancée. So we planned a whirlwind wedding during his family's annual ski trip so I could join him right after graduation."

She leaned forward and turned the page. A family gathered at the top of a ski run. Her in a wedding dress. Him in a tux. On skis. The whole thing delighted the wedding planner in Charlie. It was cute and personal. It had meaning—as evidenced by the entire family gathering at what looked to be the same lodge that featured in several pictures.

"We've come back every year."

Cherished family memories were not something Charlie had personal experience with, but she was always happy to help others craft their own. She looked around the room again —the older kids had gone back to their game, the twins had stopped running in circles and were instead sitting with their dad as he read them a book. It looked like a Hallmark commercial.

Until she spotted Deke facing off in animated

conversation with two of his sisters and one brother-in-law. Marisol was chatting with their dad as if all of this was normal.

When Charlie was younger, she'd spent more time with Ryan's family than her own. The Grants weren't perfect, no family was, but they were better than her parents—until Ryan came out and things changed.

At work, she saw families through the inevitable conflicts and breakdowns the stress of a big event brought. In the end, the thing that held everyone together was love.

It was the same thing she felt here. And the same failing in her own and Ryan's families.

"Think we ought to be heading in for dinner." Thomas Wallace stood and everyone seemed to take that as their cue to stop what they were doing and follow as he headed toward the entry. Deke tucked Charlie's hand into his and they fell in behind his sisters.

"There are four units connected to the main lodge. These places have don't have full kitchens—just a little kitchenette. Everyone eats in the dining hall."

Charlie didn't even want to think about the logistics of such a set up. The dining hall turned out to be a buffet with a seating area overlooking the mountains. And one very large table reserved for them.

Her hopes of a buffet meaning she'd be spared the whole family dinner experience were dashed once everyone had filled their plates and gotten seated. Thomas stood and clinked his knife against his glass.

"I know you all hate this moment, so I'll keep it brief."

A collective groan went up around the table. A sure sign this was his typical introduction. Charlie reached under the table and clasped Deke's hand. His fingers were warm and reassuring around hers.

"We chose to get married here because family mattered—

to both of us. And as we built our lives together, those are the same values we've tried to pass on to our children." He nodded at each of the siblings.

"We've been thrilled to welcome new members in the form of sons-in-law, and later grandchildren." He turned to face his son. Deke's hand went rigid and his entire body radiated tension. Thomas smiled at Charlie and she wasn't sure she liked where this was going.

"For years, we've waited for our boy, our youngest, to find the right person. This is the first time he's introduced us to someone special in his life. So, Charlie—welcome!"

There was some clapping, a few cheers, and a whistle or two and Charlie leaned in to Deke.

"That wasn't as bad as it could have been."

He shook his head as his father cleared his throat and everyone quieted back down.

"Deke—you said you'd consider getting serious after thirty. You're a year away, so let's hope this means this lovely lady has knocked some sense into you. We wouldn't complain about another grandchild or two."

A rock dropped in Charlie's stomach as more clapping erupted and Thomas sat. Everyone dug into their food and conversation returned to normal.

Except Deke, who sat still as stone. The whole "time to get reproducing" was nothing new to her. She'd heard some variation of that at more family occasions than she cared to think about. Engagement parties, bridal showers, weddings, even holiday brunches—any time extended family gathered, it seemed to come up.

She squeezed Deke's hand and he turned to her, shaking his head. He mouthed "I'm sorry" and Charlie shrugged.

This is what family does.

DEKE

Deke poured two glasses of whiskey and nearly dropped the bottle when his dad's hand landed on his shoulder.

"Charlie's pretty amazing. I can see why she turned your head."

It took every ounce of willpower to not groan. After the awkward start to dinner, everything else had gone smoothly. Or at least, not too bad. Sure, Charlie was bombarded with questions, but she'd smiled and chatted the whole meal as if she'd been around for years.

"I'm assuming you two are serious if you're bringing her here."

That wasn't a topic Deke wanted to discuss with his father. Or anyone. He'd tried to convince himself that his impromptu invite had been post-coital bliss, nothing more. It was too soon to be thinking anything else. She wasn't planning to stick around Baltimore and she'd made her lack of interest in serious relationships clear.

None of that mattered. No matter how much he tried to reason with himself, he came to the same conclusion every time—he wanted Charlie in his life.

He held up the glasses and shook them so the ice clinked, hoping his dad would drop the subject.

"I uhh…" What could he say? His dad stopped him, turned to the bar and grabbed an orange. He made quick work of peeling off two long strips of zest and twisting one over each glass before dropping it in.

"If it's worth doing," he said. He didn't have to finish the second half. Deke smiled and made his way back to the main room where Charlie sat by the fire, chatting with his mother and sisters.

"So, how did you two meet?" Sarah leaned forward with a

dreamy expression on her face. She was in love with love and romance, despite having married for stability more than excitement.

Oh shit. He should have anticipated that question. They'd never talked about how to answer it. Stupid oversight on his part. He sat next to Charlie and handed her a drink. She took the glass with what looked like an adoring smile, then took a slow sip and shot daggers at him over the rim. When she lowered the glass and turned back to Sarah, she was all smiles again.

"It's a bit of a whirlwind, actually," she said. "We met on New Year's Eve and I don't know how to describe it except to say it was like magic. It felt like we were the only two people in the world."

Deke nearly choked on a swallow of whiskey. He sure as shit hadn't cared who else was around when he'd had his mouth on her nipples and his fingers in her pussy. But his family didn't need to hear that part.

"I knew it." Sarah's starry-eyed look hadn't changed. "I knew it had to be something like that to get this one to change his tune. Did you move back to Baltimore for him? That was you in the car the day I had to take Jacob to the hospital."

Oh god of course his sister would bring that up. It seemed like he'd missed some conversation where Charlie shared some of her history.

"Not at all," Charlie replied. "I had a job offer here that I couldn't pass up. Deke and I ran into each other again entirely by chance."

That little tidbit sent Sarah into a deep sigh as she sank back into her chair. Even the always practical Lizzie looked love struck. Charlie's sanitized version of how they met was the absolute truth, minus the more salacious side of things. The result was a fit-for-Hallmark love story.

He had to hand it to her—she'd landed on the perfect way to appease his family's curiosity that almost guaranteed they wouldn't pry for more. Marisol might, but everyone else would prefer to hold on to the illusion of sweet romance and not think about what two adults might have been getting up to.

The downside was that it opened him up to later interrogation about her. Where'd she go? What happened? What did you do?

That was on him. He hadn't thought to make plans and come up with some generic and acceptable how-we-met story. Charlie pulled it off with ease, leaving him staring at her in admiration. Which he supposed fed the whirlwind romance picture she'd painted.

He looked smitten.

I am smitten.

Which meant he had a month to change her mind on the whole no-relationships thing and convince her to stay in Baltimore.

"It's an early day tomorrow. Time to tuck the babies in." Sarah rose and stretched, then turned to Charlie. "I hope you ski. We get a little competitive in this family."

A thread of panic wove its way into Deke. He was certain Charlie could ski. He may have even asked, but he couldn't recall. He'd assumed, considering she'd worked at a lot of ski resorts. What he didn't know was how good she was or if she'd roll with his siblings.

He stopped caring about any of that when Charlie's hand squeezed on his thigh.

"Honestly, a good night's sleep sounds like a plan." She rose and took their empty glasses to the kitchenette, rinsed them and stuck them in the dishwasher. Deke said his goodnights and climbed the stairs with her.

Behind the closed door of their room, she slipped into his arms like she belonged there and any lingering shred of doubt Deke had fell apart. When she drew him in for a kiss, she tasted like forever.

After they showered, after he'd made her come and she held her hand over her mouth to stifle the noises, when he slipped on a condom and sank into her warmth, he had to bite his tongue on the words of love that wanted to spill out.

Later, with her sleeping curled in his arms, Deke pressed his lips to her forehead and whispered against her skin.

"I love you."

EARLY THE NEXT MORNING, SHE WASN'T LOOKING AT him oddly, so Deke figured she'd been sound asleep and hadn't heard him utter those three little words. When she pulled out well-worn ski gear, his worries about her skills on the slopes evaporated. They grabbed a quick breakfast in the dining hall and Charlie looked around the empty table.

"Where is everyone?"

Deke shrugged. His family was full of morning people. "Half of them have probably done a few runs already."

He didn't think anything more of it until they exited the lodge and he got pelted with a snowball halfway down the walk. *Shit.* He moved to protect Charlie from the long-standing family tradition—the last person out the door got hammered. Fighting back was encouraged, but he couldn't do that and shield her.

Then she surprised him. She slid farther behind Deke, squatted and in what felt like seconds, stood and fired off two snowballs before ducking down again.

"Y'know you're supposed to be making more while I'm

throwing mine, right?" Charlie leaned to the side and tossed a snowball at Marisol.

They held their own until his parents joined the fray, then his sisters sent their kids in as distraction. Even Jake and Olivia came toddling over, forcing Deke and Charlie to stop as they were tackled by a pile of his nieces and nephews.

Everyone was laughing as they dropped the kids at a children's program then headed to the ski lift. It was time for the competitions to begin.

"I think we should exempt Charlie," Deke suggested as the family gathered at the top.

"Which run?" She arched an eyebrow at him.

Deke pointed at the course, designed to be similar to the 1994 women's Olympic downhill. Charlie stepped up to the plaque that outlined the run—a just over 700 feet drop over a 1.6-mile course and filled with curves, a handful of jumps, and plenty of opportunities to take an easier, but slower, path.

And opportunities to wipe out.

"I think I'll manage. What's the goal?"

"Fastest time wins bragging rights," his dad replied. "The two slowest take a turn watching the kids on the bunny slopes. After that it's just fun and games until lunch. Then everyone does their own thing until dinner."

Charlie nodded and eyed the slope. "Cool. Who's timing it, and who goes first?"

"Oh, this is a long tradition here. There's staff on either end of the course and they have a timing system." Deke's mom pointed at the staff member wearing a bright yellow jacket, then she held out the same green bag they'd been using since before Deke was born. "Take a tile and don't show it until everyone has theirs. We go in order. Guests draw first."

Charlie reached into the bag and pulled out a tile. Her

eyebrows went up and she smiled then palmed the tile. Deke reached in and pulled out number nine. *Last. Shit.*

"Okay. Remember, this is all in fun. Don't be foolish. Let's see 'em." His dad held out his down-turned fist and waited for everyone else to do the same before flipping his hand and opening his fingers to display his tile.

Charlie turned her gloved hand palm up. The number one clear and crisp on the cream tile. Maybe they could swap or talk someone else into swapping. Deke wasn't sure whether he was more worried about them being on opposite ends of the lineup, or her having to go first.

"Don't even think about it." Charlie rolled her eyes and shook her head. "I can deal."

After some excited chatter, everyone got out of the way. Charlie lowered her goggles and got herself settled at the top of the run. She paused, rolled her shoulders, then her neck, then bent into position, looked at the crew member and nodded.

Charlie took off like a shot, slicing down the hill so fast she was a blur. She took the first curve tight and rather than cutting around it, went straight for the first jump, catching air and nailing a perfect landing before leaning into the next curve and zooming out of sight.

Deke whirled to watch the ski staff, who would give the all clear for the next person.

"Holy shit." Marisol elbowed him. "You didn't tell me you brought a ringer. Dammit. She fits right in."

Marisol's ex had hated the competition and bowed out. It wasn't until a few years in Deke realized it was because he had mediocre skills at best and wasn't willing to admit it.

A green flag waved and Marisol whistled.

"That had to be a record time." She stepped up and got ready for the run. Deke had no patience for the usual banter that happened while everyone waited their turn. His sister was right, the green flag had come fast. Rick went next, then Sarah and it took a long time to get a green flag.

"I have to give you credit. When you finally decided to bring someone home, you did it right." His mom gave him a big hug before getting ready for her turn down the hill. The competition had lost some of its edge over the last few years as both parents had slowed down and were usually the ones watching the kids.

Whether that was aging bodies, or grandparents choosing to spend time with their grandchildren, Deke didn't know. He suspected they'd bow out as the older kids reached a point where they could ski the course.

Chris took his turn, fast as always. He and Deke were usually the two best times. Lizzie often came in third or fourth.

"What are you worrying about?" His dad scanned the slope, as if he could read the tracks and decide which way to go. Maybe he could. Even in his early sixties, his dad was still fluid and graceful on skis, handling difficult courses with ease.

"Nothing." That wasn't true, and his dad would know it, but Deke was already struggling with his emotions. The last thing he wanted to do was have a heart to heart with his dad while the rest of the family stood at the base of the mountain waiting for them.

With Charlie stuck there.

"You'll talk when you're ready." His dad pushed off down the slope, taking the turn tight, but skipping the jump. Deke waited, keeping an eye out for the green flag and trying not to think about what kinds of questions his family were putting to his... what? Girlfriend? Fuck buddy?

When his turn came, he sailed down the path, pushing hard like he always did. One good thing about skiing like this,

his brain was so occupied with navigating the course that he couldn't think about much else.

At the bottom, Charlie greeted him with a hug and a solid kiss.

"Congrats, you took the silver." She nodded to the board set up at the base, where her name was in the number one slot.

"And here I was worried about you." Deke held her around the waist and laughed. This felt good. Too good. He didn't want to give it up. Not ever.

Chris came up and shook Charlie's hand, his face beaming in a wide grin. "That was impressive. Normally, this guy and I are trading off first and second. Technically, Sarah and Mom came last, but Dad says he'll take Sarah's place. Congratulations—I don't know that any of us will ever beat that time."

Deke looked back at the board and let out a low whistle. Charlie had come in fifteen seconds faster than Deke and twenty faster than Chris. She leaned closer and pressed her cheek against Deke's.

"Wanna know a secret?" Her breath was warm against his skin and all Deke wanted to know was how quickly they could get back to their room. "I worked a season at Kvitfjell during college. I've skied the Olympiabakken many times. This run was a bit easier."

Marisol was right. He'd brought a ringer. *And I don't want to let her go.*

Shit.

CHAPTER 17

CHARLIE—MONDAY, MARCH 3

"I need your approval on the Adams contract."

Charlie glanced up from her desk and tried to recall the woman's name. She was one of the junior event planners and while she was inexperienced, she was a fast learner and terrific with the guests.

Lucille. Her name is Lucille.

"Sure." Charlie pulled up the account and scanned through the details. "Looks solid. This is your first time doing it all yourself, right?"

Lucille gave a nod and Charlie looked over the final page. She added her digital signature and closed the window.

"Great job. How's it feel?" When she'd accepted the job, she hadn't realized how much of her time would be spent on staff management. Sometimes she missed working with clients, but the job was growing on her. *Good thing, since this is what I'll be moving to next month.*

"It's a small wedding, so it wasn't too difficult, but it feels really good to know I got the couple everything they wanted and stayed in their budget."

Music to Charlie's ears. After Lucille left, Charlie finished her paperwork and closed down for the day. Management was the last thing she'd imagined herself doing, but here she was, and she was enjoying it—so long as there was a mix of the admin stuff and actually doing the work she loved.

For now, she had a dress fitting to get to. She'd never been in anyone's wedding party before, but she'd always known she'd be there if Ryan ever got married. Seeing how happy he was with Bradly gave her the warm fuzzies. The same feeling she got when she made a couple's wedding happen the way they dreamed.

She loved love and romance—from a distance.

At the dress shop, she slipped into a sage green silk dress and stepped onto the little platform for the tailor to make final adjustments.

"Will you be wearing flats?"

The tiny woman pointed at Charlie's feet, clad in a pair of fluffy socks but no shoes. *Shit, I left my shoes at Ryan's.*

"Sorry, no, but I don't have my shoes with me."

She knew better than this. The wedding was just over two weeks away. This was supposed to be the last fitting. The shoes were important. It wasn't like her to forget.

"What height are the heels? It won't be perfect, but we can come close. Unless you can call someone to bring them."

Maybe Ryan was free. Or Bradly. She could text.

"No call needed." Ryan sailed in, brandishing the sparkly silver and gold heels. He set them on the fitting platform, then held one of Charlie's hands as she hiked her skirt up and stepped into the shoes. As soon as she let go, he was pressing a glass of champagne into her hand.

"You are a goddess." Ryan raised his own glass and winked. Charlie had grown up always hearing that she was too much—too tall, too heavy, too curvy. Ryan had been the one telling her she was beautiful—it had taken years, but eventually, she started believing him. Then Jonathan had nearly undone it all.

It wasn't until after college, when she started working in hospitality, that the little seeds planted by her bestie had grown into real confidence.

"Are you sure you want to wear something this high?" The tailor held the hem of Charlie's skirt in her fingers as she eyed the four-inch heels. Charlie braced for the comment on her height. "You'll be on your feet a lot and that can be tiring, even if you're used to heels."

Well, that was unexpected.

"It's okay," Charlie replied. "I'll stick with these."

Ryan stifled a laugh behind his hand, then clinked his champagne glass against hers. Charlie finally took a sip. She'd been to plenty of parties and events wearing sky high shoes and never taken them off. Then again, she made sure even her highest heels were reasonably comfortable.

She was already eye-to-eye with men of average height and saw no reason to pretend to be anything less than she was. The heels stayed. If a guy couldn't handle that, well... there were plenty of other men around who could.

Like Deke.

"Oh, that's a nice smile," Ryan cooed. "How are things with Mr. Wallace?"

She flipped her middle finger at her best friend and swallowed another mouthful of bubbly liquid. Though, he'd just given her the perfect way to bring up the fact that she'd be leaving town two weeks after the wedding.

"You know me. I like things casual, and he's perfect for that. You heard his friend, Ty—Deke doesn't do relationships.

Neither do I." She sipped champagne and smiled. "And before you go getting romantic ideas, I have news and you're not going to like it."

Ryan rolled his eyes and sighed. "You're not staying."

It wasn't a question. He of all people knew her. As much as she loved Ryan, and would love to be closer to him, and now Bradly, who'd become like a second-best friend, there was nothing else for her here.

"I got offered a job at L'hôtel Majesté," she replied. "It pays more than I've ever made, plus housing and it means living in the Cotes d'Azur. I'd be foolish to pass it up. And you and Bradly can come visit."

The tailor stood and gave Charlie's skirt a little shake, then stepped back with a satisfied look.

"Let me know how that length feels."

The green silk glowed in the shop lights, making Charlie feel like a painting on display—an effect she was certain was intentional, considering the way the lights were all trained on the fitting platform.

"See? Goddess." Ryan's smile beamed at her from the mirror.

The dress draped and hugged her body in all the right places, and the tailor had done a masterful job ensuring the neckline laid just so. Charlie had seen her fair share of bridal party attire and had always preferred seeing groups where the dresses were all similar but suited the individual. Better yet, if the colors were a palette rather than a single color guaranteed to flatter almost no one.

Ryan and Bradly had managed to offer their bridal party several options and a range of colors including cream, oatmeal, and several shades of green—ensuring everyone could find something that flattered, and would look harmonious.

"It's gorgeous, and I love it." Charlie stepped off the

platform and gave a twirl. She might hem it shorter after the wedding, but she'd absolutely wear this dress again. The tailor stepped closer and fussed with the straps, then gave a curt nod.

"It's perfection on you and I think the hem is the only thing left to do. Is that good?"

Charlie nodded and stepped back onto the platform so she could finish marking.

"Look, it's no secret I'd hoped you'd stay. Maybe find a permanent job here, or launch your own business or something, but I get it." Ryan topped off their champagne glasses. "So don't feel bad, okay? Have you told Deke yet?"

She hadn't. Not in so many words.

"I don't think I need to," she replied. "Not really. I mean, he knew this was a temporary job. It's not like we're in a normal relationship or looking to get married or anything."

Though after the weekend with his family, she wasn't so sure about Deke. She'd heard enough of the stories and his "not till thirty" policy. The fact that he'd brought her to meet his parents hinted he was maybe thinking of them as something more than fuck buddies.

Not like I haven't had similar thoughts. In passing, anyway.

That was not where she needed her brain to be going. At all.

"You need to at least tell him you accepted a job."

Ryan was the only person on earth who could chide her like that without making her want to fight back.

"I know, and I will. I promise."

She still had a month. Well, almost a month. There was no rush.

DEKE—SUNDAY, MARCH 9

The hot water stung as it hit his back and Deke hissed. He popped his eyes open when Charlie giggled. She palmed the bar of soap and dangled a washcloth in her fingers.

"You sure you want me to wash your back?"

They'd spent the weekend together, rarely leaving his house. The sex felt like they were making up for keeping it tame while they were at the ski lodge.

Or maybe it's because our expiration date is approaching.

Charlie hadn't given him dates yet, but he'd known the job in Baltimore was temporary and almost over. He caught her wrists in his and pulled her under the water with him.

"I've become convinced that you're part cat," he said. If her hands were free, it was pretty much a guarantee she'd dig them into his back. Or shoulders. Or ass. Or legs. Not the first few times she came, but somewhere after the third orgasm, it was like she'd lose all sense of restraint.

"You weren't complaining at the time," she replied.

"I'm not complaining now. I like it when you lose control. I just need to remember to restrain your hands more often."

Charlie tipped her head to the side and smiled. The thought of pinning her to the wall and fucking her in the shower crossed his mind and his cock pulsed as if in agreement. Instead, he lowered his head and kissed her neck gently, then released his grip on her wrists and turned his back to her.

The first swipe of the washcloth was gentle, then Charlie started scrubbing and Deke gritted his teeth. It didn't really hurt, but it wasn't comfortable. After the things she let him do to her body, he was more than willing to put up with some paybacks. The washcloth dragged over his shoulder blade and the soap stung.

"Try to leave some skin on, please."

Her chuckle was absolute evil, but the next swipe of soapy cloth was a little softer. She finished and turned him to rinse, then handed him the soap and her washcloth. Tempting as it was to torture her the way she'd done him, Deke took his time and kept his touch soft and delicate as he slid soapy hands between her legs.

Charlie's ass cheeks were still pink from him bending her over the arm of his couch and alternating between smacking her ass and fingering her pussy. He was pretty sure the worst of his back scratches were the result of the sex that followed that.

After, she sat on the couch, wrapped in his thick terry robe, with her feet tucked up under her while he opened the door to the delivery driver. He'd long ago accepted the idea of marriage that was more about friendship than passion, but Charlie had him thinking maybe both were possible.

Maybe the folks would be happy with one kid. There were plenty of other grandkids after all. If they had a boy...

He shook his head. *Not going down that path.*

"You said you have an early morning meeting tomorrow, and I've got to be in the office by nine. Would it be better for me to go home tonight?"

Deke nearly dropped the takeout containers he was carrying. He could see her point, and any other time in his life, he'd have already made it clear. But nothing with Charlie had been his usual and he didn't want her to leave.

Ever.

He sat the containers down, handed her a pair of chopsticks and settled onto the couch next to her.

"Only if you need to," he replied. "I'll be out the door about the time you wake up, so it's not like we'll be in each other's way in the bathroom."

Charlie popped open a container of lo mein and inhaled.

He still wasn't sure whether eating noodles straight from the container was a comfort thing, part of her aftercare, or what. Probably a combination of lots of things, but he always found it adorable. She'd curl up in a blanket, or more lately, his robe, and her face would be sheer bliss as she dug into the container.

She scooped a bite and shrugged as she chewed. Deke didn't bother saying anything else. She'd eat a few bites, then she'd respond. He dunked an eggroll into the sauce, bit into it and waited.

Eventually, she balanced her chopsticks on the side of the container and scrunched up her nose.

"It's wet and gross out tonight. I'll stay, if that's okay by you."

She went back to eating as if it was no big deal either way, but Deke's bite of food felt stuck in his throat. He swallowed hard and nodded, unable to trust his voice.

"But I'm going to warn you now," she continued, "I'm tapping out. I'm sore and I need sleep."

Deke put his food down, then took hers as well. He pulled her closer until she was snug against his body with her hips between his legs. He kissed her forehead and chuckled.

"We'll call that one a mutual tap out," he replied. "Much as I'd love more, I'm right there with you."

What's more, he was sated. If she'd said she needed more, he'd deliver. Always. But while he relished the feel of her in his arms, and his cock might twitch at the thought of sliding into her delicious softness again, there was no hunger to it. Just the pleasant desire to be close to her and make her feel good.

"Huh. Good to know." She shot him a wink then picked up her food, but she toyed with the noodles. "My time is going to be really tight for a while. The wedding is next weekend and I've got a pile of things to take care of before I wrap this job up at the end of the month."

There it was. The reminder that she wasn't sticking around. What Zach called the built-in expiration date. A thing that should have thrilled Deke. Instead, thinking about it created a sinking hole in his stomach.

"It's all good," he replied. "I get it. We'll grab time when we can."

She laid her head back until it rested on his shoulder. "You could be my plus one at the wedding. Dinner. Dancing. Then the rest of the night free and I don't have to work the following day. Or that Monday, actually."

They'd have all of that Sunday together. Maybe instead of spending it in bed, he could find something that would make her want to stay. The idea of Charlie walking out of his life, possibly for good, didn't sit right with him.

In the couple of months they'd known each other, and without even trying, she'd managed to succeed where others had failed—Charlie had his heart in her hands. And he was terrified she'd break it.

"Sounds like a plan."

CHAPTER 18

CHARLIE—SATURDAY, MARCH 15

The crowd erupted in applause as Ryan and Bradly kissed. Charlie dabbed her eyes and crossed her fingers the happy tears wouldn't screw up her makeup. At least they'd done group photos before the ceremony so she didn't have to worry about that.

Then she was squashed between Ryan and Bradly as they crushed her in a giant hug before they and the entire wedding party danced their way through the guests in a chaotic rush. Just the way the grooms had wanted. The entire wedding was a seamless mix of tradition and throwing it all to the wind and it was perfect.

The venue's coordinator swooped in as they exited the main space and she and Charlie got the happy couple sequestered in a small room so they could enjoy a few moments of privacy. They had eschewed the idea of a receiving line, instead preferring to go straight to dinner and dancing.

Charlie made her way to the hall where dinner would be served and quickly found her place next to Deke. Another thing Ryan and Bradly had skipped was the idea of a big head table with the entire wedding party at it. In keeping with their wedding-in-the-round theme, they'd instead opted for a small platform with a table for two in the middle of the room. Their attendants were seated at the first row of circular tables, but instead of being grouped together, they were seated with their dates or partners, along with a mix of guests.

"You look amazing," Deke said as she sat down. "And I look forward to peeling that dress off of you later."

She shushed him as the DJ welcomed the bridal couple and Ryan and Bradly came in to raucous cheers mixed with some wolf whistles. They looked amazing in matching champagne tuxedos, Ryan's accented with the same true sage green Charlie wore, while Bradly sported a deep evergreen hue that looked amazing against his rich, dark skin.

Dinner service began as soon as the two were seated and Charlie twisted her napkin in her lap. Her speech was next up, scheduled as the first course was cleared and the next brought out. Deke's arm landed on her shoulders and his lips pressed against her ear.

"You'll be fine."

She wished she had his confidence. Still, she held on to his words as the DJ's assistant handed her a wireless microphone. Charlie rose and brought the mic up.

"When Ryan asked me to say a few words here, my first thought was to write something down so it would be special and poignant—hey, I'm a wedding planner, it's what I do. But he insisted I speak instead from the heart. So..." She spread her hands wide, showing her lack of written notes. A few chuckles rippled through the room.

"He also said to keep it semi-short, because no one really likes sitting through long speeches." More laughter and Charlie took a deep breath. "And Ryan always gets what he wants. Witness..." She pointed toward Bradly, who had the grace to at least try to look mildly embarrassed. Charlie knew better. That turned the laughter into a roar and she waited for it to die down before continuing.

"I could get sentimental or tell embarrassing stories. But I'll skip that—mostly because Ryan has just as much dirt on me as I have on him. Instead, I will say this."

She took another slow breath and faced Ryan and Bradly, then swallowed against the lump in her throat, praying she could do this without crying.

"Ryan, you are the brother I never had. My forever best friend. And you deserve every happiness this world can offer and then some. When you told me about Bradly, I saw the love in your eyes and I knew he was special. Then I met him."

Almost there. She just had to hold it together a little longer.

"You two are perfect for each other." A collective sigh echoed through the room and Charlie forced herself to continue. "You complement and complete each other. It sounds trite, but I feel like I've gained another bestie. My wish for you is simple—more.

"More of this. More of the everyday love you show each other. More of the partnership, the friendship, the genuine caring and concern you both have, seemingly without effort. I wish you more—never ending."

She raised her glass and waited as everyone else did the same.

"Ryan and Bradly—blessings. From all of us who love you both."

Charlie took a sip and dropped to her seat, swiping furiously at her leaking eyes. Both Bradly and Ryan were wiping their own eyes, as were a few guests.

"You missed your calling," Deke whispered. "That was sweet."

The rest of the dinner passed in a blur until it was time for the first dance. As Ryan and Bradly took the floor, Ty Lake clapped a hand on Deke's shoulder, then nodded to Charlie.

"Good to see you again." He squatted next to Deke with an ear-to-ear grin. "Do you have any idea how much restraint it's taking to not give you the same kind of shit you gave me?"

Charlie had no clue what Ty was talking about, but Deke must have.

"Oh fuck off. Not the same at all." The laughter in Deke's tone and the big smile on his face pegged the conversation as friendly ribbing, but Charlie sensed something deeper.

"You say that now, but I'm betting that tune changes before you hit that magic age." Ty rose and flashed his bright grin. "And you two are next."

That shed a whole lot of light on the teasing banter and Charlie shook her head. "My contract ends this month, so you might lose that bet."

Ty laughed and walked away, calling "we'll see" over his shoulder. Deke looked stricken, or like a kicked puppy. Neither were things she associated with him. Then she blinked and the look was gone, replaced with his normal just-cocky-enough smirk.

"I suppose we should be glad that was Ty and not Zach. He's a lot less tactful." Deke leaned in close and wrapped his arm over her shoulders. "I knew this was a short-term contract, but you hadn't said anything about a specific end date. Wanna let me in on that?"

His words were light but like the banter with Ty, there was something in his tone that hinted at more. Ryan was right, she had to tell Deke, and now was as good a time as any.

"I was offered a permanent position, but it's not in Maryland." She scanned his face, trying to gauge his response, but Deke looked the same as always—sinfully hot. "In fact, it's not state side."

He shifted in his seat, bringing his body closer to hers.

"I'd rather not have to ask the right questions for you to get me up to speed."

There was no question in his words, but his brow furrowed and his gaze bored into her. His face was full of all the things he said he didn't want to ask. Charlie sighed. It wouldn't be right to say nothing.

"I leave in two weeks. There's a new hotel opening in the Côtes d'Azur."

It was a step up the ladder. A great opportunity that got her back to Europe. And she'd be on the French Riviera. She should have been thrilled. Instead, she felt like shit.

DEKE

Her words landed like a punch to the gut. He'd known this was coming and thought he was ready for it. *Wrong.* He was about to open his mouth and say something when the DJ called the wedding party to join in the dancing. Charlie stood and snagged Deke's hand, pulling him to stand with her.

Memories of the night they'd first met flooded his brain as they stepped onto the dance floor. He leaned close and whispered in her ear.

"May I touch your waist?" That seemed like so long ago. Another lifetime. Charlie rolled her eyes, but she stepped into his arms with a bright smile.

"You can touch anything you'd like."

How about your heart?

He ached to say it, but how could he expect her to open up when he hadn't. He pulled her close and gave silent thanks that in her heels, she matched his height. It made talking while dancing easier. He figured he had one song before the DJ went with something more up tempo.

"I guess I'm surprised you're leaving so soon," he said. He'd been on the receiving end of this type of conversation and he knew how it would likely go, but he had to try. "Charlie, I... Uhh..."

He'd never said the words he wanted to say—not romantically, anyway. He took a deep breath, maneuvered them to the edge of the dance floor, and tried again.

"I never imagined I'd meet someone who made me want to settle down. I never dreamed I'd find a romantic love. Then I met you."

Charlie's hand stiffened in his. Her back tensed under his fingers. She shook her head, curls bouncing and tickling against his cheek.

"I don't believe in romance."

"How? You're a wedding planner—romance is your business. And I've seen how you look when talking about weddings and engagements. Or about them." He tipped his head toward Ryan and Bradly, still wrapped around each other on the dance floor.

"Oh, I think it's wonderful for others, just not for me. Life has proven that's not in my cards."

What the hell had happened to make her so cynical? Charlie was an intelligent, vibrant woman who seemed to love love and all the trappings that came along with it—so long as it was someone else, and not her.

"Well, life is wrong."

If he could find a woman who made him look forward to marriage, then love had to be in her cards. She lifted a shoulder and shook her head.

"Not in my case. I've been burned twice and that was two times too many."

He'd never heard such bitterness in her voice before. Nor had he ever seen her eyes look so cold. Whatever had happened, she'd picked up the broken pieces of herself and surrounded them with a wall so thick and high that no one could get through.

But I'm gonna try.

"Yeah, and I'm the one who figured I'd marry for duty. That settling down meant settling, like my sisters. But here we are, and Ty was right."

Charlie's head tipped to the side and she arched an eyebrow. "How so?"

Just say it. Fuck it. Take the leap.

"You know my rule—not before I'm thirty. Ty bet I'd change my tune before then." Deke could lose himself in the depths of her cool blue eyes. "I love you, and I believe we have something special."

The slightest flicker of warmth crossed Charlie's face, but she blinked and it was gone. Maybe it had been wishful thinking on his part. All the times he'd given Ty shit about his emotional state around Nicky swirled in his head. He owed his friend an apology because he was every bit as fucked up as Ty had been. Maybe more.

"You can't know that," Charlie replied. "It's too soon to know that."

"Is that what you tell someone who wants to plan a surprise engagement event? Or a couple who wants to get married quickly?"

He knew it wasn't. She'd talked about some of her favorite experiences. How sweet and romantic they were. Maybe she didn't believe she deserved happiness, just like he'd believed he'd never find someone like her.

"It's not the same thing," she said.

"Isn't it?" They'd stopped moving and instead stood at the

edge of the dance floor, still locked in an embrace as if they were swaying to the music. "You admire loving families, even if they're fucked up and not perfect. Your favorite part of your job revolves around love—engagements, weddings, anniversaries, it's all about romantic love. You don't have a cynical bone in your body when it comes to other people's families and romantic relationships."

It would have been easy to miss the tears gathered in the corners of her eyes, or the way her lips compressed at the sides as if she was struggling to maintain composure. He could drop the conversation. Give up. Accept that she didn't return his feelings.

Or he could give it one last try.

"Don't you deserve that same happiness?"

A single tear cascaded down her cheek and she sniffed. Her eyes darted around the room and Deke realized his mistake. He'd put her on the spot in a very public place, when she was obligated to not just be there physically, but be entirely present.

"Shit, I'm sorry, I..."

Charlie's fingers clenched, stopping his words. She flicked her eyes toward the door and gave him a bright, if tremulous smile, then turned and started walking. He took the hint and moved with her. Once through the door, she continued down a hall, until she pushed open another door and they stepped into a restroom, where she promptly locked the door.

"Drop it." Charlie whirled on him before he could open his mouth. "You knew from the beginning what was on the table here."

Her breasts rose and fell on a long sigh. Deke wanted to argue. He wanted to convince her to give them a chance. But time was not on his side and he'd said the same or similar to women in his life. He nodded.

"I'm sorry," he repeated. "You're right. That was out of bounds. I would still like to see you, while we have time and I promise I'll behave. But I understand if you're pissed at me."

He'd said it and he meant it—he'd behave if it killed him. No matter how much he wanted her to be a part of the rest of his life, he'd keep that to himself if that's what it took to have a little more time with her.

Charlie reached out, grabbed his tie and pulled him closer to her. She rested her forehead against his and a small chuckle escaped her lips.

"If you were any other man, I'd be walking away right now."

Deke took that as a positive sign. She proved him right when she shrugged and leaned in to kiss him. It was achingly sweet and her body was practically vibrating with tension. He dared to hope that the idea had been planted and maybe would grow.

"My job is to make people's dreams come true."

She'd said the same thing the night they'd met. It had made him smile then, even as it had triggered a yellow warning flag—he'd learned to avoid women who were all about love and romance. Now, he was wishing she was that type.

"But you don't buy into the whole fairy tale thing?"

"Fairy tales are pretty dark when you think about them," she replied. "Besides, what do you think all the side characters are doing while the newlywed Charmings ride off into the sunset?"

She wasn't wrong. Deke held his hands up in surrender.

"Well, maybe you can show me what you get up to once you send your couple off on that sunset ride."

Her laughter rang clear and bright in the small room. She leaned close and winked.

"You already know. I've got a few more wedding party

duties. After that, I don't think Ryan would miss me if we skipped out. I'll see them off following the wedding brunch tomorrow."

She'd stepped smoothly back into their easy flirtation and banter and Deke breathed a sigh of relief.

"I think I need a refresher course," Deke replied, then pulled her in for a kiss. Her lips parted under his and he breathed her in. He planned to enjoy every moment he could with her. And maybe figure out how to break through the walls she had up.

CHAPTER 19

A purple suitcase thudded to the entryway tiles. She looked from the bag to Ryan and arched an eyebrow at him. As flamboyant as he could be, his travel bags were always basic black or gray—like the ones already stacked near the door.

"It's Bradly's," he said before she could ask. The man in question came down the stairs hauling another bright purple bag that he added to the pile. Apparently, neither of them believed in traveling light.

"Don't judge," Bradly said. "They're easy to find in baggage claim."

Charlie had to give him that. She'd watched Ryan fumbling through every virtually identical black bag as it came down the belt.

"I'm so glad you could be here for more than just the wedding. Even though it wasn't all happy circumstances that made it possible, but..." Ryan shrugged, then wrapped Charlie in a bear hug. "You will never convince me that it wasn't all for the best."

He held her at arm's length and looked her up and down. "I'm not convinced you're making the right choice here, either. But I love you, I believe in you, and I'll stand beside you no matter what. Through thick and thin."

Tears prickled Charlie's eyes at his words. He was echoing what she'd said to him when he'd first come out to her. She'd wiped the tears from his face and told him she'd always be there for him, through thick and thin. Over the years, even with distance and jobs, they'd stayed true to that promise.

Bradly handed over a set of keys. "My sister will come over before you leave. She'll stay in our place and take care of the plants. Glenda just called and they don't have a new tenant lined up yet, so you don't need to rush packing."

He hugged her tight and kissed her cheek. "Ryan is a very lucky man to have a friend like you. And I count myself even luckier that you're a part of our lives." His grip loosened, then he bit his lip and nodded as if in agreement with something in his head.

"One more thing," he said. "I'll tell you the same thing I said to Ryan when I realized how shitty his family was. Blood doesn't make family. You're part of us—you've got Ryan, and me, and all of my family. Remember that, okay?" He gave her another squeeze, then started hauling suitcases out the door.

Charlie swiped at the tears trickling down her face. Ryan ran his thumb over her cheeks and shook his head.

"He's right. I know it's not the same, but chosen family is what we have. This is your home, Charlie. It's not just you and me anymore. It's us. I hope you find everything you want and need, but no matter what, you can always come home to us."

He gave her one last rib-crushing hug before grabbing the remaining suitcases just as their car pulled up. Charlie stood on the stoop, waving after them until they were out of sight. She gathered her jacket around her and sank to the step.

The last few months had been a rollercoaster, leaving her spinning and confused. Deke's declaration of love at the wedding had her questioning everything. It didn't help that it had come when she was already doubting everything, including the new job.

She closed her eyes and drew in a shuddering breath. Deke's question echoed in her head.

"Don't you deserve that same happiness?"

She'd thought she'd found it. First with Jonathan, then with Noah. Both had proven her wrong. The breakup with Jonathan nearly caused her to derail at college. It shattered her fledgling self-esteem and left her questioning everything outside of her school and professional goals.

She'd pursued casual relationships in an effort to avoid being hurt again. Then came Noah, and look where that got her.

Now Deke.

He didn't seem like the others. Then again, they hadn't either.

She pushed herself up and went back inside, climbing the stairs slowly. She had a busy week on the calendar, getting everything ready to turn back over to DeeDee, plus a couple of corporate events and small weddings.

And Deke.

The man who seemed to get her in ways no one, not even Ryan, ever had. The one who could go from quiet cuddles on the couch to fucking her in ways she'd be embarrassed to admit. Except she wasn't with him. Ever.

He said he loved me.

So had Jonathan. So had Noah.

Words were meaningless. Anyone could say the words.

Inside the apartment, she flopped onto the bed and stared at the painting on the wall.

Nicky and Ty. What had he said at the wedding? Something about not giving Deke the same kind of shit. She hadn't understood what that meant, but friends had inside jokes. She'd assumed it was all just friendly banter about Deke's well-known stance that he wouldn't get serious with anyone until he'd turned thirty. But that didn't feel right. She was missing something.

Her phone buzzed and Charlie swiped at the screen.

Speaking of Deke.

> How are you holding up?

Leave it to him to ask. All along, he'd shown incredible sensitivity to her moods and needs. She'd just chalked it up to him being experienced. Now she wondered if she was missing something there as well. She tapped her screen again.

> Holding it together.

Was she really? The rollercoaster that her life had become felt like it was careening in a direction she hadn't intended. She should be ecstatic over the new job. Instead, all she could think about was how much she enjoyed being back in Baltimore—Ryan and Bradly. Deke and even his family.

Sure, she'd put the final nail in the coffin with her parents. Or at least her mother. But the last two and half months had been filled with more love and friendship than she'd known in years.

> Anything I can do?

Charlie read the text several times. Each time she'd start to type out a response, then quit and erase it all. She could tell him she needed to forget her name. He'd make sure she did just that. Of that, she had no doubt.

The couple in the painting seemed to mock her. Her first impression of the piece was one of passion. After she'd met Ty and Nicky, that seemed like an understatement. She'd never known that kind of all-consuming passion with anyone.

Until Deke.

Charlie shoved those thoughts aside. Having sex was one thing, but she'd learned her lessons on falling for a guy. It never ended well.

> What did you have in mind?

Three little dots appeared and Charlie stared at her phone, willing him to type faster. This was the behavior she didn't like in herself. Anxiously waiting for the guy she liked to say something.

> I'm swamped this week and babysitting this weekend. You're welcome to join me for that. G-rated, sorry. Late next week is open. If that's not pushing your schedule too tight.

Charlie forced herself to stop after three readings. She was obsessing over every possible hidden meaning. Was he really that busy, or was he just saying that? Maybe it his way of breaking things off slowly. Was the G-rated comment because he thought all she wanted was sex? And wasn't that the message she'd given him?

Fuck it.

She tapped out a response.

As cute as your sisters' kids are, I'll leave the babysitting to you. But I'm sure we can find a lunch or two, or even a dinner hour here and there. And I'm free last weekend of the month if that works for you.

She hit send and put her phone down. The next two weeks were going to be non-stop busy. She might as well get some of the easy stuff done now. Bonus points, it would keep her mind off Deke for a while.

CHAPTER 20

CHARLIE—SUNDAY, MARCH 30

Two weeks. Charlie had barely seen Deke in fourteen days, and what time they'd had felt like scraps. Or maybe that was how she was seeing it. The last time they'd had sex was the night of Ryan and Bradly's wedding. Since then, it had been a quick lunch here, a dinner there. Never more than an hour or two, and never anywhere private.

She supposed it made sense—Deke had made his feelings clear and she'd rejected him. She couldn't blame him for losing interest. Just because she still wanted him didn't mean the feeling was mutual.

They'd made plans for this weekend, but Saturday had fallen through. He'd suggested lunch today and she'd been surprised when he said to come to his place. She'd showered and dressed and then sat watching the clock until it was time to call an Uber.

She picked up her phone and tapped the button to summon a car. Her stomach bounced with nerves all the way over to Deke's. She had no idea what to expect and the possibilities ripped at her.

The car pulled to the curb and Charlie climbed the steps. Deke pushed open the storm door and ushered her inside, his face an impassive mask. He closed the door and leaned against it while Charlie bent and pulled off her shoes.

"I ordered your favorite noodles. Food got here just before you did." He pushed away from the door and headed for the dining area. The smell of food set her stomach even more on edge. Charlie sat, but didn't open the containers. Instead, she looked down at her hands, held tight in her lap.

"I'm sorry for the things I said to you at the wedding. I could have been a lot more sensitive to your feelings."

She'd been kicking herself over it for two weeks. The bottom line was that she owed Deke an apology.

"I invalidated your feelings, and that's fucked up."

She looked up as Deke sank into the chair across from her, a small smile playing at his lips. "I suspect it doesn't matter how you phrase it, the outcome is still the same."

"Yeah, sorry." She'd tried to wrap her head around it, but always came to the same conclusion—she wasn't willing to risk her heart again. "You're amazing, but you want things that I can't give."

Deke nodded as if he'd been expecting her to say exactly that.

"What do you want right now, Charlie?"

The question hung in the air, a reminder of things shared and things lost. Charlie gave a weak laugh and shook her head.

"I want you." She whispered the words, afraid if she voiced them any louder, she'd crumble apart. She craved to feel his touch one last time. To get lost in his kisses and drown in his arms.

Silence stretched, then Deke scraped his chair back and

stood. He took her hands and pulled her up, then came behind her and wrapped his arms at her waist. His chin rested on her shoulder and his breath tickled her neck.

"Go upstairs, get undressed and lie back on the bed. I'll be up in a minute." He released her and Charlie didn't question his instructions. She obeyed. Upstairs, she stripped and laid her clothes on the chair in the corner, then arranged herself in the middle of the bed and waited.

Deke came up after a few minutes and sat a glass of water near the bed. He bent and retrieved a bag from the under the bed storage.

"Tell me your safe word."

"Café."

"Good girl." His voice was so soft she barely heard him. "I want to tie you to the bed, then take my time kissing and touching every inch of your body. I want to tease you until you beg me to fuck you. When you've begged me enough, maybe I will fuck you. Or maybe I'll spank your ass for being such a naughty girl, then start all over again. Anything is possible."

Deke slid a finger along her collarbone, then down her sternum before stopping at her bellybutton.

"Do you want that? Yes or no?"

"Yes, please." She hadn't expected her voice to be so breathy, but there was no denying she was turned on. Deke opened his rope bag and put the first loop over her wrist, then pulled her arm over her head and secured it to the bedframe. He did the same with her other arm, then both feet.

He stroked his fingers over her toes, her feet, then up her ankles. He kept going over her calves and thighs, then her hips, her belly, and around her breasts, then down her arms. Her skin prickled in goosebumps and a gasp escaped her lips.

"You are so beautiful." His words were a caress against her

skin, as tangible as the feel of his fingers smoothing down her sides. "This spot right here."

He placed the pad of his index finger over the faint white scar low on her hip. "I've kissed it dozens of times. But I don't know how you got it. Tell me."

He bent his head and peppered her hip with tiny kisses.

"Not much to tell. I was in high school. We went water skiing. It was rope burn."

His tongue traced the edge of her hipbone, then continued up to her belly button. "This, I can guess. You had a piercing. Why'd you give it up?"

His fingers dug into her hips, massaging tight muscles into relaxed looseness. Teeth grazed her belly, gently nibbling at where her piercing used to be. That one wasn't as easy to answer.

"I was a teenager when I did it. Act of rebellion. Guess I just grew out of it."

"No." Deke maneuvered himself between her legs. "Your whole body tightened when I mentioned it. Can't be that simple."

She expected him to move down, instead, he levered up, holding himself over her and dipping his head to kiss her breasts. His tongue traced one nipple with agonizing tenderness.

"Why, Charlie?"

She could lie to him. Or try to make less of it. But it was like Deke was so in tune with her and her body that he'd know. And when the hell did that happen? How was it this man she'd known for a matter of months knew her body better than anyone?

"Because they don't look good on bigger girls."

Deke sat back so quickly, she worried she'd said something wrong. Charlie struggled to sit up, but the ropes held her tight to the bed. Deke's scowl melted as he laid a hand in the middle of her chest, urging her to relax.

"What asshole told you that?"

Charlie had lost count, so she shrugged. Jonathan had been the first to say it. Noah the last, except he didn't settle for making it about size alone. No, he had to add age—she'd just turned thirty, wasn't she too old for that? And class—he didn't see himself dating anyone with more than their ears pierced. It was tacky.

"Lots of people," she replied.

"They're wrong. You're stunning, and if you like it, that's all that matters." He shifted and touched his lips to the inside of her elbow. Then down her arm. True to his word, Deke covered her body in soft kisses and gentle touches.

When his fingers slid between her legs, she trembled with need. But Deke wasn't rushing. He eased one finger along her labia, then up to brush her clit with the softest of touches. It was delicious. It was maddening. And it didn't stop.

Tension ratcheted up in her body and Deke kept to slow, gentle strokes. When he lowered his head, Charlie nearly shouted for joy. But his mouth was as soft and gentle as his fingers. Every time she'd think she was on the edge of orgasm, he'd switch to massaging her legs, or her arms. Then he'd take his time before returning his attention to her pussy.

By the third or fourth round, she was ready to scream. Her clit throbbed, pulsing in time with her heartbeat.

"Deke, please!"

His chuckle sent vibrations along her sensitized flesh. "What do you want, Charlie?"

"I want you inside me. Now!"

He sat up and ran his hands up her legs, cupping her hips then gliding over her waist to settle just under her breasts.

"Oh, is that all?"

One hand trailed down her belly and dipped between her legs. He slid one finger between her labia and into her pussy then stroked slowly.

"Like this?"

"Oh. My. God. Deke, fuck me. Please."

"It's tempting to make you keep begging, but..." Deke sighed and moved back. The bed shifted as he stood and reached into the nightstand where he kept condoms. He rolled one down then knelt between her legs. The heavy weight of his dick rested on her pubic bone and Charlie arched up to him, desperate to fill him inside her.

Instead of pushing into her, Deke ran his thumbs up the creases of her thighs, then back down, stroking closer to her labia with each pass. Finally, he trapped her clit between his thumbs and applied soft pressure, rolling along the base of her clit until she was breathless with need.

The head of his dick slid down and Charlie arched as much as the ropes and Deke's legs pressing against her would allow, but she couldn't get the angle right.

"Did you want something?"

"I want your dick in me."

She didn't see any reason to be coy. Deke chuckled and on the next breath, he pushed in. Slow and steady, he kept going until his body ground against hers. Then he rocked his hips in an easy grind. No pounding thrusts.

Instead, Deke did something different. He made love to her with a slow, deliberate tenderness that somehow felt more intense than anything they'd done before. The world faded away until all Charlie knew was Deke—his touch bringing her to new heights of pleasure, his voice urging her on. Her orgasms were different, too—like a rolling tide that kept going. Endless. Relentless. An ebb and flow of passion that had her shaking.

Then Deke buried his face in her neck and his body stiffened. She wanted to wrap her arms and legs around him, but the ropes held her still as he came. He withdrew, then slid down her body and treated her to oral with the same gentle intensity and slow build. He did not stop until she was shaking from an orgasm so intense it brought tears to her eyes.

Charlie turned her head, trying to keep Deke from seeing the tears spilling down her cheeks. But he was already stroking her hair from her face as his other hand worked to undo the ropes. He kept one hand on her the whole time, never letting her go, even as he stretched to free her feet. Once the last rope tumbled off the bed, Deke folded her in his arms, cradling her against his chest.

"I've got you, baby. And I always will."

She wished she could believe him, but painful lessons had taught her otherwise. From her parents to the two men who'd claimed to love her—they had all been the same. No amount of hoping Deke was different would make it so.

"Hey, look at me." Deke's voice was soft, but there was an unmistakable note of command. Charlie tipped her head back. He traced his fingers along her face, gently brushing the last of her tears away.

"Let's jump in the shower then heat some food, because I'm starved."

She had expected something deep or serious. Instead, he'd focused on the practical. Charlie smiled and nodded. In the shower, his tender touch continued and almost sent Charlie into a fresh spate of crying.

Deke popped their lunches into the microwave while Charlie set the table. Halfway through the food, Deke caught her hand and kissed her knuckles.

"Do you think you're up for round two? Because I really

liked the idea of making you beg for my cock, then smacking your ass for being so naughty. And speaking of ass..."

His raised eyebrows and the lifting tone made it a question. This was the Deke she'd spent so many hours with. Cocky and sexy.

"Yes, and yes," she replied. After the emotionally wrenching sex they'd just had, the idea of some hard fucking and his dick in her ass sounded like heaven.

"Good." He planted another kiss on her knuckles, then nibbled his teeth along one finger. "I hope you're ready for it rough because I plan to make sure you have a hard time sitting down on that plane tomorrow."

That sent a flood of warmth through her, and tension coiled in her gut. *How can I be horny again so soon?*

Whether it made sense or not, that was the reality. One word from Deke and Charlie would be happy to leave their half-finished food on the table, all to have him inside her again.

CHAPTER 21

"**Y**ou are a godsend!" Marisol pushed through the door, a half-rolled sleeping bag in one hand, and a steaming travel mug of coffee in the other. *Leave it to Marisol to be chugging high octane before dinner on a Friday.*

Jaime came in, hugged Deke, then went straight to the dining table and started spreading out books. Deke's eyebrows went up, and he looked back at his sister.

"His dad was supposed to get him, but something came up. Again. He does this about every other scheduled visit. Last time I canceled my plans but I don't want to do that again, so thanks for helping."

Deke shook his head. "Yeah, no problem, but I wasn't looking for that rundown. More like—what's up with that?" He hooked his thumb toward Jaime, now hunched over his schoolbooks like it was his job.

"Well, that's a long story. Short version—Jaime had a book report due last month. He'd gotten it about half done before his dad picked him up. I should have known better, but...

whatever. Jaime says he got stuck and asked his dad for help. I can't get a straight answer outta the man. Bottom line, his 'help' consisted of quoting directly from Wikipedia."

Marisol's eyes rolled up and she took a deep breath. "Anyway. After a long conference, his teacher agreed to let Jaime redo the book report—properly. And I insisted he work on it tonight, so if he has any problems, we can tackle them together over the weekend. Besides, I figured it would make babysitting easier."

Which would have been great, except Deke didn't want easier. He wanted something that would keep his mind off Charlie. Zach had called and tried to convince him to go out, but Deke refused. The last thing he wanted to do was think about another woman. Marisol's panicked phone call felt like a lifesaver.

"Yeah, sure. I mean, I could probably help him with any issues, then you won't have to. At least you know I won't use a fucking wiki to do it."

Marisol hugged her son, then eyed Deke up and down. On the surface, he was fine—he'd showered, his laundry was done, and he'd even caught up on his grading. In fact, he'd completed his lesson plans for the rest of the year.

"What's going on? You being free on a Friday is unheard of. Is Charlie working or something?"

Deke tried to maintain a poker face. He even thought he succeeded until Marisol's eyes went wide and her mouth went into a big, round O.

"Oh shit, I'm sorry. I know you really liked her. What happened?"

Nothing. Everything.

"Don't you have a date to get to?"

His sister smacked his shoulder. Hard. "Fuck that, he can wait a minute or two. What did you do?"

Of course she assumed he'd fucked up.

"It's not like that. Tables got turned on me, that's all."

Her shocked expression turned to glee and she laughed. "I'm sorry, but that's funny. So, you caught feelings, and she gave you the can't we just be fuck buddies routine?"

"Something like that," Deke muttered. He didn't want to think about it. He sure as hell didn't want to examine the whole thing with his sister. "Go on. Jaime and I will be fine. Have fun."

Marisol waved at her kid, then headed out the door, cackling the whole time. Deke had no doubts the news would travel fast and he'd likely be fielding texts or calls from his other sisters and possibly his mother. Everyone had loved Charlie and asked when he was bringing her around again.

At this point, the twelfth of never.

He waited until the door clicked behind his sister then checked on Jaime. The kid had his head in a book and was studiously writing notes. Had he had to do book reports in fourth grade? Probably. Deke picked up the instruction sheet and chuckled. He could see why a nine-year-old might get stumped, but why a grown man thought plagiarizing an online encyclopedia was a good plan was beyond him.

"Is this the same book you did the first time?" He couldn't imagine the teacher requiring the kid to read a whole new book, but stranger things had happened. Jaime nodded and Deke held out his hand for the page he was working on.

"Okay, you've got the right idea, but you're overthinking it." He sat the sheet down and walked through the instructions with his nephew. Somewhere along the way, the lightbulb clicked on and Jaime's face lit up in a grin.

"Oh that's easy!" He tore out a new sheet and started writing, occasionally stopping to ask Deke a question about spelling. Half an hour later, Deke helped him proofread then re-write the piece neatly, or as neatly as he could.

"Great job!" Deke high fived the kid. "Do you have more homework?"

Jaime shook his head. "Mom said I could play games or watch a movie, or whatever you say once I was done with that."

Smart mom. Deke pointed at his collection of games and movies. He kept the non-kid-friendly ones in the bedroom. They played some games, then Deke made dinner. They watched some anime and Jaime's eyes started to drift. Deke tucked him into the sleeping bag and checked his phone.

Sure enough, there was a string of texts from his siblings. And one from Ty. He clicked on that one.

> Lunch. Tomorrow. No fucking excuses.
> You're getting your ass out of the house.

Deke sent a thumbs up and considered looking at the other texts. *No. I don't want to dissect the relationship and what went wrong.*

He turned the volume down on his TV and spent the next hour in one of Jaime's games—some edutainment thing that was actually pretty engaging and required some logic and math skills to navigate.

When Marisol texted that she was out front, he opened the door and helped her get her sleeping son buckled into the car, then hugged her goodnight. Back inside, his phone buzzed with another text.

Mom. Shit.

> What happened? What did you do?

He rolled his eyes. The universal question. Of course he

was to blame. By the time he cleaned up from dinner and got his living room back in order after several hours of a rambunctious nine-year-old, Deke was ready for bed. Maybe tonight he'd actually sleep.

He woke to bright sunlight streaking across his face and the distinct impression that he was in the wrong place. Deke shifted to his side and everything made sense. He'd fallen asleep on the couch. Again. But he'd drawn his blinds, so why was the sun in his face?

A cup of coffee landed on the table in front of him. Zach dropped into the cushy chair and propped his elbows on his knees. With his height, the move made him look like a troll or a giant bug and Deke bit his tongue to keep from laughing.

Maybe I'm losing it.

He'd spent the entire week in some weird state where laughter seemed to be right below the surface. And not the good kind of laughter. Deke swiped a hand over his face, sat up and grabbed the coffee.

"Time's it?"

Zach flicked his wrist and glanced down. "Not quite eleven. Ty suggested I stop by."

Great. The last thing Deke wanted was Zach's insistence that getting laid would solve all his problems.

"She broke up with you?"

Deke shook his head. "Dunno that I'd call it a breakup. Not really. We were friends with benefits. Fuck buddies. I wanted more. She didn't."

Zach nodded, then pointed at the coffee table where the picture from New Year's Eve sat.

"Which is totally why it looks like this isn't the first time you slept on your couch and you're staring at a pic of the night you met." Zach clapped his hands together and stood. "Drink your coffee. Get your ass up and get showered. We're getting out of here."

"Can't," Deke answered. "Supposed to meet Ty for lunch."

The look Zach shot him was the same look he reserved for annoying customers who were about to be asked to leave. It was a last chance to straighten up and fly right before the big, bearded dude got unpleasant.

"Who the fuck do you think we're meeting?"

"I'm not spending lunch discussing this with you two." Deke snatched up the photo and took the stairs two at a time, determined to tuck the thing away in his desk drawer or something. He might spend lunch getting pleasantly drunk. That sounded a hell of a lot more fun than examining a situation he couldn't change.

He was halfway to that goal in the backroom at Cold Bottom when his phone blew up with more texts from his family. He silenced the damn thing and went for another pitcher. They stayed through dinner, and at least his friends seemed to recognize Deke's need to avoid any painful subjects. He'd pay for the heavy drinking, but for the moment, it felt good to be numb.

By the time Ty dropped him off, Deke was well and truly drunk—a state he hadn't been in for a very long time.

He'd barely made it in his door when his mother texted. Again.

> I expect you at the house tomorrow for brunch.

He'd been summoned. That was not something to be refused. She didn't need to include details. All the Wallace siblings knew. Sighing and swiping a hand over his face, Deke replied he'd be there.

He groaned and looked at the time. He'd been looking forward to spending Sunday sleeping in and nursing a well-deserved hangover. Instead, he'd be prying his ass out of bed to make it to his parents' house at ten.

Better shower and sleep, then.

Deke woke on the couch again with barely enough time to shower and dress before brunch. He grabbed his darkest sunglasses and still flinched at the bright light when he left his house. No surprise, his mother snatched them off his face the second he walked in the door.

"Really? Are you back in college?" She sighed and tossed the shades on the side table. "You still smell like a brewery. Go take a seat. I'll get you coffee."

He was an adult with a college degree, a good job, and his own home, but his mother could still make him feel like a teenager coming home drunk from a party. Deke slid into his spot at the same table where he'd done his homework and been lectured about too many things to count.

"Oh, you've got it bad." His dad chuckled as he grabbed a plate and filled it with quiche and some fresh fruit then sat it at his wife's place. It was a quiet ritual Deke had seen all his life —his mom was the cook and his dad would always fix her plate. He also took charge of supervising the siblings as they cleared the table and washed up.

"I expect you to eat." His mother placed a full coffee in front of him, kissed her husband's cheek, then sat. After a quick grace, they dug in. Deke poked a fork at the food on his plate.

"So, what happened?"

The lack of 'what did you do' made Deke look up to find both his parents staring at him with expressions of deep concern. He could put off his friends and ignore his sisters, but not his parents.

"Fell in love with the wrong person, I guess."

That's what it boiled down to. He'd gone and fallen head over heels for Charlie, and she didn't want that. There was no big ugly breakup, and in a way, that was worse. If he'd done something wrong, he could figure out how to make up for it. How to fix it.

"Oh, I don't believe that," his mother chided. "Not for an instant."

Deke dropped his fork and shook his head. "She doesn't want marriage. Or kids. What else would you call it?"

His mother snatched up her napkin and dabbed her mouth. A move he'd seen all his life and only realized after watching her with his nieces and nephews that she was hiding a smirk. His dad outright laughed. Loudly.

"How is that a bad thing? We were under the impression you didn't want marriage and kids, either."

Hold up. What the fuck alternate dimension have I landed in?

"But that's what's expected. How else do we carry on the Wallace name and all that. I figured I'd have to settle."

His mother let out a strangled sound and waved her napkin like she'd swallowed something spicy. She cleared her throat and took a sip of water.

"Darling, what we want is for all our children to be happy. Sure, to us, that means marriage and babies." She reached over and took Deke's hand, squeezing hard. "If that's not what works for you, then why on earth would you think you had to settle?"

It was Deke's turn to nearly choke. "What do you call Sarah and Lizzie's relationships? Or the shit over Marisol's divorce?"

Her head tilted to the side and her lips pressed together,

then she glanced across the table at her husband, her expression clear—you deal with him.

"We encouraged them to go to counseling. Marisol didn't tell us about him cheating until later. The church didn't grant an annulment because, for some unknown reason, she had sex with him after she found out."

Well shit. There were whole layers that Deke had never imagined. Including having discussions about sex with his parents.

"Sarah absolutely chose security," his mother added. "She'd been hurt enough in the past, and Chris knows that. They have a good relationship and they're both getting what they want from it. What's wrong with that?"

She refilled everyone's coffee and shook her head. "As for Lizzie and Rick, well... They're both very duty driven. He's the oldest of his siblings as well. Whether you agree with it or not, that's the life they chose."

Deke had spent his adult life looking at his sisters and their relationships as if they were prisons—things they hadn't wanted, but did for duty, or security, or desperation. He'd never considered that at least Lizzie and Sarah were living lives of their choosing.

Why would anyone want that?

"You met a woman who seems to be your perfect match. If that's what makes you happy, it doesn't matter what that relationship looks like. Or whether you have kids or not." His dad rose and clapped a hand on Deke's shoulder.

"Figure out what you really want. Then see if she wants the same. That's the only way to be true to yourself."

Some great weight lifted from Deke's shoulders and he sucked in a rush of air. This was not what he'd expected to hear from his parents. Ever.

He didn't have to figure out what he wanted. He knew.

Charlie.

CHAPTER 22

CHARLIE—WEDNESDAY, JUNE 18

Sparkling sunshine painted the world in shades of gold as Charlie climbed the steps back to the main hotel building. She was done for the day and it was time to go home.

"Pardon!"

Charlie moved aside as a young woman who had to be a photographer's assistant rushed down the steps carrying a light reflector. Sure enough, a young couple stood in the surf, the sun dancing off the salt spray and turning the couple into magical creatures as the photographer gestured wildly for her assistant to hurry.

Golden hour is fleeting.

Just like happiness. This was supposed to be her dream job. Instead, it was everything she didn't want. She no longer worked with guests seeking to hold an event at the hotel. Her entire job revolved around managing the staff who did see guests. She taught others how to make the magic happen and she hated it.

Charlie grabbed her things, locked up her office and opted to walk the short distance to the furnished employee apartment she got at a decent rate. Housing options near the hotel were ridiculously expensive and usually meant getting a room with no kitchen. She'd have to drive to Nice to find a place of her own. Nothing about this place felt like she belonged. It didn't feel like home.

She keyed in her door code and kicked off her shoes the moment she was in the door, then tossed the food container in the apartment size fridge to reheat later. If she got to it before falling asleep. Her evening routine—Hang up her purse. Plug in her electronics. All the things that made up her life.

She talked to Ryan and Bradly every week, and they had imagined her living a charmed life—swimming in the French Riviera on her days off or cycling into town to shop at the open-air market and spending her days organizing fabulous events.

The truth was far less picturesque.

She spent most days inside reviewing policies, or conducting training for new employees. Orientation days were her favorite. At least she was out of her tiny cubby of an office and in the hotel proper. She was out the door by seven most mornings and didn't get home until eight each night. Sometimes later.

Her phone buzzed, nearly vibrating itself off the table.

Weekly FaceTime.

The bright spot in her life. She tapped the screen and immediately felt better when Ryan and Bradly's smiling faces appeared.

"Ooh, bad day?" Ryan's forehead creased with worry. Leave it to him to spot something off right away.

"Same same," she replied. "I feel like an asshole

complaining, but this is soul sucking. And if I feel like that now, what's it going to be like in a year?"

The two men exchanged a look and Charlie squinted at them. "You both look like you're up to something."

Ryan tried to appear innocent. Bradly didn't bother. He leaned in, braced his elbows on his knees, and stared at her through the video.

"Come home."

She wasn't sure she heard him right. Then Ryan repeated what his husband had said.

"Quit if you have to. Come back. You can stay with us until you find something. Anything. Just get out of there." Ryan had his big puppy dog eye thing going on and Charlie almost laughed. He'd pull that out when he was trying to get his way and everything else had failed.

"I'm immune to that look, remember?"

He stuck his tongue out at her and flopped back on the couch. Bradly patted his knee, then turned back to the camera.

"I don't know you like Ryan, but it's easy to see you're miserable. You've been miserable. And he's right—come home. If you don't want to do that, go anywhere else. Do anything else."

"I ran into Deke at the grocery." Ryan dropped that bomb like someone would mention the weather.

Charlie sucked in a breath and willed herself to count to ten before saying anything. She got to five.

"And that means what, exactly?"

Ryan the hopeless romantic. He'd never change. She'd never admit to anyone that she thought of Deke every day. Somewhere over the last two and a half months, she'd come to grips with the fact that she was in love with him. Which was just about as fucked up a thing as could possibly happen.

"Oh come on. You can pretend you don't care, but I know better. He said to tell you hi. I thought you parted as friends."

A trickle of warmth settled into Charlie's chest, like a cold hearth being lit.

"We did," she whispered. "We just wanted different things."

"I'm confused," Bradly spoke up. "Did you ghost him? Or did he ghost you? Or what?"

"Neither, really."

They'd had a night of amazing, mind-blowing sex and barely slept all night. He even drove her to the airport. At the entrance to security, he'd pulled her into his arms and kissed her so thoroughly they gathered a crowd of onlookers. He told her again he loved her, then he let her go.

"He told me he understood my position and that he'd like to stay friends, but that he needed some time first."

That had been in a phone call when she'd landed in France.

"That was the last I heard from him, and I figured he'd moved on."

"He hasn't," Ryan replied. "Have you?"

There was no sense in lying to Ryan. He'd never believe her.

"No."

"Come home." Ryan and Bradly spoke at the same time, then both started saying something else until Charlie waved her hands at them to stop.

"Okay, okay, I get it. I have options. And you're right, this isn't working out. I'll figure this out in the morning. I promise."

After that, they updated her on all the rest of the news. Ty and Nicky had set their wedding date—October 31. *Quelle surprise.* The couple that owned Ryan and Bradly's place was planning to sell the unit, so they either had to move, or they could buy it—they'd decided to buy it.

"The neighborhood is amazing, it's between his work and mine, and the building is gorgeous. Besides, imagine what we can do with this place when it's ours!"

Ryan's enthusiasm always made Charlie smile, and today was no different. She didn't want to let them go. They were her lifeline to an existence beyond this—in theory, she should have been in heaven. Her reality, though, was hell.

When they hung up, Charlie got ready for bed and resolved to tackle the big questions in the morning. Starting with the hardest one: what did she really want in life.

But instead of going to bed, she pulled out her laptop and drafted an email to her manager about seeking a more guest-centric role.

She gave it a quick read then hit send. It wouldn't be seen until morning, but she imagined she'd get a fairly quick response. It was a shot in the dark, but for the first time since she'd arrived, she slipped into bed with hope in her heart.

CHAPTER 23

The laptop bag weighed heavy on Charlie's shoulder. The mirrored walls of the elevator were supposed to make the small space feel bigger, but all she saw were the signs of exhaustion etched on her face. The doors opened and she took a deep breath before walking the carpeted hall to the manager's office.

"He's out. You can leave everything here and I'll sign for it."

The secretary spoke in heavily accented English, even though she knew Charlie was fluent in French. None of the senior staff had been thrilled to have an American in management.

Fine. She wants to be like that. Whatever.

"Laptop, keys, and there's a folder in here with a full summary, file names, everything I've done since I started."

The morning after sending the email, she'd woken up to a meeting request. They couldn't offer her anything at this hotel, but they could offer her a role at their sister location—in Geneva.

The idea of being down the street from Noah was bad enough. The fact that it was a junior concierge position paying less than she'd been making five years ago was worse. Charlie refused and they'd elected to terminate her employment, effective today.

"Need anything else?" Charlie signed the paperwork the secretary thrust at her.

"No. We will call you if we do."

Charlie knew a dismissal when she heard one. She headed back to the elevator. The had at least arranged her flight back to the States and even allowed her to stay in employee housing until her departure Saturday morning.

Less than twenty-four hours till I'm headed back home.

Home. It felt odd to be thinking that about Baltimore, but Ryan and Bradly were there. As was Deke.

Nope. Not thinking about him.

Outside the hotel, the sound of the surf beckoned and Charlie cast her gaze to the beach below. Nearly three months here and she'd spent almost no time in the sand.

Fuck it. I'll pack tonight.

Everything had happened so fast, she'd barely had time to text Ryan the details and they kept missing each other by phone. The only thing she knew for sure—Ryan had texted her to come home. They'd worry about the rest later.

She waved at the attendant and had just settled on an empty lounge chair when her phone rang.

Speaking of Ryan.

Charlie tapped to answer and stuck her EarPods in.

"I figured I might get you now. How'd it go?"

Ryan's voice soothed her frayed nerves. Whatever happened, she at least had her bestie.

"About like you'd expect," she replied. "I'm sitting here staring at the Mediterranean, wondering why I couldn't just make this work. This is gorgeous."

Soft waves caressed the shore and even the early afternoon sun felt magical.

"Because you're not happy. And you can always go there on vacation."

He wasn't wrong. But first she'd have to find work. And rebuild her savings. And a whole lot of other things.

And would I enjoy it without Deke?

"Yeah, whatever. Are you sure you're okay picking me up tomorrow? I can Uber. Really."

She already felt like she was asking a lot of Ryan and Bradly.

Like staying in their guest room rent free until I get back on my feet.

"Stop it."

Ryan rarely sounded stern, so his tone made Charlie sit up and take note.

"Stop worrying. This is what friends and family do. You taught me that, and Bradly and his family proved it to me. So stop it. Also, fuck this. Switch to FaceTime."

Charlie moved to a shady spot just as Ryan's face popped up on her screen.

"That look, right there? That's how I knew you weren't happy. Before you even opened your mouth. This isn't you. Now turn the camera around and show me the damn view before I have to leave for work."

She switched the camera and panned around for Ryan to see. L'hôtel Majesté sat right on the edge of the Baie des Fourmis. A sliver of sand separated the blue waters from the lush plantings and vacation spaces that perched at the base of craggy hills. She swung back around to show the hotel—not that there was much to see from this angle. Beach loungers and umbrellas. A stone path leading up to the swimming pool. The hotel itself was barely visible from this angle.

"Beautiful, but so what? Flip it back."

Charlie moved farther into the shade as a family with several children came bounding onto the sand, headed for the water adventures tent. On her screen, Bradly appeared, waved at her, handed Ryan a coffee cup and kissed his cheek, then disappeared.

"You looked happier here in Baltimore." Bradly's singsong tone carried even without being right in front of the phone.

Ryan covered his mouth like he was hiding laughter. Combined with Bradly's snarky comment, it all sent Charlie into a fit of giggles. It felt like the weight of the last few months shifted—a little, anyway.

"Real talk." Ryan cradled his coffee cup and stared into the phone like they were face to face on his couch and not thousands of miles apart. "You think you might try again with Deke?"

All of her old arguments bubbled to the surface. *I'm not interested in a relationship. I don't do love. I'm not looking for forever.*

And it all echoed hollow and empty. She'd fallen for Deke. Hard.

"I don't know." She couldn't bring herself to say yes. Not even to Ryan. "It's not like we had some ugly breakup. But the things he wants? Marriage. Kids. All of that? Not for me. Especially not the kids."

She'd decided that long ago. Kids were terrific, when they were someone else's.

"So, you don't want the cookie-cutter cis-het relationship thing. And it sounds like he does." Bradly popped back into view with his own coffee cup and settled next to Ryan. "Did you have a conversation about what a relationship might look like? Or if either of you was open to compromise?"

"Yes, we di..." *Except, we didn't. Not really.* He'd said he loved her and thought they had something special. He challenged her on her cynicism, but they hadn't talked about what a relationship would mean. She assumed—because he'd made comments about his family's expectations. Because his family had made comments about grandkids. But Deke had never come right out and said that was the only thing on the table.

"No," she whispered. She sniffed back the tears that were threatening to spill over. The last thing she wanted to do was sit on the beach, in view of hotel staff and guests, crying.

"I stand by my question." Ryan looked like he wanted to reach through the phone and hug her. And right now, she needed that, because her world had just been turned upside down.

"And I still don't know," she replied. "That's a conversation I'd have to have with him."

The smiles on Ryan and Bradly's faces could have lit up several rooms. More importantly, they drove Charlie's tears away.

I'm going home.

DEKE—FRIDAY, JUNE 20

The empty classroom echoed the way Deke felt—like something was missing. Nearly three months and he still couldn't get her out of his mind. He'd thrown himself into work. Spent more time with his family than usual—that was a mistake, since they all asked about Charlie. He'd even gone out drinking and dancing with Zach—an unmitigated disaster that ended when Zach told him to get lost because he was ruining the vibes.

Everyone told him it would take time, but the ache was just as bad as the day she left. It hadn't helped that Deke had run into Ryan at the grocery store, and from what her bestie shared, it sounded like Charlie wasn't happy in her new job.

Deke grabbed his bag and crossed the room in a rush. In the car, he cranked up his music and sang along, anything to keep from second guessing himself.

The doubts crept in as he strode down the hall to Ty's office. He ignored them and kept walking. His best friend looked up before Deke could knock.

"Come in and close it." Ty closed his laptop and came around the desk to sit in one of the cushy chairs in the corner. Deke dropped into the other one and shoved a hand through his hair.

"So, what are your options?"

Deke hadn't said a word. Didn't need to. Ty got it.

"Suck it up and get over her," Deke replied. "What else is there?"

Ty blew out a breath and laughed. "Well, you could start by calling or texting. Which I'm betting you haven't done since she left."

Deke hadn't. He'd been waiting. Hoping she would reach out. Then he'd convinced himself it was better this way.

"Because it's so great when you tell a woman you just wanna be fuck buddies when she wants more, and then she keeps calling. Right?"

"How is that the same thing? You told her you needed time. You're kinda the one who has to say: okay, I've had time to think about it and here's where I'm at."

Ty sprawled back in his chair. "I thought you parted on good terms. So again, what are your options? And no, suck it up and get over her isn't the only one. What would you have told me if this had happened between me and Nicky?"

Deke laughed. He'd given Ty immeasurable hell, but once he'd figured out that his friend was serious, he'd encouraged him and called him on his bullshit. Just like Ty was doing now.

"Call, text, write a letter, whatever," Deke replied. "What difference does it make when she doesn't want the same..."

Deke stopped himself. She didn't want marriage and kids. More than that, she rejected the idea of love and romance for herself. She was afraid of being hurt.

"Shit." She'd met his family. Seen the focus on marriage and kids, and even though Deke was reluctant, he'd been clear he would do what was expected of him—get married and have a kid. Then he'd gone and mentioned love.

What he should have told her was how much he loved her and wanted her in his life—and he didn't care what that meant. All he cared about was sharing his life with Charlie.

"Someone have an epiphany?"

Deke flipped his middle finger at his friend.

"Had that courtesy my parents, along with discussions of shit I'd rather not know about my sisters. You just added a layer to it." Deke sat back and groaned. "I need to take a vacation."

"It's summer break. Aren't you already on vacation?" There was laughter in Ty's tone and any other time, Deke would be giving him shit right back.

"No, I mean, I need to go to France. I know she's at a hotel on the Riviera, pretty sure I have the name in a text. I'm damn sure I could get it from Ryan. I just don't know if showing up unannounced is a good idea."

A knowing look crossed Ty's face and he reached for his phone. "Hang on. Time to get an informed opinion." His fingers tapped the screen in a flurry. The whoosh of a sent message seemed loud in the quiet office. He smiled when an incoming message pinged, then pocketed his phone and crossed to the door.

"Give it a minute." Ty had his hand on the knob. Deke had no clue what was going on, or what Ty was waiting for but after less than a minute, his friend swung open the office door and Bradly walked in. Deke had forgotten that he worked with Ty.

"Huh." Bradly nodded at Deke, then settled into the chair Ty had vacated. "Let me get Ryan on FaceTime."

Deke shot Ty a questioning look, but his friend just waved his hand and pulled up another chair.

Bradly propped his phone on the table so they could all see Ryan, clearly sitting at his desk at work.

"What's this about?"

"Charlie." All three men responded at once and Ryan's face lit up.

"Are you... Wait, what's the plan?"

Bradly and Ty both looked at Deke and he let out a slow breath.

"It's not even a plan yet. Just a wild idea. I think... I hope that maybe, if I show up where she is, show her I'm invested, and that we can be whatever she wants us to be... I don't know... maybe..."

"No." Ryan blurted the word out. He waved his hands and shook his head.

How bad can it be to make Ryan act like this? Shit. I fucked up.

"I think maybe that needs explanation," Bradly said. Deke couldn't agree more.

"I meant, don't go to France," Ryan said. His lips curled up and Deke had the distinct impression that things weren't as bad as he feared.

"You planning to tell me why not?" Charlie had mentioned Ryan's flair for the dramatic, and Deke guessed he was seeing a bit of that now.

"Well, of course," Ryan replied. "You need to be at the airport tomorrow. I'll text you all the details."

Wait. She's coming back? That has to be what he means.

"Done. Now, what else are you thinking?" Deke leaned forward, forgetting Ty and Bradly. His entire focus was on Ryan—the man who knew Charlie best.

"I'm gonna go get a cup of coffee." Ty rose and grabbed his suit coat from a hook. "Text when you're done."

The door snicked closed behind him and Bradly shifted in his seat and gave Deke a serious look.

"If you're serious, you need to be ready to talk about all of that—what you want, what she wants, and whether you two can be on the same page."

On the screen, Ryan nodded and Deke felt like he'd just gained some secret knowledge. If these two were encouraging him, it had to mean Charlie was willing to talk. He left the unexpected meeting in Ty's office with new hope and a plan. He'd been ready to drop everything and fly to France. Instead, he just had to show up at the airport and cross his fingers Ryan knew his best friend as well as he thought he did.

And that we can find some common ground.

CHAPTER 24

CHARLIE—SATURDAY, JUNE 21

Exhaustion and worry warred for dominance as Charlie deplaned in Baltimore and made her way through customs. It was hard not to feel like a huge failure—years of building her career up only to have it fall apart thanks to her shitty relationship choice.

No. The only fault I had was trusting Noah. The rest is on him and management.

She had to get over her past mistakes if she hoped to have a chance of anything with Deke. Not that she had any idea if they could work things out, but she was willing to risk it all to find out.

She hefted her bags onto a luggage cart and down the last stretch of hallway. At least she hadn't been forced to call her parents. Not that they would have helped. Not after the way she'd spoken to her mother in the coffee shop. And if they did offer help, there would have been strings and judgements.

Nearly a decade of her life potentially down the tubes. All

those years of busting her ass, working her way up, only to wind up back in Maryland.

Maybe Ryan was right. Maybe here is where I'm meant to be.

Ryan said he'd pick her up. Once again, her bestie rescuing her from an emotional mess of her own making.

She stuttered to a stop as she turned the last corner and exited the secure area, sure she was seeing things. The tall man with the sweep of dark hair staring at the arrivals board looked a lot like Deke. That was all it was. Same build. Same broad shoulders and remarkable ass.

The man raised a hand and swept his fingers through his hair.

Was that a flash of ink? No, I'm seeing things. Gotta be.

He turned around and there was no mistaking that smile. Or the look in his eyes. That was Deke.

He closed the distance in a few long strides then stopped barely an arm's length from her, his arms open as if asking for a hug. Charlie stood frozen in place. The care and stress she'd seen in her own reflection was mirrored on his face and somehow, just looking at him made her knees weak. She loved this man. Heart and soul.

She'd been worried he wouldn't give them another chance, but here he was.

I think I owe Ryan and Bradly dinner for this. The two romantics were the only way Deke could have known when she was coming in.

Charlie shoved all her old fears aside and stepped into his embrace. The moment he wrapped his arms around her, she knew what home meant. He bent his head and his lips tasted of salt, or maybe that was from her tears.

"You're here." There was so much more she wanted to say.

So much to ask. But she didn't want to do any of that standing in the airport.

"Welcome home." Deke took over the luggage cart as they wound their way through the terminal to the parking garage. At his car, he pulled her into his arms again, crushing her body to his as his lips claimed hers.

He was perfect. They were perfect.

At least this part is.

It was too sobering a thought and Charlie broke the kiss. "Can we go somewhere and talk? Please?"

Deke dropped a kiss on her forehead. "Thought you'd never ask."

He got her settled in the passenger seat, then loaded her luggage before sliding into his seat and pulling out of the lot. She texted Ryan that she'd arrived and saved the rest for later. When she could think straight. Once on the road, Deke reached for her hand, squeezing gently. Charlie forced herself to just be—tempting as it was to launch into everything. Sitting here with Deke felt too good to risk ruining it with questions.

"You okay with my place? I know you're staying with Ryan and Bradly, but I figured you might want a bit more privacy than that."

"Yeah, that works." Never mind the fact that they'd probably wind up in bed and not doing much talking. She was fine with that. The ride passed quickly and Deke pulled up in front of his house.

"What do you need to bring in?"

"Just my bag." Charlie hefted the leather backpack at her feet. Everything else could stay in the car for now.

Deke led the way up the steps and held the door for her. Once inside, he swept her into his arms before she had a chance to kick off her shoes. His lips pressed against hers and she wound her arms around his neck, reveling in the feel of him.

He backed her against the wall, and she lifted her legs around his waist. Months of missing him had her so on edge she nearly came when he cupped her ass and ground against her.

The wild rush stopped as quickly as it had begun. Deke lifted his head and she let her legs slide down. He stepped back and pushed his hand through his hair.

"I've uh... missed you." He let out a soft chuckle. "And as much as I want to, I don't have a condom."

What?

"Aren't you the one who claimed you always had them?"

He shrugged and shook his head. *Well fuck.* She didn't have condoms, either. Charlie pushed away from the wall, kicked out of her slip-on loafers and stepped into the living room, suddenly nervous.

Deke shucked his own shoes, then settled on the sofa and beckoned her over. Sitting next to him was a dangerous prospect, but she couldn't imagine doing anything else.

The moment she sat, Deke took her hands in his. The smile he gave her sent her heart soaring even as her brain tried to exert some degree of control.

"I don't know if Ryan told you, but I was about to fly to France to see you." Deke let out a slow breath, then focused those gorgeous brown eyes on Charlie and stared directly into her soul. "I don't care what it looks like, or what you call it. I want you in my life."

Deke had put himself out on a limb again, risking it all. This time, she could meet him there.

"You were right," Charlie said. "We have something special."

He'd bared his soul, told her he loved her, even challenged

her to overcome her fears and she'd rejected him. And yet, he'd been ready to fly to another country just to give them another shot.

"I love you." Charlie whispered the words, afraid if she said it too loudly, her world would crumble apart like it had before. "I'm still not keen on the idea of kids, but I love you, and if you're willing, I'd like to try this again."

Deke slid her into his lap, held her face in his hands and kissed her until she was breathless before he pulled back.

"I have nieces and nephews. I'm content being Uncle Deke. And believe it or not, I recently discovered my parents are more interested in me being happy than in me giving them more grandchildren."

"Is that a yes, let's try again?" Charlie hoped it was. She might not have a job, or know what in the hell she was going to do next, but there were things she did know—she had family in Ryan and Bradly, and maybe, if she was lucky, she had Deke—and those were more important than all the rest, and more powerful than her fears.

The truth had finally settled in her heart—she was safe with Deke.

"That's a yes," he replied.

Charlie moved to kiss him, but he held her away.

"If I kiss you, I'm not going to want to stop. Why don't you go upstairs and shower while I run to the drugstore?"

That familiar glint was in his eyes. She needed a shower, but she didn't want to shower alone. She wriggled around until she straddled his hips, then braced her hands on Deke's chest.

"Unsexy sex talk." Charlie tapped her fingers and waited for Deke to pull his eyes up from her cleavage. "I haven't been with anyone else and I'm on the pill. If you haven't, and aren't planning to, or..."

She stopped when Deke grabbed her ass and stood.

"Wrap your legs around me." Deke carried her up the stairs and didn't stop till they reached the bathroom. He sat her on the counter, then untucked her blouse.

"I'm not interested in seeing anyone else." He popped the first three buttons loose, exposing the lace cups of her bra. He undid the last buttons and slid the silky fabric down her shoulders, then he turned his attention to her belt buckle.

"I guess if you want to talk about some type of open thing, or threesomes, or something like that, we can have that conversation, but I gotta warn you, I'm feeling downright possessive." He grabbed both ends of her belt and pulled forward until she slid off the counter, then he turned on the shower.

"Funny, monogamy never appealed to me before," Deke said as he turned to her. "But back to the point I think you were about to make."

He hooked his fingers in her waistband and with a few quick movements had her pants undone and puddling around her ankles, leaving her standing in his bathroom in nothing but a lace bra and panties.

He stepped back and his gaze traveled her body up and down, then settled back on her face with a smile. His arms wrapped around her and her bra joined the rest of her clothes on the floor. He made equally quick work of her panties.

"Get in the shower."

The note of command was unmistakable and Charlie didn't hesitate. She stepped under the warm spray and turned back to Deke. He'd braced himself on the counter and was watching her.

"Say the word, and I'll run to the store for condoms." He pushed up from the counter and stepped closer, his hands on the open shower door. "Or invite me in. Just know if you do, we are fucking. In the shower. Raw."

Charlie reached out and caught his shirt in her hand, then tugged until he stepped in with her, fully clothed. Deke took the hint and in an instant, backed her against the wall. He cupped her head in his hands and took her mouth in a savage kiss. Charlie worked her hands down his chest, relishing the ripple of muscles under the wet fabric.

She tugged at his belt, then the buttons on his jeans. A whimper tore from her as Deke moved to her neck, grazing his teeth over sensitive skin. Another tug and the familiar weight of his dick filled her hands.

"Miss me, baby?" Deke's lips moved against her collarbone as he kissed his way back up to her mouth. He cupped her chin in his fingers. "I want my cock in this beautiful mouth."

Charlie slid down the wall until she could wrap her lips around his heavy dick.

"That's my girl." Deke coiled a hand in her hair as she sucked. "I love the way you take my cock. Finger your pussy for me. I want you wet and ready."

She was already wet and more than ready. Sex had never been like this before. She'd played kinky games, but Deke was the only one who made her feral for it. She moaned around his dick as her fingers slid over her swollen clit.

"Fuck yes, just like that." Deke held her head and thrust into her mouth until she nearly gagged. He pulled out and tugged her to stand, then hooked an arm under one of her legs and stepped close. Charlie let out a gasp at the feel of his dick pulsing against her pussy.

"Tell me what you want," he commanded.

"Fuck me." She lifted her other leg and wrapped it around him, pulling him into her. The intense pressure made her cry out, but she clung to him, urging him deeper. She'd forgotten how big he was. How hard he got and how he filled her.

"That's my good girl." Deke's words washed over her, filling her heart like he filled her body. He rocked his hips, grinding himself against her clit. Whether it was Deke, or the way his half-undone jeans added to the sensations, she didn't know and didn't care. She liked it.

The tension built until Charlie felt like she would explode. Deke cupped her ass in both hands and lifted, levering himself deeper. She threw her head back as the orgasm hit like a freight train.

As soon as she could speak, Charlie kissed him and smiled. "Yeah, I missed you."

DEKE

Those words were a balm to Deke's soul. He'd been determined to do whatever it took to convince her to give them a chance. When he found out she was coming home, it felt like a hint he was on the right path. Her body pulsed and twitched around him, making him keenly aware he was still fully dressed. And soaking wet.

He did not care.

But he did want to get more comfortable. He kissed her again and stepped back, letting her slide back down the wall as gently as possible. Once he was sure she was steady on her feet, he worked his way out of his sodden clothes and hung them up in the stall to be dealt with later.

As much as he wanted to take the time to soap them both up, the urge to be back inside of her was greater. He shut off the water, stepped out and grabbed a towel to wrap her in, then tucked another around his waist before drying her off.

Charlie had other plans.

"We're not finished." She pulled his towel off and wrapped her fingers around his cock. "Do you want me on my knees right here?"

"Tempting, but..." Deke turned her to face the mirror, then guided her hands to rest on the bathroom counter. "Spread your legs, baby."

Once Charlie did as told, he knelt and buried his face between her ass cheeks. She gasped and arched her back, giving him greater access. Deke flicked her clit with his tongue as he slid two fingers into her pussy. She'd already come once, and he knew from experience that was just the beginning.

"Deke, please! I want you."

Any other time, he'd make her wait. Tease her. Draw the experience out. But he'd missed her, too. He stood and positioned his cock at her entrance, slippery with her juices and his spit. He took his time easing into her, prolonging the sensation and relishing each gasp and tremble from her.

Their eyes locked in the mirror and she smiled, then arched back, giving him access to cup her breasts. He'd intended to pound into her hard and fast, just the way she liked it. Instead, he ground against her slowly, stroking deep and smooth. Charlie's moans got lower, and she slid a hand down her belly.

"That's it, baby. Make yourself come while I fuck you." Deke was counting backwards and doing equations in his head to keep from tipping over the edge himself. He wasn't ready for this to end. Charlie's fingers sped up, and she pushed her ass back against him. He knew that move—she wanted it harder.

He lowered his hands to her hips and held her tight, then gave her what she craved—hard, deep thrusts that sent her into a gasping, panting orgasm. Coppery curls cascaded over her face and lifted with each breath she blew out.

Deke reached and caught a handful of her hair, pulling her head up and forcing her to arch even further.

"You are so fucking beautiful." He trailed kisses along her neck, then sank his teeth into her shoulder, barely noticing the feel of her fingernails digging into his thigh. They'd both have marks.

Not for the first time. Or the last.

"Look at us." He waited until Charlie opened her eyes and looked in the mirror. The expression on her face said she was drunk with pleasure—just the way he liked it. "I want all of you, Charlie. You've given me every bit of your body, but I want it all."

He thrust into her hard. "Body."

Another deep, pounding thrust. "Soul."

Deke pressed her against the counter and drove into her hard enough it stung. "Mind."

He reached around her, bracing his hands on the counter, and delivered another stinging thrust. "Heart."

Charlie's eyes closed, and she let out a soft moan.

"Open your eyes." Deke ground the words out as he switched to hard and fast. "I want all of you, Charlie. Everything."

Her eyes opened, and he saw it—raw vulnerability. All of her fears and insecurities painted on her face and mixed with the pleasure he was giving her.

"Fuck my ass, please." It was a whisper so soft, Deke might have missed the request had he not been fixated on her reflection. Maybe she was asking in the hopes of avoiding the emotional road he'd just gone down, or maybe it was her way of saying yes. Either way, he wasn't about to disappoint.

He didn't even want to stop to retrieve lube from the bedroom. Deke reached into the cabinet for the coconut oil, then slowly worked a finger into her ass. Charlie smiled and bent forward more. As soon as he could slide three fingers in, he pulled out of her pussy, stroked oil over his cock and laid the head against her asshole.

"You want this?"

Charlie nodded. Her entire body was vibrating with tension. He could make her beg for it, or tell her to fuck herself on his cock. They'd played those games before and she loved them all. He pushed the head of his cock in slowly and Charlie's eyes went wide. She sucked in a sharp breath and exhaled. Deke put more oil on, but held himself still.

"Tell me what I want to hear."

She could take that so many ways, and he'd be cool with any of them.

"I'm yours. All of me. Everything. I love you." Charlie pushed back, taking his cock in her ass in one smooth motion. Deke thought he was prepared to hear any response, but that one floored him. And sent his heart soaring. But Charlie was grinding her hips against him, sliding her ass up and down his cock, and he had a promise to deliver on.

He wrapped his arms around her body and pulled her against him, then cupped her pussy with one hand and her breasts with the other. Charlie liked it rough, and as hard as they'd gone, he'd always held back, at least a little.

"When I pull out, I want you on my bed, face down, ass up so you can look in the mirror." He let go and did the hardest thing ever—withdrew. Charlie didn't miss a beat. She turned for the bedroom and scrambled onto his bed.

Deke grabbed lube from the nightstand and poured it over her ass, then lubed up his cock. For what he had in mind, he wanted to be slippery as fuck. He knelt behind her and caught her hair in his hand, then looked at their reflection in the mirror.

"You're mine." He pushed his cock into her ass, ramming in

balls deep in one stroke. Her eyes fluttered and her mouth opened in a long, low moan, but she didn't flinch or wince. "And I'm yours. Everything. All of me. If that's what you want."

He'd never offered himself to anyone. Never wanted to. Until Charlie.

"I want it all, Deke."

That was what he needed to hear.

"What's your safe word?"

Charlie laughed so deep he felt it around his cock. "Café."

"Good girl."

Deke drove himself into her ass hard, again and again. Their harsh breathing punctuated by the slapping of skin on skin and Charlie's cries of pleasure. Deke pulled out and flipped her over, then reached into the nightstand for her favorite toy—the replica of his cock. He lubed it up and slid it into her pussy as Charlie's eyes went wide.

Deke pushed her legs together, then back so her knees were on her chest and he could slide his thighs under her ass. She'd be taking him deep in this position, and his thrusts would have the cock in her pussy pounding into her as well.

Charlie wrapped her arms around her legs, holding them tight against her body and freeing Deke to position himself over her.

"Don't be gentle." There wasn't a trace of uncertainty in her voice, and it drove Deke wild. He added more lube and slid into her ass.

"Your wish is my command." Deke gave her what she wanted. Hard, fast, deep strokes. When her moans turned to cries of pleasure, he pulled her legs wide apart, tightening her ass around his cock, and giving him even deeper access. He thrust hard, then ground against her so his body rubbed against her clit and the dildo in her pussy.

"Oh fuck yes!"

That was all the encouragement Deke needed. He alternated hard strokes with deep grinds, keeping it up until they were both sweat slicked and breathing hard. Charlie matched him stroke for stroke.

He managed to reach the nightstand drawer and grab the little palm vibe. It took seconds to get it wedged against her clit, then he lowered his head and pulled a nipple into his mouth and sucked as he turned the vibe on.

The effect was electric. Charlie let out a wail and her ass lifted off his legs. Deke shifted closer so she couldn't lower back down and drove himself into her ass hard, not stopping. He grazed her nipple with his teeth and Charlie begged for more, harder. And Deke gave.

Her hands clutched at him, and her nails raked his skin. He sucked and pinched and used his teeth and fingers everywhere he could reach. Then Charlie did the impossible.

She grabbed her ankles and pulled her legs back even more, exposing herself completely for him. Deke tapped the vibrator remote to a higher setting, then closed his fingers over her nipples, pinching and rolling the tight buds in time with his strokes.

And Charlie exploded. Words turned to gibberish and a gush of wetness flowed onto his legs. Her body twitched and spasmed and Deke kept going, riding the wave of her orgasm as it wound down, then back up, cresting again and again until her eyes rolled back and the only sounds coming from her were inarticulate moans.

She let go of her legs and clutched at him, gripping his shoulders as he continued to fuck her senseless. Deke released her nipples and leaned down, wrapping her in his arms as if they could merge into one flesh. She tipped her head back, and he caught her lips with his as she cried out another orgasm into his mouth.

Fire ignited in his veins as he stroked into her one last time, pushing deep as he came so hard the world went gray. He turned off the little vibrator and braced himself so she wasn't bearing his full weight. His cock was in no hurry to go soft, and she still had the dildo in her pussy.

"Ready for more?" Deke gave her a slow stroke.

Charlie blinked as if waking from a dream. "Are you serious?"

"That wasn't a no." Another slow stroke. Yep. His cock was still rock hard.

"You're right, it wasn't." She smiled and her muscles clenched around his cock, as if encouraging him to get back at it.

"You sure?" Even after the sex they'd just had, years of experience taught Deke to take it easy. Go slow. Hold himself back. With Charlie, he didn't need to, and it felt amazing. "I want more of this ass, and later, more of your sweet pussy. And I want it disrespectfully hard and rough. I plan on changing the way you walk, baby."

He kept up slow strokes in her ass, loving the feel of lube, his cum, and no condom between him and her silken skin. The slow smile spreading over her face made it even better.

"Bring it on."

"Careful what you ask for," Deke whispered, then flipped the vibrator back on before bracing his hands on the headboard for leverage. "You just might get more than you bargained for."

EPILOGUE

DEKE—WEDNESDAY, DECEMBER 31

Loud music pumped through the brick building and a crowd pulsed on the dance floor. The big clock on the wall said it was getting close to midnight. Deke wove his way through the throng to find Ryan and Bradly, sitting at a table next to a kinetic sculpture of a giant pink poodle. Deke had learned tonight that her name was Fifi. He grabbed an empty chair and pulled it up to the table.

"Ty and Zach are at the park, staking out space." Bradly peered across the crowded floor then pointed. "Charlie is with Nicky and Sabrina over there."

"Anne is wrangling the champagne," Ryan added. "The rest of us are on porter duty as soon as you grab Charlie. So, get your ass out there."

Shades of Ty and Nicky.

One weekend morning over breakfast, just before school started back up for fall, Deke had blurted out the suggestion that Charlie move in with him—he'd been just as surprised as she was, but it felt right. It was Halloween before she agreed.

After spending Thanksgiving with his family, he knew he wanted to propose—just not at Christmas.

There was only one date that felt right—New Year's Eve.

He was reasonably confident she'd say yes, but there was a nagging doubt. He'd gone to her best friend for advice and Ryan, true to everything Charlie had ever said about him, had switched into Romance Engineer mode and helped Deke orchestrate everything.

To say he was nervous would be an understatement.

Deke stood and navigated the dance floor until he reached Charlie. Last year, she'd been in a sparkling mini dress that shimmered and shifted when she moved. Tonight, she was in some slinky thing that looked like gold mesh and hugged all of her curves just right. It had taken every shred of willpower to get out the door tonight instead of pinning her against the wall and hiking the dress around her hips.

Sabrina shot him a wink, leaned in to Charlie and kissed her cheek, then headed off. Nicky stayed for a minute longer, then excused herself to find Ty. She hugged Charlie and mouthed 'don't fuck this up' at Deke over her shoulder.

Deke snagged Charlie's hand and she turned, threw her arms around his neck and laughed.

"Last year, if you'd told me we'd be together on New Year's Eve, in Baltimore, I'd have laughed." She was practically shouting to be heard over the music. This wasn't the place to talk, but he had a plan. He tugged her hand and smiled.

They grabbed their coats, and he insisted Charlie swap out her sparkly sandals for warmer shoes. Then he led the way into the garden out back.

"I needed a break." Deke pulled Charlie down onto a bench near one of the patio heaters. She settled against him and he wrapped his arm over her shoulders. "Everybody's gone to the park to get ready for the fireworks, but I wanted a minute of quiet with you."

Deke was torn. Part of him wanted to propose now, in private. Another part wanted to wait until the fireworks because that was their first kiss.

She reached across him and entwined her fingers in his. "I was serious back there. I never imagined... well... all of this."

Over the past six months, Deke had watched Charlie's walls crumbling bit by bit. She'd landed a permanent job at the Four Seasons—the woman she'd been temping for got pregnant and decided to stay home—and Charlie found the family she so desperately craved. She'd even insisted on having Zach over for dinner. In that moment, he knew what was right.

"Let's go find everyone."

They walked hand in hand out the back, across the street, then around to the stairs. Federal Hill Park was crowded with groups and he worried about finding theirs. Then he spotted Zach, towering above the crowd.

Right up front. Shoulda known.

"What, no date?" Charlie greeted Zach with a hug.

"Are you serious? No way. New Year's Eve is the perfect night for a hookup. Already made plans for later." He leaned in and kissed Charlie's cheek. "I knew he was a goner way back in January. Welcome to the family."

Even Zach sees it. Huh.

Deke stood behind Charlie and wrapped his arms around her waist, then leaned in to whisper in her ear.

"He's not wrong. We're a family—Ty and Nicky, Sabrina and Anne, Bradly and Ryan, you and me, plus Zach and who knows. And you've got Bradly's family. And mine."

He kissed her cheek. "I first laid eyes on you one year ago, and I think some part of me knew then."

Anne and Zach handed out plastic flutes of champagne and the countdown began.

"Ten!"

Charlie looked over her shoulder and winked at Deke.

"Nine!"

She grabbed his jacket collar and pulled him closer.

"Eight!"

Her lips brushed his ear, then her tongue.

"Seven!"

Deke pressed himself against her ass so she could feel him growing hard.

"Six!"

She picked her head up and raised her eyebrows at him.

"Five!"

This was the longest ten seconds Deke had ever experienced, but he had the love of his life in his arms.

"Four!"

Charlie turned to face him, her eyes dancing with happiness.

"Three!"

Someone blew a horn nearby, and Deke's stomach clenched with nerves.

"Two!"

Please let her say yes.

"One! Happy New Year!"

Deke kissed Charlie as the fireworks exploded in the harbor. Then he pulled her tight against him and whispered in her ear.

"I love you, and I want to spend the rest of our lives together. If you'll have me. Marry me?"

CHARLIE

The world moved in slow motion and the sounds of cheering crowds and booming fireworks faded into the background. Charlie blinked, sure she'd misheard Deke. Her champagne flute tumbled from her fingers. She watched in a blur as Deke bent and sat his down in the winter grass. He straightened and took her hands, his face a mask of concern.

They'd talked long term relationship. They'd even beaten around the bush on marriage—in the most abstract terms. Over the last six months, Deke had broken down her emotional barriers, worked with her through her fears, and brought her into his world of friends and family.

Plain and simple, Deke was home to her.

"Yes."

The worried look on Deke's face started to ease and Charlie reached up, wrapped her arms around his neck, and kissed him.

"Yes!"

Deke lifted her off her feet in a crushing hug and kissed her again, long and hard, as the fireworks continued to explode overhead.

She was dimly aware of hoots and hollers that had nothing to do with New Year's Eve. Then Deke let her down and he sank to one knee on the ground.

"Since you're all about the fairy tale." Deke took her hands in his and slipped a ring on her finger as the fireworks finale began.

"I love you with all my heart. I'm yours, Charlie—body and mind, heart and soul."

She didn't look at the ring. It could be a candy ring pop for all she cared. Deke had given her a fairy tale of her own, and he was both Prince Charming and the darkness that lurked in the shadows. The perfect man for her.

"I love you!" She tugged him up to stand and threw herself at him. Deke's strong arms held her, making her want to leave. Right now.

"All right, show it off!" Ryan poked her shoulder.

"What, like you haven't seen it? Don't think I don't recognize your hand in planning shit."

Ryan gave her a theatrical pout. "Sure, I helped plan, but he did the shopping. And yeah, I saw it. But not on your finger. You can't get engaged and not flash the new jewelry at your friends."

Deke's laughter rumbled against her chest. "He's not wrong."

"Fine." Charlie held out her left hand and gasped. Deke had put a rock on her finger. Everyone gathered around, making oo and ahh noises about the emerald-green bling she now wore.

"Like it?" Deke stood behind her and whispered in her ear. "I'd planned on waiting, then taking you ring shopping. But someone convinced me to be more romantic about it. So, here's hoping I got it right—emerald because it's your birthstone, and it goes with your red hair, and you don't strike me as the diamond type. If I was wrong, well... we've got till the end of January to exchange it."

Charlie shook her head, stunned at how much thought he'd put into it all. "I'm not a diamond type, and it's perfect. Just like you."

BREWED AWAKENING

Here's a quick peek at **Brewed Awakening**, book 3 of Charm City Connections.

Note: this text is rough and unedited.

♥

SAM—FRIDAY, APRIL 3

The door latch clicked into place and Sam Crowley flipped the sign to say 'closed' then turned to face the shop. A flower garden with legs came in from the back and Sam rushed to help. She took an armload of roses and laughed as a stem caught in Carla's curls.

"Hold still. Let me just..." Sam disentangled the wayward bud then the two of them got to work arranging flowers. Carla, Sam's best friend and business partner, had wanted to put up streamers and other spring-theme decor for their first Books and Brews event, but Sam had convinced her that lots of flowers and a balloon bouquet for the front door were enough.

"What did you do? Buy out the entire florist shop?" Sam surveyed the assortment of roses, carnations, lilies, and who knew what all else, as well as piles of greenery and filler.

"You said abundant." Carla shrugged as she stuck a handful of eucalyptus in a waiting vase. "I figure we can get the flowers done and have time to grab a late lunch before the team from Cold Bottom gets here to set up the beer station."

The flowers took longer than Carla had planned and they wound up ordering takeout to save time. Sam had just dropped their leftovers in the fridge when the back buzzer rang. Voices carried through the storeroom as Carla let the team in and showed them through to the front. Sam went to the office figuring she had time to get a little work done, but before she could turn on her laptop, Carla was back and looking like she was up to something.

"C'mon. You need to meet the crew. Especially the brewmaster." Carla dragged Sam to the shop floor where a small team in pristine Cold Bottom tees bustled around setting up a bar. *Wow. They're going all out.*

"Coming through." The deep voice rumbled through the air and Sam hurried out of the way as a giant Viking wheeled a cart laden with kegs toward the front corner. Lines of colorful ink traced biceps that bulged under the pushed-up sleeves of his T-shirt. His arms were a display of corded muscles that flexed and moved as he shifted kegs from the cart and into place behind the bar.

A sharp poke in her own bicep broke whatever strange thing had taken over Sam's brain and brought her back to the present. Carla smirked and said something. At least Sam assumed she said something. Her mouth moved, but all Sam heard was a gravelly voice near the bar talking about tasting order.

"I'm sorry, what was that?" She forced herself to focus on Carla.

"You were right. I was wrong. Zach agrees the food station should go in the reading area."

Who's Zach? Is that the Viking?

"Oh? Sure. That makes sense. I uh..." Weeks ago, when they'd planned the layout, Sam had suggested that very thing, but Carla proposed that having the food up front by the bar would be better visibility.

"Been a minute since I've seen that look on your face. Wow." Carla tipped her head and looked over her shoulder toward the team finishing the bar set up. "Yeah. I figured you'd notice him. Totally your type. Or at least your type before the stick in the mud. Also, about time you came out of that shell."

Carla turned and waved an arm in the air. "Hey, Zach. Come meet my business partner."

Sure enough, the Viking lifted his head and nodded. He said something to the rest of the crew, then straightened, pulled off his gloves and swiped a hand through the sandy hair that had fallen over his forehead. He crossed to them and Sam sucked in a sharp breath.

Her best friend was right. He was Sam's type, pre Preston, but she had no interest in repeating her college mistakes.

And what exactly was Preston if not a seven-year-long mistake?

The Viking's hand swallowed hers as he gave a firm, but somehow gentle, handshake as Carla introduced her to Zach Muir, Cold Bottom's brewmaster and the tasting guide for tonight.

"Nice to meet you, Sam." A perfectly groomed beard covered the lower half of a face that looked as if it could have been chiseled by the gods. Then he broke into a dazzling smile and Sam smiled right back. "Carla said you'd know where to set up the food station. We passed an open space near the back."

Oh. Yeah. The event. Shit.

"Perfect. Follow me." She led the way to the back of the shop. "We use this as a reading area, or when we've hosted community meetings, or classes. It's very flexible and we have folding tables and stackable chairs we can put out."

Zach paced along the borders of the space, then stood in the middle, arms crossed and eyes narrowed as he looked around. As if Sam needed more opportunities to admire the man. He looked like exactly what you'd expect of the brewmaster at a craft brewery. A heady combination of Viking mixed with lumberjack, biker, and bad boy all rolled into one package.

Catnip.

And exactly what Sam did not need.

"Show me where you keep the tables and chairs and I'll get the staff setting everything up."

She went down the short hall and opened the storeroom. Zach braced a hand on the doorjamb and leaned past her to peer into the room. And Sam bit her tongue to keep from asking what cologne he was wearing. He smelled like a campfire on the beach at sunset—smoke and warm skin mixed with a salty ocean breeze.

"I'm guessing those right there." He hooked his finger toward the stacks of chairs in the corner of the room, then straightened. "Catering should arrive any minute. We've got the food and beverages handled. You and Carla can focus on running the rest of the event, and if you need anything, I'll be manning the bar all night."

He headed back into the shop, and Sam leaned against the wall, trying to catch her breath. She hadn't looked twice at a man since the breakup with Preston. First because she was too busy figuring out how to rebuild her life. Then because she was too busy with getting the bookshop up and running. Besides, she had toys, and they didn't come with the problems men brought.

"Why are you hiding back here?" Carla grabbed Sam's elbow and steered them to the kitchen where she shut the door then turned on the overhead fan before crossing her arms and fixing Sam with a look that said she was up to no good.

"That man is gorgeous." Carla waved one hand toward the front of the shop. "It's time to get out and do something. I know you haven't dated in what? Two years?"

It had been twenty-one months, not that Sam was counting. She didn't bother answering Carla's question. It wasn't necessary. She'd been there for all of it.

"Even if I were interested, he's at work. It would be inappropriate to flirt." Sam reached past her friend and switched off the fan. "I'll get the swag bags if you'll check with the Cold Bottom crew. We've got about fifteen minutes till the event starts."

Sam didn't wait for Carla's response. She marched from the kitchen, dodged around a pair of catering staff carrying insulated containers down the hall, and picked up the bundle of balloons and the bin of goody bags she and Carla had assembled.

There was a quiet hum of energy in the shop as she passed the catering set up, that shifted to a more festive feel in the front where the bar sat across from the register.

Shit. I'm gonna have to look at him all night.

Sam shook her head and focused on storing the goody bags. She could avoid the register tonight. They had an employee coming in for that so Sam and Carla would be free to mingle. Sam checked the till and double checked the VIP list.

Suck it up and deal.

She grabbed the clipboard and marched across the shop to where Zach was laying out what looked like drinks menus while the rest of the staff assembled small, bar height tables around the room. Zach looked up as Sam laid the clipboard on the bar.

"That the list?" He picked it up and scanned the single page before bringing his eyes back to hers and Sam couldn't look away from those sparkling blues. "Just a reminder—you don't need to worry about checking IDs. That's on us. And to confirm—the VIP list gets a purple wristband and open bar. Everyone else gets an orange band and they pay for their drinks. Food is on the house. I get that right?"

"Yes. Perfect." Sam tried to breathe, or look away, or something. She wasn't even sure she was capable of blinking.

"Kinda going all out for the kickoff. This an anniversary or something? I know it's not a grand opening. Carla said you'd been in business six months."

"Shelf Indulgence opened the first Friday in September," Sam replied. "We never did a big grand opening thing. Just some sales and lots of ads, but we hit the ground running and business has been good. The Books and Brews event has been our dream forever. So, in a way, this is our grand opening, which is why we're kinda going all out tonight. The weekly events won't be this big."

Zach leaned down, elbows on the bar and getting eye level with Sam. "You can always tell when someone loves what they do. Their passion shows. Cool shop name, by the way. Really clever. Sounds a tiny bit naughty."

He winked and straightened. Sam tried to tell herself that wasn't flirting. It was the type of friendly, mildly flirty banter people in customer-facing jobs often employed. Nothing more. She was sure of it. None of that changed the fact that his wink sent her thoughts careening into places she didn't want to go. No matter how hard she tried, she couldn't think of an appropriate response. She didn't want to sound pissy or prudish, but she didn't want to seem like she was misinterpreting friendly as something more.

"Thanks." Sam tore her eyes away from him and hurried to get the balloons to the front door. She was saved from dwelling on it too much when she found a line of about a dozen people waiting outside. She pushed open the heavy glass door, propped up the A-frame sign and anchored the balloons to it then gave the group her best smile and stepped out of their way.

"Welcome to Books and Brews at Shelf Indulgence! Thank you for coming."

ZACH

Books and beer were never a combination Zach expected. Wine? Sure. Hell, even whisky. He'd never imagined bookish people to be into beer. Especially women. The event had been packed from the moment the doors opened and it had stayed steady for three solid hours. Things hadn't slowed down yet, and with an hour left, he surveyed the crowd.

"I'm gonna take a break." Zach whipped off his apron and hung it on a peg under the collapsible bar. "Text if you need me."

The crew waved him away and Zach eased through the clusters of people happily drinking, munching on food, and talking books. From the covers, it looked like mostly romance and fantasy. Stuff Deke's sister Sarah liked.

"Zach? Since when do you work events?"

Speaking of. He turned around and gave her a big hug. "You just get here? Hubby got the twins?"

She tipped her head toward the bar where Chris stood chatting with one of the crew. "They're with my folks for the weekend. I twisted his arm into coming with me to this. We've got concert tickets tomorrow night."

Chris came over with two drinks, handed one to Sarah then shook Zach's hand. "Good to see you. Been a while. Thought you were strictly in the brewhouse these days."

Zach hooked a thumb toward the back. "There's still munchies, if you're hungry. And yeah. I usually am, but Ryan couldn't be here tonight and Mom insisted I'd be a better choice than Reg. She talked me into it."

Looking around the room, he got her reasoning. Lynn Abell was an award-winning brewmaster, and she also knew business. Like any good bartender, Reg had the gift of gab, but he gave off dad vibes. Great for a bar setting. Maybe not so great at an event that seemed catered to women. They'd given out more discount cards tonight than usual.

Correction: I've given out more cards than usual.

"Oh, yeah, I'm sure working this event was a huge burden to you. How many numbers have you gotten tonight?" Sarah jabbed an elbow into his ribs and Chris laughed along.

Zach took it in stride. He was an only child, but then he'd met Deke in college and gotten to know his family and suddenly he had three older sisters.

"Believe it or not, none. A little flirting goes with the territory, but even I understand professional boundaries."

He wasn't going to discuss the disaster that was his January. He'd tried going out a time or two since, but the mindless conversations left him flat. Never mind that he never wanted to wake up next to someone who couldn't remember they'd been fucking for three weeks.

"Seriously? Wow. Who the hell are you and what did you do with the real Zach?"

He flipped his middle finger up then grabbed Sarah's shoulders and steered her toward the food. "Feed her before she gets hangry or something."

Sarah shot him a dirty look, but thankfully went along with Chris to find the food. Leaving Zach stuck in the middle of the shop, unable to go to the front where the bar was, and not wanting to keep hanging around with Sarah and Chris in the back.

"This shop is designed to get lost in." Sam crooked her finger and beckoned him between the bookshelves before disappearing. He'd caught her staring at him a few times through the night, but then she'd look quickly away. Behavior that often said a woman was interested, but shy or uncertain. He stepped between the shelves and realized there was a gap about halfway down the aisle. He turned and there she stood in a small area ringed with bookshelves. Two cushy looking chairs filled most of the hidden room.

"Folks don't always find this reading nook." Sam stepped sideways, giving him room to get to the chairs. "You looked like you needed some place quiet."

"More like a break from being on." Zach suspected she'd understand that feeling. Socially, he was the life of the party, but work was a different game. She tossed her head back and let out a soft laugh.

"So grab a seat. Pick up a book if you want. That's what this spot is for." She slipped between the bookshelves, leaving Zach alone.

He stuck his head out, but she'd disappeared. *Weird.* The hum of conversation seemed distant. Quieter. Maybe all the books muffled sound, or the event was winding down. He'd forgotten how draining working a bar could be. Especially doing guided tastings. Zach eyed the chairs; in his experience, furniture like this wasn't meant to accommodate his height.

The crew would text if they needed him. He settled carefully, then leaned back with a smile, surprised at how comfortable he was.

Sam must look like a kid in these. She's tiny. She was also not his usual type, but there was no denying she was cute, in a hot librarian kind of way. Fuck. He needed to get out more if he was thinking shit like that.

"I don't know if you're a tea drinker, but this is one of my favorites when I've had a stressful day." Sam placed a steaming mug on the little table next to him. "If you don't want it, or don't like it, that's fine."

Zach caught her hand before she could turn away. "Thank you. There's a sort of... I dunno... weird sound distortion happening here or something."

Sam smiled and slid into the other chair. He'd been wrong. She didn't look like a kid. Maybe it was the whole librarian vibe.

"We wanted the shop to feel a little magical. Like something outside of time. Some of the shelves can be moved —they create nooks like this one or change the flow. When I left earlier, I moved the shelf at the end of the row. Makes this space harder to find. I'm sure that dampened sounds."

At least he hadn't been imagining that shit seemed quiet. He picked up the tea and took a cautious sip, afraid it would be too hot. It wasn't, and it was delicious.

"I'm dying to know. Why beer?" Zach took another sip of tea and shook his head. "Not wine? Or I dunno, brandy?"

Another soft laugh whispered in the cozy space and Sam shrugged. "Carla and I both like beer." She shifted sideways, leaning one elbow on the back of the seat so she was looking directly at him.

"You think bookish folks are pretentious." It was a statement, not a question.

"No, I don't... well, maybe?" This wasn't the usual type of conversation he had with attractive women. *And maybe that's a good thing.* "Would it surprise you to know I have a dual degree in chemistry and brewing microbiology as well as a graduate degree in brewing science and operations?"

Most people didn't think about the science behind a successful beer, and trotting out his CV wasn't in his usual flirting tactic. Sam didn't look surprised.

"And you're asking me why beer? Let's do a tasting." Her head tipped at an angle and her lips curled into a smile that kept his attention riveted on her face.

"What? Now?" He checked his watch. They had time. "Okay. Let's go. Lead the way."

Sam rose and led him out of the reading nook, taking a different path then how they'd come in so they came out next to the bar.

"How did you..." Zach shook his head. She wasn't kidding about the shop feeling a little magical. He pointed her to a stool at the end of the bar then donned his apron and set up a row of their plastic tasting glasses.

"You've done a tasting with us before?"

"Of course. With Lynn Abell before we contracted for this event."

No pressure then. Great. His mother knew every brew inside and out. She'd created most of them. His were the newer ones. He removed three of the tasting glasses and Sam raised an eyebrow.

"You'll know all about the colors, the flavors, the nose. So let's deep dive on three of my favorites. One's from the keg— the pilsner you included in your selection for tonight. Two from cans. We bring those to events to pad out the choices, but they're not available for the tasting flight. For you, I'll make an exception."

He winked at her, easily flowing into the banter and routine of being behind the bar. Sam rolled her eyes but propped her chin on her hands as he pulled two cans from the cooler. He filled the first glass with the classic pilsner from the keg and placed it in front of her.

"Looks like your typical beer, but this is better. And I'm not just bragging. I never brag without reason."

That earned him another eye roll, bigger this time, but her smile grew.

"It's our biggest seller and has won several awards."

Zach leaned down and braced his elbows on the bar so he could see her face better. "Pick up the glass and close your eyes, then tell me what you smell."

Her eyes narrowed but she smiled and lifted her chin from her hands then scooped up the glass. Her gaze shot back to him and held as she lifted the glass to her chin level. *Hazel. Her eyes are hazel.* No. They were a starburst with spikes of green and gold and brown. Her lids closed and Zach felt like he could breathe again.

What the fuck was that?

"Citrus." The single word pulled his attention to her lips. Pink and plump. "Toast! It smells like toast."

"Don't open your eyes." He wasn't sure what had just happened between them but he knew if she looked at him like that right now, he'd have a hard time not kissing her. *Not on the clock. Nope.* "Take a slow sip. Take your time before swallowing then breathe out through your nose."

"You talk to all the girls like this?"

She tipped the glass and drank then made a little humming sound. It was barely noticeable in the still busy room, but Zach heard it clear as day. *What was in that tea?*

Sam sat the glass down and opened her eyes. Whatever the

weird thing was from before was gone. *No. Still there. Just mellowed. Huh.*

"Amazing. And I don't usually care for lighter beers. So, why is this one of your favorites?"

"So glad you asked." Zach shifted the glass to the side and cracked open the can of amber lager. "You can pair beer with food, just like you do wine. And that one is what you reach for when you don't want a heavy drink, but you're having a burger. Or a steak. Or it goes really great with a grilled cheese, bacon, and tomato sandwich."

"Because it's crisp and would cut the fattiness. And for the record, that sandwich sounds delicious."

"It is and it's on the menu." He slid the glass of red over to her and she leaned in, chin in her hands again and her gaze fixed on him. The rest of the world disappeared as Zach explained the flavors of the new beer.

Sam laughed at the usual jokes he peppered into any tasting, her smile wide and bright and her laugh soft. He was mesmerized by her every move as she tucked a strand of blonde hair behind her ear, or tapped a short, pink nail against the beer menu in front of her. When she licked her lips after tasting the second beer, the urge to kiss her reared up again and Zach shook himself.

"That one is more my style," she said. "I like the flavors and it's not too heavy. The hint of toffee is nice. It's got a nuttiness."

That last wasn't something most people picked up, and it wasn't in the tasting notes. "Final one, and it may be a bit adventurous. Did you try the stout during your tasting?"

"No. We stuck to the most popular selections."

He opened the can and poured the dark brew into the last glass then reached for a second glass and poured one for himself.

"I wondered when you'd join me."

"I don't usually drink when working, but it's the end of the night, I'm not driving, and I'm a little fond of this one."

He raised his glass and tapped it against hers, but didn't drink. He watched as she closed her eyes and inhaled. Her eyebrows lifted and she inhaled again, then her eyes opened wide and she looked up at him.

"Coffee and something smoky."

"You have a remarkable nose. Taste and tell me what else there is."

Sam took a slow slip and Zach nearly dropped the glass in his hand as her lips parted on a sigh before she took another taste.

"It's woody. And there's another layer to the bitter. A little sweet. Maybe chocolate."

Zach swallowed hard then tipped his glass back, finishing in one swallow. Anything to get his brain on its usual path. Something about her flipped his world into some alternate reality. Maybe it was the shop, but Zach suspected it was her. He took a deep breath and forced himself back to his routine.

"Great palette. Most people catch the bitter, but can't identify it. You're right. Coffee and cocoa." He topped off her glass before she said anything. It was the only one she'd taken a second drink of and that was usually a sign someone liked the brew.

"Over the Barrel generates a lot of interest, even though it's not to everyone's taste. Aged in bourbon barrels. That's the smoky and woody you picked up."

Sam closed her eyes as she took another drink and Zach was struck by how immersed in the sensual she was.

"That last one was your creation."

"Yep. Launched at Christmas."

She finished her glass and Zach offered to pour more but

she shook her head. He tipped the rest of the can into his glass then leaned back down. Maybe he'd get her number. Sam was easy to talk to and there was some chemistry or something between them.

"Hey Zach, time for last call. You want me to handle the till?"

Shit.

"Guess it's back to work." Zach straightened and shoved a hand through his hair. Flirting was one thing, but pursuing when he was supposed to be working was stepping into a gray area. Sam leaned in and placed a hand on his arm. The contact brought his swirling thoughts to a single point of focus—her.

"Yeah, duty calls." She shifted off the stool and her hand slid away. "You know we're doing this event every Friday for a month."

She turned away and disappeared behind the small crowd that clustered around the bar to get another drink. Zach cleared their glasses and wiped the bar, throwing himself into the rhythm of end-of-night tasks and trying not to dwell on whatever had happened between them.

Maybe I just need to get laid. Been a while. That's gotta be it. This is what happens when I'm fucking horny.

ABOUT THE AUTHOR

Roxanne Blackhall is the alter-ego of a former magazine and newspaper editor from San Diego, California, now living in the heart of Baltimore, Maryland. When not at her desk coming up with new ways to torment her characters, she can often be found in the kitchen, glass of wine in hand, cooking a meal for friends.

 bsky.app/profile/roxyblackhall.bsky.social

 facebook.com/roxanneblackhall

 instagram.com/roxanneblackhall

 threads.net/@roxanneblackhall

 goodreads.com/Roxanne_Blackhall

ACKNOWLEDGMENTS

This book was a labor of love and a lot of help from friends.

Shout out to some awesome Baltimore folk who helped make sure I got the vibes right. Christa, Zoe, and Trey. Y'all rock!

Many thanks to Jo, Michael, and Blaire for guidance when it came to beer and breweries. Y'all helped me craft one of my fave scenes.

The anonymous-by-choice folks who helped ensure certain scenes (mostly) stayed in the realm of healthy, consensual adult fun times.

My kids, Gabe and Marcie, are always on hand to help ensure my characters read like 20- and 30-somethings.

And a dizzying number of beta readers, editors, proofreaders, artists, designers, etc. You are so appreciated!

And always, my husband–my real-life romance hero!

This could not have happened without every single one of y'all!

AUTHOR'S NOTE

While this series is set in Baltimore, and features many famous institutions in the city, the people and specifics are fictional. It's not about real, behind-the-scenes details.

Why?

Because this is a work of fiction, not an insider's look at those places and events. Because they are the setting and framework for a story about people who do not exist and things that never happened.

I am a huge fan of all of the places mentioned in this story, and this whole series is something of a love letter to my adopted hometown.

Book 1 was drafted pre-pandemic and faced with the options of "fixing" it all, and the resulting changes to the narrative, or leaving them and letting this story exist outside of time, I chose the latter. Again, because this is a work of fiction and not a Baltimore tour book. Books 2 and 3 exist in that same world—outside of time.

Go to the link at the end and you'll find links to many of the places featured in the serie—if they still exist, of course, sadly, many closed during the pandemic.

If you ever find yourself in Baltimore—look these places up. They're worth a visit!

In short, any negatives, or "inaccuracies" are entirely works of my imagination and there for the purpose of the story— they are not reflections of the amazing events, places, and people who make Baltimore what it is—a surprisingly wonderful, and very quirky, city that I am happy to call home.

www.RoxanneBlackhall.com/locations

ALSO BY ROXANNE BLACKHALL

Charm City Connections

Book 1 ~ Complementary Colors

Book 2 ~ Intersecting Paths

Book 3 ~ Brewed Awakening (October 2025)

Logan County Love Series

Book 1 ~ Rekindled

Book 2 ~ Scorched

Book 3 ~ Arrested

Bristol Park Series

Book 1 ~ Abbeydon Attraction

Book 2 ~ Abbeydon Academy

Book 3 ~ Abbeydon Abandon